Frederik Pohl was born in New York in 1919. His first contribution to an SF publication was a poem, 'Elegy to a Dead Planet: Luna', in *Amazing* (1937). He edited *Astonishing* and *Super Science Stories* 1940–41, and *Star Science Fiction Stories* for Ballantine Books 1953–59. He then edited *Galaxy* and *If* for several years. His partnership with C. M. Kornbluth produced *The Space Merchants* (1953), one of the major SF classics of the 50s, depicting an over-populated world dedicated completely to consumerism and dominated by brain-washing advertising. Kornbluth died in 1958, but Pohl continued writing and is established as one of the classic writers of hard-core science fiction.

D0727014

Frederik Pohl

Survival Kit

PANTHER
GRANADA PUBLISHING
London Toronto Sydney New York

Published by Granada Publishing Limited
in Panther Books 1979

ISBN 0 586 04963 0

First published with *The Man Who Ate the World* as one volume,
The Frederik Pohl Omnibus, by Victor Gollancz Ltd 1966
Copyright © Frederik Pohl 1966

Survival Kit copyright © Galaxy Publishing Corporation 1957
The Knights of Arthur copyright © Galaxy Publishing
Corporation 1957
Mars by Moonlight copyright © Galaxy Publishing
Corporation 1958
The Haunted Corpse copyright © Galaxy Publishing
Corporation 1956
The Middle of Nowhere copyright © Galaxy Publishing
Corporation 1955
The Day of the Boomer Dukes copyright © Galaxy Publishing
Corporation 1956
I Plinglot, Who You? copyright © Galaxy Publishing
Corporation 1958

Granada Publishing Limited
Frogmore, St Albans, Herts AL2 2NF
and
3 Upper James Street, London W1R 4BP
866 United Nations Plaza, New York, NY10017, USA
117 York Street, Sydney, NSW 2000, Australia
100 Skyway Avenue, Rexdale, Ontario, M9W 3A6, Canada
PO Box 84165, Greenside, 2034 Johannesburg, South Africa
CML Centre, Queen & Wyndham, Auckland 1, New Zealand

Made and printed in Great Britain by
C. Nicholls & Company Ltd
The Philips Park Press, Manchester
Set in Intertype Plantin

Granada ®
Granada Publishing ®

Contents

There was three of us – I mean if you count Arthur. We split up to avoid attracting attention. Engdahl just came in over the big bridge, but I had Arthur with me so I had to come the long way round.

When I registered at the desk, I said I was from Chicago. You know how it is. If you say you're from Philadelphia, it's like saying you're from St. Louis or Detroit – I mean *nobody* lives in Philadelphia any more. Shows how things change. A couple years ago, Philadelphia was all the fashion. But not now, and I wanted to make a good impression.

I even tipped the bellboy a hundred and fifty dollars. I said: 'Do me a favour. I've my baggage booby-trapped –'

'Natch,' he said, only mildly impressed by the bill and a half, even less impressed by me.

'I mean *really* booby-trapped. Not just a burglar alarm. Besides the alarm, there's a little surprise on a short fuse. So what I want you to do, if you hear the alarm go off, is come running. Right?'

'And get my head blown off?' He slammed my bags onto the floor. 'Mister, you can take your damn money and –'

'Wait a minute, friend.' I passed over another hundred. 'Please? It's only a shaped charge. It won't hurt anything except anybody who messes around, see? But I don't want it to go off. So you come running when you hear the alarm and scare him away and –'

'No!' But he was less positive. I gave him two hundred more and he said grudgingly: 'All right. If I hear it. Say, what's in there that's worth all that trouble?'

'Papers,' I lied.

He leered. 'Sure.'

'No fooling, it's just personal stuff. Not worth a penny to anybody but me, understand? So don't get any ideas –'

He said in an injured tone: 'Mister, naturally the *staff* won't bother your stuff. What kind of a hotel do you think this is?'

'Of course, of course,' I said. But I knew he was lying, because I knew what kind of hotel it was. The staff was there only because being there gave them a chance to knock down more money than they could make any other way. What other kind of hotel was there?

Anyway, the way to keep the staff on my side was by bribery, and when he left I figured I had him at least temporarily bought. He promised to keep an eye on the room and he would be on duty for four more hours – which gave me plenty of time for my errands.

I made sure Arthur was plugged in and cleaned myself up. They had water running – New York's very good that way; they always have water running. It was even hot, or nearly hot. I let the shower splash over me for a while, because there was a lot of dust and dirt from the Bronx that I had to get off me. The way it looked, hardly anybody had been up that way since it happened.

I dried myself, got dressed and looked out the window. We were fairly high up – fifteenth floor. I could see the Hudson and the big bridge up north of us. There was a huge cloud of smoke coming from somewhere near the bridge on the other side of the river, but outside of that everything looked normal. You would have thought there were people in all those houses. Even the streets looked pretty good, until you noticed that hardly any of the cars were moving.

I opened the little bag and loaded my pockets with enough money to run my errands. At the door, I stopped and called over my shoulder to Arthur: 'Don't worry if I'm gone an hour or so. I'll be back.'

I didn't wait for an answer. That would have been pointless under the circumstances.

After Philadelphia, this place seemed to be bustling with activity. There were four or five people in the lobby and a couple of dozen more out in the street.

I tarried at the desk for several reasons. In the first place, I was expecting Vern Engdahl to try to contact me and I didn't want him messing with the luggage – not while Arthur might get nervous. So I told the desk clerk that in case anybody came inquiring for Mr. Schlaepfer, which was the name I was using – my real name being Sam Dunlap – he was to be told that on no account was he to go to my room but to wait in the lobby; and in any case I would be back in an hour.

'Sure,' said the desk clerk, holding out his hand.

I crossed it with paper. 'One other thing,' I said. 'I need to buy an electric typewriter and some other stuff. Where can I get them?'

'PX,' he said promptly.

'PX?'

'What used to be Macy's,' he explained. 'You go out that door and turn right. It's only about a block. You'll see the sign.'

'Thanks.' That cost me a hundred more, but it was worth it. After all, money wasn't a problem – not when we had just come from Philadelphia.

The big sign read 'PX,' but it wasn't big enough to hide an older sign underneath that said 'Macy's.' I looked it over from across the street.

Somebody had organized it pretty well. I had to admire them. I mean I don't like New York – wouldn't live there if you gave me the place – but it showed a sort of go-getting spirit. It was no easy job getting a full staff together to run a department store operation, when any city the size of New York must have a couple thousand stores. You know what I mean? It's like running a hotel or anything else – how are you going to get people to work for you when they can just as easily walk down the street, find a vacant store and set up their own operation?

But Macy's was fully manned. There was a guard at every door and a walking patrol along the block-front between the entrances to make sure nobody broke in through the windows. They all wore green armbands and uniforms – well, lots of people wore uniforms.

I walked over.

'Afternoon,' I said affably to the guard. 'I want to pick up some stuff. Typewriter, maybe a gun, you know. How do you work it here? Flat rate for all you can carry, prices marked on everything, or what is it?'

He stared at me suspiciously. He was a monster; six inches taller than I, he must have weighed two hundred and fifty pounds. He didn't look very smart, which might explain why he was working for somebody else these days. But he was smart enough for what he had to do.

He demanded: 'You new in town?'

I nodded.

He thought for a minute. 'All right, buddy. Go on in. You

pick out what you want, see? We'll straighten out the price when you come out.'

'Fair enough.' I started past him.

He grabbed me by the arm. 'No tricks,' he ordered. 'You come out the same door you went in, understand?'

'Sure,' I said, 'if that's the way you want it.'

That figured – one way or another: either they got a commission, or, like everybody else, they lived on what they could knock down. I filed that for further consideration.

Inside, the store smelled pretty bad. It wasn't just rot, though there was plenty of that; it was musty and stale and old. It was dark, or nearly. About one light in twenty was turned on, in order to conserve power. Naturally the escalators and so on weren't running at all.

I passed a counter with pencils and ball-point pens in a case. Most of them were gone – somebody hadn't bothered to go around in back and had simply knocked the glass out – but I found one that worked and an old order pad to write on. Over by the elevators there was a store directory, so I went over and checked it, making a list of the departments worth visiting.

Office Supplies would be the typewriter. Garden & Home was a good bet – maybe I could find a little wheelbarrow to save carrying the typewriter in my arms. What I wanted was one of the big ones where all the keys are solenoid-operated instead of the cam-and-roller arrangement – that was all Arthur could operate. And those things were heavy, as I knew. That was why we had ditched the old one in the Bronx.

Sporting Goods – that would be for a gun, if there were any left. Naturally, they were about the first to go after it happened, when *everybody* wanted a gun. I mean everybody who lived through it. I thought about clothes – it was pretty hot in New York – and decided I might as well take a look.

Typewriter, clothes, gun, wheelbarrow. I made one more note on the pad – try the tobacco counter, but I didn't have much hope for that. They had used cigarettes for currency around this area for a while, until they got enough bank vaults open to supply big bills. It made cigarettes scarce.

I turned away and noticed for the first time that one of the elevators was stopped on the main floor. The doors were closed, but they were glass doors, and although there wasn't any light inside, I could see the elevator was full. There must have been thirty or forty people in the car when it happened.

I'd been thinking that, if nothing else, these New Yorkers were pretty neat – I mean if you don't count the Bronx. But here were thirty or forty skeletons that nobody had even bothered to clear away.

You call that neat? Right in plain view on the ground floor, where everybody who came into the place would be sure to go – I mean if it had been on one of the upper floors, what difference would it have made?

I began to wish we were out of the city. But naturally that would have to wait until we finished what we came here to do – otherwise, what was the point of coming all the way here in the first place?

The tobacco counter was bare. I got the wheelbarrow easily enough – there were plenty of those, all sizes; I picked out a nice light red-and-yellow one with rubber-tyred wheel. I rolled it over to Sporting Goods on the same floor, but that didn't work out too well. I found a 30-30 with telescopic sights, only there weren't any cartridges to fit it – or anything else. I took the gun anyway; Engdahl would probably have some extra ammunition.

Men's Clothing was a waste of time, too – I guess these New Yorkers were too lazy to do laundry. But I found the typewriter I wanted.

I put the whole load into the wheelbarrow, along with a couple of odds and ends that caught my eye as I passed through Housewares, and I bumped as gently as I could down the shallow steps of the motionless escalator to the ground floor.

I came down the back way, and that was a mistake. It led me right past the food department. Well, I don't have to tell you what *that* was like, with all the exploded cans and the rats as big as poodles. But I found some cologne and soaked a handkerchief in it, and with that over my nose, and some fast footwork for the rats, I managed to get to one of the doors.

It wasn't the one I had come in, but that was all right. I sized up the guard. He looked smart enough for a little bargaining, but not too smart; and if I didn't like his price I could always remember that I was supposed to go out the other door.

I said 'Psst!'

When he turned around, I said rapidly: 'Listen, this isn't the way I came in, but if you want to do business, it'll be the way I come out.'

He thought for a second, and then he smiled craftily and said: 'All right, come on.'

Well, we haggled. The gun was the big thing – he wanted five thousand for that and he wouldn't come down. The wheelbarrow he was willing to let go for five hundred. And the typewriter – he scowled at the typewriter as though it were contagious.

'What you want that for?' he asked suspiciously. I shrugged.

'Well –' he scratched his head – 'a thousand?'

I shook my head.

'Five hundred?'

I kept on shaking.

'All right, all right,' he grumbled. 'Look, you take the other things for six thousand – including what you got in your pockets that you don't think I know about, see? And I'll throw this in. How about it?'

That was fine as far as I was concerned, but just on principle I pushed him a little further. 'Forget it,' I said. 'I'll give you fifty bills for the lot, take it or leave it. Otherwise I'll walk right down the street to Gimbel's and –'

He guffawed.

'What's the matter?' I demanded.

'Pal,' he said, 'you kill me. Stranger in town, hey? You can't go any place but here.'

'Why not?'

'Account of there *ain't* any place else. See, the chief here don't like competition. So we don't have to worry about anybody taking their trade elsewhere, like – we burned all the other places down.'

That explained a couple of things. I counted out the money, loaded the stuff back in the wheelbarrow and headed for the Statler; but all the time I was counting and loading, I was talking to Big Brainless; and by the time I was actually on the way, I knew a little more about this 'chief.'

And that was kind of important, because he was the man we were going to have to know very well.

I locked the door of the hotel room. Arthur was peeping out of the suitcase at me.

I said: 'I'm back. I got your typewriter.' He waved his eye at me.

I took out the little kit of electricians' tools I carried, tipped the typewriter on its back and began sorting out leads. I cut them free from the keyboard, soldered on a ground wire, and began taping the leads to the strands of a yard of fortyply multiplex cable.

It was a slow and dull job. I didn't have to worry about which solenoid lead went to which strand – Arthur could sort them out. But all the same it took an hour, pretty near, and I was getting hungry by the time I got the last connection taped. I shifted the typewriter so that both Arthur and I could see it, rolled in a sheet of paper and hooked the cable to Arthur's receptors.

Nothing happened.

'Oh,' I said. 'Excuse me, Arthur. I forgot to plug it in.'

I found a wall socket. The typewriter began to hum and then it started to rattle and type:

DURA AUK UKOO RQK MWS AQB

It stopped.

'Come on, Arthur,' I ordered impatiently. 'Sort them out, will you?'

Laboriously it typed:

! ! !

Then, for a time, there was a clacking and thumping as he typed random letters, peeping out of the suitcase to see what he had typed, until the sheet I had put in was used up.

I replaced it and waited, as patiently as I could, smoking one of the last of my cigarettes. After fifteen minutes or so, he had the hang of it pretty well. He typed:

YOU DAMQXXX DAMN FOOL WHUXXX WHY DID YOU LEAQNXXX LEAVE ME ALONE Q Q

'Aw, Arthur,' I said. 'Use your head, will you? I couldn't carry that old typewriter of yours all the way down through the Bronx. It was getting pretty beat-up. Anyway, I've only got two hands –'

YOU LOUSE, it rattled, ARE YOU TRYONXXX TRYING TO INSULT ME BECAUSE I DON'T HAVE ANY QQ

'Arthur!' I said, shocked. 'You know better than that!'

The typewriter slammed its carriage back and forth ferociously a couple of times. Then he said: ALL RIGHT SAM YOU KNOW YOUVE GOT ME BY THE THROAT SO YOU CAN DO ANYTHING YOU

WANT WITH ME WHO CARES ABOUT MY FEELINGS ANYHOW

'Please don't take that attitude,' I coaxed.

WELL

'Please?'

He capitulated. ALL RIGHT SAY HEARD ANYTHING FROM ENGDAHL Q Q

'No.'

ISNT THAT JUST LIKE HIM Q Q CANT DEPEND ON THAT MAN HE WAS THE LOUSIEST ELECTRICIANS MATE ON THE SEA SPRITE AND HE ISNT MUCH BETTER NOW SAY SAM REMEMBER WHEN WE HAD TO GET HIM OUT OF THE JUG IN NEWPORT NEWS BECAUSE

I settled back and relaxed. I might as well. That was the trouble with getting Arthur a new typewriter after a couple of days without one – he had so much garrulity stored up in his little brain, and the only person to spill it on was me.

Apparently I fell asleep. Well, I mean I must have, because I woke up. I had been dreaming I was on guard post outside the Yard at Portsmouth, and it was night, and I looked up and there was something up there, all silvery and bad. It was a missile – and that was silly, because you never *see* a missile. But this was a dream.

And the thing burst, like a Roman candle flaring out, all sorts of comet-trails of light, and then the whole sky was full of bright and coloured snow. Little tiny flakes of light coming down, a mist of light, radiation dropping like dew; and it was so pretty, and I took a deep breath. And my lungs burned out like slow fire, and I coughed myself to death with the explosions of the missile banging against my flaming ears . . .

Well, it was a dream. It probably wasn't like that at all – and if it had been, I wasn't there to see it, because I was tucked away safe under a hundred and twenty fathoms of Atlantic water. All of us were on the *Sea Sprite*.

But it was a bad dream and it bothered me, even when I woke up and found that the banging explosions of the missile were the noise of Arthur's typewriter carriage crashing furiously back and forth.

He peeped out of the suitcase and saw that I was awake. He demanded: HOW CAN YOU FALL ASLEEP WHEN WERE IN A PLACE LIKE THIS Q Q ANYTHING COULD HAPPEN SAM I KNOW YOU DONT CARE WHAT HAPPENS TO ME BUT FOR YOUR OWN SAKE YOU SHOULDNT

'Oh, dry up,' I said.

Being awake, I remembered that I was hungry. There was still no sign of Engdahl or the others, but that wasn't too surprising – they hadn't known exactly when we would arrive. I wished I had thought to bring some food back to the room. It looked like long waiting and I wouldn't want to leave Arthur alone again – after all, he was partly right.

I thought of the telephone.

On the off-chance that it might work, I picked it up. Amazing, a voice from the desk answered.

I crossed my fingers and said: 'Room service?'

And the voice answered amiably enough: 'Hold on, buddy. I'll see if they answer.'

Clicking and a good long wait. Then a new voice said: 'Whaddya want?'

There was no sense pressing my luck by asking for anything like a complete meal. I would be lucky if I got a sandwich.

I said: 'Please, may I have a Spam sandwich on Rye Krisp and some coffee for Room Fifteen Forty-one?'

'Please, you go to hell!' the voice snarled. 'What do you think this is, some damn delicatessen? You want liquor, we'll get you liquor. That's what room service is for!'

I hung up. What was the use of arguing? Arthur was clacking peevishly:

WHATS THE MATTER SAM YOU THINKING OF YOUR BELLY AGAIN Q Q

'You would be if you –' I started, and then I stopped. Arthur's feelings were delicate enough already. I mean suppose that all you had left of what you were born with was a brain in a kind of sardine can, wouldn't you be sensitive? Well, Arthur was more sensitive than you would be, believe me. Of course, it was his own foolish fault – I mean you don't get a prosthetic tank unless you die by accident, or something like that, because if it's disease they usually can't save even the brain.

The phone rang again.

It was the desk clerk. 'Say, did you get what you wanted?' he asked chummily.

'No.'

'Oh. Too bad,' he said, but cheerfully. 'Listen, buddy, I forgot to tell you before. That Miss Engdahl you were expecting, she's on her way up.'

I dropped the phone onto the cradle.

'Arthur!' I yelled. 'Keep quiet for a while – trouble!'

He clacked once, and the typewriter shut itself off. I jumped for the door of the bathroom, cursing the fact that I didn't have cartridges for the gun. Still, empty or not, it would have to do.

I ducked behind the bathroom door, in the shadows, covering the hall door. Because there were two things wrong with what the desk clerk had told me. Vern Engdahl wasn't a 'miss,' to begin with; and whatever name he used when he came to call on me, it wouldn't be Vern Engdahl.

There was a knock on the door. I called: 'Come in!'

The door opened and the girl who called herself Vern Engdahl came in slowly, looking around. I stayed quiet and out of sight until she was all the way in. She didn't seem to be armed; there wasn't anyone with her.

I stepped out, holding the gun on her. Her eyes opened wide and she seemed about to turn.

'Hold it! Come on in, you. Close the door!'

She did. She looked as though she were expecting me. I looked her over – medium pretty, not very tall, not very plump, not very old. I'd have guessed twenty or so, but that's not my line of work; she could have been almost any age from seventeen on.

The typewriter switched itself on and began to pound agitatedly. I crossed over towards her and paused to peer at what Arthur was yacking about: SEARCH HER YOU DAMN FOOL MAYBE SHES GOT A GUN

I ordered: 'Shut up, Arthur. I'm *going* to search her. You! Turn around!'

She shrugged and turned around, her hands in the air. Over her shoulder, she said: 'You're taking this all wrong, Sam. I came here to make a deal with you.'

'Sure you did.'

But her knowing my name was a blow, too. I mean what was the use of all that sneaking around if people in New York were going to know we were here?

I walked up close behind her and patted what there was to pat. There didn't seem to be a gun.

'You tickle,' she complained.

I took her pocketbook away from her and went through it. No gun. A lot of money – an *awful* lot of money. I mean there must have been two or three hundred thousand dollars. There was nothing with a name on it in the pocketbook.

She said: 'Can I put my hands down, Sam?'

'In a minute.' I thought for a second and then decided to do it – you know, I just couldn't afford to take chances. I cleared my throat and ordered: 'Take off your clothes.'

Her head jerked around and she stared at me. *What*?

'Take them off. You heard me.'

'Now wait a minute –' she began dangerously.

I said: 'Do what I tell you, hear? How do I know you haven't got a knife tucked away?'

She clenched her teeth. 'Why, you dirty little man! What do you think –' Then she shrugged. She looked at me with contempt and said: 'All right. What's the difference?'

Well, there was a considerable difference. She began to unzip and unbutton and wriggle, and pretty soon she was standing there in her underwear, looking at me as though I were a two-headed worm. It was interesting, but kind of embarrassing. I could see Arthur's eye-stalk waving excitedly out of the opened suitcase.

I picked up her skirt and blouse and shook them. I could feel myself blushing, and there didn't seem to be anything in them.

I growled: 'Okay, I guess that's enough. You can put your clothes back on now.'

'Gee, thanks,' she said.

She looked at me thoughtfully and then she shook her head as if she'd never seen anything like me before and never hoped to again. Without another word, she began to get back into her clothes. I had to admire her poise. I mean she was perfectly calm about the whole thing. You'd have thought she was used to taking her clothes off in front of strange men.

Well, for that matter, maybe she was; but it wasn't any of my business.

Arthur was clacking distractedly, but I didn't pay any attention to him. I demanded: 'All right, now what are you and what do you want?'

She pulled up a stocking and said: 'You couldn't have asked me that in the first place, could you? I'm Vern Eng –'

'*Cut it out!*'

She stared at me. 'I was only going to say I'm Vern Engdahl's partner. We've got a little business deal cooking and I wanted to talk to you about this proposition.'

Athur squawked: WHATS ENGDAHL UP TO NOW Q Q SAM IM WARNING YOU I DONT LIKE THE LOOK OF THIS THIS WOMAN AND ENGDAHL ARE PROBABLY DOUBLECROSSING US.

I said: 'All right, Arthur, relax. I'm taking care of things. Now start over, you. What's your name?'

She finished putting on her shoe and stood up. 'Amy.'

'Last name?'

She shrugged and fished in her purse for a cigarette. 'What does it matter? Mind if I sit down?'

'Go ahead,' I rumbled. 'But don't stop talking!'

'Oh,' she said, 'we've got plenty of time to straighten things out.' She lit the cigarette and walked over to the chair by the window. On the way, she gave the luggage a good long look.

Arthur's eyestalk cowered back into the suitcase as she came close. She winked at me, grinned, bent down and peered inside.

'My,' she said, 'he's a nice shiny one, isn't he?'

The typewriter began to clatter frantically. I didn't even bother to look; I told him: 'Arthur, if you can't keep quiet, you have to expect people to know you're there.'

She sat down and crossed her legs. 'Now then,' she said. 'Frankly, he's what I came to see you about. Vern told me you had a pross. I want to buy it.'

The typewriter thrashed its carriage back and forth furiously.

'Arthur isn't for sale.'

'No?' She leaned back. 'Vern's already sold me his interest, you know. And you don't really have any choice. You see, I'm in charge of materiel procurement for the Major. If you want to sell your share, fine. If you don't, why, we requisition it anyhow. Do you follow?'

I was getting irritated – at Vern Engdahl, for whatever the hell he thought he was doing; but at her because she was handy. I shook my head.

'Fifty thousand dollars? I mean for your interest?'

'No.'

'Seventy-five?'

'No!'

'Oh, come on now. A hundred thousand?'

It wasn't going to make any impression on her, but I tried to explain: 'Arthur's a friend of mine. He isn't for sale.'

She shook her head. 'What's the matter with you? Engdahl wasn't like this. He sold his interest for forty thousand and was glad to get it.'

Clatter-clatter-clatter from Arthur. I didn't blame him for having hurt feelings that time.

Amy said in a discouraged tone: 'Why can't people be reasonable? The Major doesn't like it when people aren't reasonable.'

I lowered the gun and cleared my throat. 'He doesn't?' I asked, cueing her. I wanted to hear more about this Major, who seemed to have the city pretty well under his thumb.

'No, he doesn't.' She shook her head sorrowfully. She said in an accusing voice: 'You out-of-towners don't know what it's like to try to run a city the size of New York. There are fifteen thousand people here, do you know that? It isn't one of your hick towns. And it's worry, worry, worry all the time, trying to keep things going.'

'I bet,' I said sympathetically. 'You're, uh, pretty close to the Major?'

She said stiffly: 'I'm not married to him, if that's what you mean. Though I've had my chances ... But you see how it is. Fifteen thousand people to run a place the size of New York! It's forty men to operate the power station, and twenty-five on the PX, and thirty on the hotel here. And then there are the local groceries, and the Army, and the Coast Guard, and the Air Force – though, really, that's only two men – and – Well, you get the picture.'

'I certainly do. Look, what kind of guy is the Major?'

She shrugged. 'A guy.'

'I mean what does he like?'

'Women, mostly,' she said, her expression clouded. 'Come on now. What about it?'

I stalled. 'What do you want Arthur for?'

She gave me a disgusted look. 'What do you think? To relieve the manpower shortage, naturally. There's more work than there are men. Now if the Major could just get hold of a couple of prosthetics, like this thing here, why, he could put them in the big installations. This one used to be an engineer or something. Vern said.'

'Well ... *like* an engineer.'

Amy shrugged. 'So why couldn't we connect him up with the power station? It's been done. The Major knows that – he was in the Pentagon when they switched all the aircraft warning net over from computer to prosthetic control. So why couldn't we do the same thing with our power station and release forty men for other assignments? This thing could work day, night, Sundays – what's the difference when you're just a brain in a sardine can?'

Clatter-rattle-*bang*.

She looked startled. 'Oh. I forgot he was listening.'

'No deal,' I said.

She said: 'A hundred and fifty thousand?'

A hundred and fifty thousand dollars. I considered that for a while. Arthur clattered warningly.

'Well,' I temporized, 'I'd have to be sure he was getting into good hands –'

The typewriter thrashed wildly. The sheet of paper fluttered out of the carriage. He'd used it up. Automatically I picked it up – it was covered with imprecations, self-pity and threats – and started to put a new one in.

'No,' I said, bending over the typewriter, ' I guess I couldn't sell him. It just wouldn't be right –'

That was my mistake; it was the wrong time for me to say that, because I had taken my eyes off her.

The room bent over and clouted me.

I half turned, not more than a fraction conscious, and I saw this Amy girl, behind me, with the shoe still in her hand, raised to give me another blackjacking on the skull.

The shoe came down, and it must have weighed more than it looked, and even the fractional bit of consciousness went crashing away.

I have to tell you about Vern Engdahl. We were all from the *Sea Sprite*, of course – me and Vern and even Arthur. The thing about Vern is that he was the lowest-ranking one of us all – only an electricians' mate third, I mean when anybody paid any attention to things like that – and yet he was pretty much doing the thinking for the rest of us. Coming to New York was his idea – he told us that was the only place we could get what we wanted.

Well, as long as we were carrying Arthur along with us, we

pretty much needed Vern, because he was the one who knew how to keep the lash-up going. You've got no idea what kind of pumps and plumbing go into a prosthetic tank until you've seen one opened up. And, naturally, Arthur didn't want any break-downs without somebody around to fix things up.

The *Sea Sprite*, maybe you know, was one of the old liquid-sodium-reactor subs – too slow for combat duty, but as big as a barn, so they made it a hospital ship. We were cruising deep when the missiles hit, and, of course, when we came up, there wasn't much for a hospital ship to do. I mean there isn't any sense fooling around with anybody who's taken a good deep breath of fallout.

So we went back to Newport News to see what had happened. And we found out what had happened. And there wasn't any-thing much to do except pay off the crew and let them go. But us three stuck together. Why not? It wasn't as if we had any families to go back to any more.

Vern just loved all this stuff – he'd been an Eagle Scout; may-be that had something to do with it – and he showed us how to boil drinking water and forage in the woods and all like that, because nobody in his right mind wanted to go near any kind of a town, until the cold weather set in, anyway. And it was always Vern, Vern, telling us what to do, ironing out our troubles.

It worked out, except that there was this one thing. Vern had bright ideas. But he didn't always tell us what they were.

So I wasn't so very surprised when I came to. I mean there I was, tied up, with this girl Amy standing over me, holding the gun like a club. Evidently she'd found out that there weren't any cartridges. And in a couple of minutes there was a knock on the door, and she yelled, 'Come in,' and in came Vern. And the man who was with him had to be somebody important, because there were eight or ten other men crowding in close behind.

I didn't need to look at the oak leaves on his shoulders to realize that here was the chief, the fellow who ran this town, the Major.

It was just the kind of thing Vern *would* do.

Vern said, with the look on his face that made strange officers wonder why this poor persecuted man had been forced to spend so much time in the brig: 'Now, Major, I'm sure we can straighten all this out. Would you mind leaving me alone with my friend here for a moment?'

The Major teetered on his heels, thinking. He was a tall, youngish-bald type, with a long, worried, horselike face. He said, 'Ah, do you think we should?'

'I guarantee there'll be no trouble, Major,' Vern promised.

The Major pulled at his little moustache. 'Very well,' he said, 'Amy, you come along.'

'We'll be right here, Major,' Vern said reassuringly, escorting him to the door.

'You bet you will,' said the Major, and tittered. 'Ah, bring that gun along with you, Amy. And be sure this man knows that we have bullets.'

They closed the door. Arthur had been cowering in his suit-case, but now his eyestalk peeped out and the rattling and clattering from that typewriter sounded like the Battle of the Bulge.

I demanded: 'Come on, Vern. What's this all about?'

Vern said: 'How much did they offer you?'

Clatter-bang-BANG. I peeked, and Arthur was saying: WARNED YOU SAM THAT ENGDAHL WAS UP TO TRICKS PLEASE SAM PLEASE PLEASE PLEASE HIT HIM ON THE HEAD KNOCK HIM OUT HE MUST HAVE A GUN SO GET IT AND SHOOT OUR WAY OUT OF HERE.

'A hundred and fifty thousand dollars,' I said.

Vern looked outraged. 'I only got forty!'

Arthur clattered: VERN I APPEAL TO YOUR COMMON DECENCY WERE OLD SHIPMATES VERN REMEMBER ALL THE TIMES I

'Still,' Vern mused, 'it's all common funds anyway, right? Arthur belongs to both of us.'

I DONT DONT DONT REPEAT DONT BELONG TO ANYBODY BUT ME.

'That's true,' I said grudgingly. 'But I carried him, remember.'

SAM WHATS THE MATTER WITH YOU Q I DONT LIKE THE EXPRESSION ON YOUR FACE LISTEN SAM YOU ARENT

Vern said, 'A hundred and fifty thousand, remember.'

THINKING OF SELLING

'And of course we couldn't get out of here,' Vern pointed out. 'They've got us surrounded.'

ME TO THESE RATS Q Q SAM VERN PLEASE DONT SCARE ME

I said, pointing to the fluttering paper in the rattling machine:
'You're worrying our friend.'

Vern shrugged impatiently.

I KNEW I SHOULDNT HAVE TRUSTED YOU, Arthur wept. THATS
ALL I MEAN TO YOU EH

Vern said: 'Well, Sam? Let's take the cash and get this thing
over with. After all, he *will* have the best of treatment.'

It was a little like selling your sister into white slavery, but
what else was there to do? Besides, I kind of trusted Vern.

'All right,' I said.

What Arthur said nearly scorched the paper.

Vern helped pack Arthur up for moving. I mean it was just
a matter of pulling the plugs out and making sure he had a fresh
battery, but Vern wanted to surprise it himself. Because one of
the little things Vern had up his sleeve was that he had found a
spot for himself on the Mayor's payroll. He was now the official
Prosthetic (Human) Maintenance Department Chief.

The Major said to me: 'Ah, Dunlap. What sort of experience
have you had?'

'Experience?'

'In the Navy. Your friend Engdahl suggested you might want
to join us here.'

'Oh. I see what you mean.' I shook my head. 'Nothing that
would do you any good, I'm afraid. I was a yeoman.'

'Yeoman?'

'Like a company clerk,' I explained. 'I mean I kept records
and cut orders and made out reports and all like that.'

'Company clerk!' The eyes in the long horsy face gleamed.
'Ah, you're mistaken, Dunlap! Why, that's *just* what we need.
Our morning reports are in foul shape. Foul! Come over to
HQ. Lieutenant Bankhead will give you a lift.'

'Lieutenant Bankhead?'

I got an elbow in my ribs for that. It was that girl Amy, standing alongside me. 'I,' she said, 'am Lieutenant Bankhead.'

Well, I went along with her, leaving Engdahl and Arthur behind. But I must admit I wasn't sure of my reception.

Out in front of the hotel was a whole fleet of cars – three or
four of them, at least. There was a big old Cadillac that looked
like a gangster's car – thick glass in the windows, tyres that
looked like they belonged on a truck. I was willing to bet it was
bulletproof and also that it belonged to the Major. I was right

both times. There was a little MG with the top down, and a couple of light trucks. Every one of them was painted bright orange, and every one of them had the star-and-bar of the good old United States Army on its side.

It took me back to old times – all but the unmilitary colour. Amy led me to the MG and pointed.

'Sit,' she said.

I sat. She got in the other side and we were off.

It was a little uncomfortable on account of I wasn't just sure whether I ought to apologize for making her take her clothes off. And then she tramped on the gas of that little car and I didn't think much about being embarrassed or about her black lace lingerie. I was only thinking about one thing – how to stay alive long enough to get out of that car.

See, what we really wanted was an ocean liner.

The rest of us probably would have been happy enough to stay in Lehigh County, but Arthur was getting restless.

He was a terrible responsibility, in a way. I suppose there were a hundred thousand people or so left in the country, and not more than forty or fifty of them were like Arthur – I mean if you want to call a man in a prosthetic tank a 'person.' But we all did. We'd got pretty used to him. We'd shipped together in the war – and survived together, as a few of the actual fighters did, those who were lucky enough to be underwater or high in the air when the ICBMs landed – and as few civilians did.

I mean there wasn't much chance for surviving, for anybody who happened to be breathing the open air when it happened. I mean you can do just so much about making a 'clean' H-bomb, and if you cut out the long-life fission products, the short-life ones get pretty deadly.

Anyway, there wasn't much damage, except of course that everybody was dead. All the surface vessels lost their crews. All the population of the cities were gone. And so then, when Arthur slipped on the gangplank coming into Newport News and broke his fool neck, why, we had the whole staff of the *Sea Sprite* to work on him. I mean what else did the surgeons have to do?

Of course, that was a long time ago.

But we'd stayed together. We headed for the farm country around Allentown, Pennsylvania, because Arthur and Vern Engdahl claimed to know it pretty well. I think maybe they had some hope of finding family or friends, but naturally there wasn't any of that. And when you got into the inland towns, there hadn't been much of an attempt to clean them up. At least the big cities and the ports had been gone over, in some spots anyway, by burial squads. Although when we finally decided to move out and went to Philadelphia –

Well, let's be fair; there had been fighting around there after the big fight. Anyway, that wasn't so very uncommon. That was one of the reasons that for a long time – four or five years, at any rate – we stayed away from big cities.

We holed up in a big farmhouse in Lehigh County. It had its own generator from a little stream, and that took care of Arthur's power needs; and the previous occupants had been just crazy about stashing away food. There was enough to last a century, and that took care of the two of us. We appreciated that. We even took the old folks out and gave them a decent burial. I mean they'd all been in the family car, so we just had to tow it to a gravel pit and push it in.

The place had its own well, with an electric pump and a hot-water system – oh, it was nice. I was sorry to leave but, frankly, Arthur was driving us nuts.

We never could make the television work – maybe there weren't any stations near enough. But we pulled in a couple of radio stations pretty well and Arthur got a big charge out of listening to them – see, he could hear four or five at a time and I suppose that made him feel better than the rest of us.

He heard that the big cities were cleaned up and every one of them seemed to want immigrants – they were pleading, pleading all the time, like the TV-set and vacuum-cleaner people used to in the old days; they guaranteed we'd like it if we only came to live in Philly, or Richmond, or Baltimore, or wherever. And I guess Arthur kind of hoped we might find another pross. And then – well, Engdahl came up with this idea of an ocean liner.

It figured. I mean you get out in the middle of the ocean and what's the difference what it's like on land? And it especially appealed to Arthur because he wanted to do some surface sailing. He never had when he was real – I mean when he had arms and legs like anybody else. He'd gone right into the undersea service the minute he got out of school.

And – well, sailing was what Arthur knew something about

and I suppose even a prosthetic man wants to feel useful. It was like Amy said: He could be hooked up to an automated factory —

Or to a ship.

Hq for the Major's Temporary Military Government — that's what the sign said — was on the 91st floor of the Empire State Building, and right there that tells you something about the man. I mean you know how much power it takes to run those elevators all the way up to the top? But the Major must have liked being able to look down on everybody else.

Amy Bankhead conducted me to his office and sat me down to wait for His Military Excellency to arrive. She filled me in on him, to some degree. He'd been an absolute nothing before the war; but he had a reserve commission in the Air Force, and when things began to look sticky, they'd called him up and put him in a Missile Master control point, underground somewhere up around Ossining.

He was the duty officer when it happened, and naturally he hadn't noticed anything like an enemy aircraft, and naturally the anti-missile missiles were still rusting in their racks all around the city; but since the place had been operating on sealed ventilation, the duty complement could stay there until the short half-life radioisotopes wore themselves out.

And then the Major found out that he was not only in charge of the fourteen men and women of his division at the centre — he was ranking United States Military Establishment officer farther than the eye could see. So he beat it, fast as he could, for New York, because what Army officer doesn't dream about being stationed in New York? And he set up his Temporary Military Government — and that was nine years ago.

If there hadn't been plenty to go around, I don't suppose he would have lasted a week — none of these city chiefs would have. But as things were, he was in on the ground floor, and as new-comers trickled into the city, his boys already had things nicely organized.

It was a soft touch.

Well, we were about a week getting settled in New York and things were looking pretty good. Vern calmed me down by pointing out that, after all, we had to sell Arthur, and hadn't we come out of it plenty okay?

And we had. There was no doubt about it. Not only did we have a fat price for Arthur, which was useful because there were a lot of things we would have to buy, but we both had jobs working for the Major.

Vern was his specialist in the care and feeding of Arthur and I was his chief of office routine – and, as such, I delighted his fussy little soul, because by adding what I remembered of Navy protocol to what he was able to teach me of Army routine, we came up with as snarled a mass of red tape as any field-grade officer in the whole history of all armed forces had been able to accumulate. Oh, I tell you, nobody sneezed in New York without a report being made out in triplicate, with eight endorsements.

Of course there wasn't anybody to send them to, but that didn't stop the Major. He said with determination: 'Nobody's ever going to chew *me* out for non-compliance with regulations – even if I have to invent the regulations myself!'

We set up in a bachelor apartment on Central Park South – the Major had the penthouse; the whole building had been converted to barracks – and the first chance we got, Vern snaffled some transportation and we set out to find an ocean liner.

See, the thing was that an ocean liner isn't easy to steal. I mean we'd scouted out the lay of the land before we ever entered the city itself, and there were plenty of liners, but there wasn't one that looked like we could just jump in and sail it away. For that we needed an organization. Since we didn't have one, the best thing to do was borrow the Major's.

Vern turned up with Amy Bankhead's MG, and he also turned up with Amy. I can't say I was displeased because I was beginning to like the girl; but did you ever try to ride three people in the seats of an MG? Well, the way to do it is by having one passenger sit in the other passenger's lap, which would have been all right except that Amy insisted on driving.

We headed downtown and over to the West Side. The Major's Topographical Section – one former billboard artist – had prepared road maps with little red-ink Xs marking the streets that were blocked, which was most of the streets; but we charted a course that would take us where we wanted to go. Thirty-fourth Street was open, and so was Fifth Avenue all of its length, so we scooted down Fifth; crossed over, got under the Elevated Highway and whined along uptown towards the Fifties.

'There's one,' cried Amy, pointing.

I was on Vern's lap, so I was making the notes. It was a Fruit Company combination freighter-passenger vessel. I looked at Vern, and Vern shrugged as best he could, so I wrote it down; but it wasn't exactly what we wanted. No, not by a long shot.

Still, the thing to do was to survey our resources, and then we could pick the one we liked best. We went all the way up to the end of the big-ship docks, and then turned and came back down, all the way to the Battery. It wasn't pleasure driving exactly – half a dozen times we had to get out the map and detour around impenetrable jams of stalled and empty cars – or anyway, if they weren't exactly empty, the people in them were no longer in shape to get out of our way. But we made it.

We counted sixteen ships in dock that looked as though they might do for our purposes. We had to rule out that the newer ones and the reconverted jobs. I mean, after all, U-235 just lasts so long, and you can steam around the world on a walnut-shell of it, or whatever it is, but you can't store it. So we had to stick with the ships that were powered with conventional fuel – and, on consideration, only oil at that.

But that left sixteen, as I say. Some of them, though, had suffered visibly from being left untended for nearly a decade, so that for our purposes they might as well have been abandoned in the middle of the Atlantic; we didn't have the equipment or ambition to do any great amount of salvage work.

The *Empress of Britain* would have been a pretty good bet, for instance, except that it was lying at pretty nearly a forty-five-degree angle in its berth. So was the *United States,* and so was the *Caronia.* The *Stockholm* was straight enough, but I took a good look, and only one tier of portholes was showing above the water – evidently it had settled nice and even, but it was on the bottom all the same. Well, that mud sucks with a fine tight grip, and we weren't going to try to loosen it.

All in all, eleven of the sixteen ships were out of comission just from what we could see driving by.

Vern and I looked at each other. We stood by the MG, while Amy sprawled her legs over the side and waited for us to make up our minds.

'Not good, Sam,' said Vern, looking worried.

I said: 'Well, that still leaves five. There's the *Vulcania*, the *Cristobal* –'

'Too small.'

'All right. The *Manhattan*, the *Liberté* and the *Queen Elizabeth*.'

Amy looked up, her eyes gleaming. 'Where's the question?' she demanded. 'Naturally, it's the *Queen*."

I tried to explain. 'Please, Amy. Leave these things to us, will you?'

'But the Major won't settle for anything but the best!'

'The *Major*?'

I glanced at Vern, who wouldn't meet my eyes. 'Well,' I said, 'look at the problems, Amy. First we have to check it over. Maybe it's been burned out – how do we know? Maybe the channel isn't even deep enough to float it any more – how do we know? Where are we going to get the oil for it?'

'We'll get the oil,' Amy said cheerfully.

'And what if the channel isn't deep enough?'

'She'll float,' Amy promised. 'At high tide, anyway. Even if the channel hasn't been dredged in ten years.'

I shrugged and gave up. What was the use of arguing?

We drove back to the *Queen Elizabeth* and I had to admit that there was a certain attraction about that big old dowager. We all got out and strolled down the pier, looking over as much as we could see.

The pier had never been cleaned out. It bothered me a little – I mean I don't like skeletons much – but Amy didn't seem to mind. The *Queen* must have just docked when it happened, because you could still see bony queues, as though they were waiting for customs inspection.

Some of the bags had been opened and the contents scattered around – naturally, somebody was bound to think of looting the *Queen*. But there were as many that hadn't been touched as that had been opened, and the whole thing had the look of an amateur attempt. And that was all to the good, because the fewer persons who had boarded the *Queen* in the decade since it happened, the more chance of our finding it in usable shape.

Amy saw a gangplank still up, and with cries of girlish glee ran aboard.

I plucked at Vern's sleeve. 'You,' I said. 'What's this about what the *Major* won't settle for less than?'

He said: 'Aw, Sam, I had to tell her something, didn't I?'

'But what about the Major —'

He said patiently: 'You don't understand. It's all part of my plan, see? The Major is the big thing here and he's got a birthday coming up next month. Well, the way I put it to Amy, we'll fix him up with a yacht as a birthday present, see? And, of course, when it's all fixed up and ready to lift anchor —'

I said doubtfully: 'That's the hard way, Vern. Why couldn't we just sort of get steam up and take off?'

He shook his head. '*That* is the hard way. This way we get all the help and supplies we need, understand?'

I shrugged. That was the way it was, so what was the use of arguing?

But there was one thing more on my mind. I said: 'How come Amy's so interested in making the Major happy?'

Vern chortled. 'Jealous, eh?'

'I asked a question!'

'Calm down, boy. It's just that he's in charge of things here so naturally she wants to keep in good with him.'

I scowled. 'I keep hearing stories about how the Major's chief interest in life is women. You sure she isn't ambitious to be one of them?'

He said: 'The reason she wants to keep him happy is so she *won't* be one of them.'

The name of the place was Bayonne.

Vern said: 'One of them's *got* to have oil, Sam. It *has* to.'

'Sure,' I said.

'There's no question about it. Look, this is where the tankers came to discharge oil. They'd come in here, pump the oil into the refinery tanks and —'

'Vern,' I said. 'Let's look, shall we?'

He shrugged, and we hopped off the little motor-boat onto a landing stage. The tankers towered over us, rusty and screeching as the waves rubbed them against each other.

There were fifty of them there at least, and we poked around them for hours. The hatches were rusted shut and unmanageable, but you could tell a lot by sniffing. Gasoline odour was out; smell of seaweed and dead fish was out; but the heavy, rank smell of fuel oil, that was what we were sniffing for. Crews had been aboard these ships when the missiles came, and crews were still aboard.

Beyond the two-part super-structures of the tankers, the sky-line of New York was visible. I looked up, sweating, and saw the Empire State Building and imagined Amy up there, looking out towards us.

She knew we were here. It was her idea. She had scrounged up a naval engineer, or what she called a naval engineer – he had once been a stoker on a ferryboat. But he claimed he knew what he was talking about when he said the only thing the *Queen* needed to make 'er go was oil. And so we left him aboard to tinker and polish, with a couple of helpers. Amy detached from the police force, and we tackled the oil problem.

Which meant Bayonne. Which was where we were.

It had to be a tanker with at least a fair portion of its cargo intact, because the *Queen* was a thirsty creature, drinking fuel not by the shot or gallon but by the ton.

'Saaam! Sam *Dunlap*!'

I looked up, startled. Five ships away, across the U of the mooring, Vern Engdahl was bellowing at me through cupped hands.

'I found it!' he shouted. 'Oil, lots of oil! Come look!'

I clasped my hands over my head and looked around. It was a long way around to the tanker Vern was on, hopping from deck to deck, detouring around open stretches.

I shouted: 'I'll get the boat!'

He waved and climbed up on the rail of the ship, his feet dangling over, looking supremely happy and pleased with himself. He lit a cigarette, leaned back against the upward sweep of the rail and waited.

It took me a little time to get back to the boat and a little more time than that to get the damn motor started. Vern! 'Let's not take that lousy little twelve horsepower, Sam,' he'd said reasonably. 'The twenty-five's more what we need!' And maybe it was, but none of the motors had been started in most of a decade, and the twenty-five was just that much harder to start now.

I struggled over it, swearing, for twenty minutes or more.

The tanker by whose side we had tied up began to swing to-wards me as the tide changed to outgoing.

For a moment there, I was counting seconds, expecting to have to make a jump for it before the big red steel flank squeezed the little outboard flat against the piles.

But I got it started – just about in time. I squeezed out of the trap with not much more than a yard to spare and threaded my way into open water.

There was a large, threatening sound, like an enormous slow cough.

I rounded the stern of the last tanker between me and open water, and looked into the eye of a fire-breathing dragon.

Vern and his cigarettes! The tanker was loose and ablaze, bearing down on me with the slow drift of the ebbing tide. From the hatches on the forward deck, two fountains of fire spurted up and out, like enormous nostrils spouting flame. The hawsers had been burned through, the ship was adrift, I was in its path –

And so was the frantically splashing figure of Vern Engdahl, trying desperately to swim out of the way in the water before it.

What kept it from blowing up in our faces I will never know, unless it was the pressure in the tanks forcing the flame out; but it didn't. Not just then. Not until I had Engdahl aboard and we were out in the middle of the Hudson, staring back; and then it went up all right, all at once, like a missile or a volcano, and there had been fifty tankers in that one mooring, but there weren't any more, or not in shape for us to use.

I looked at Engdahl.

He said defensively: 'Honest, Sam, I thought it was oil. It *smelled* like oil. How was I to know –'

'Shut up,' I said.

He shrugged, injured. 'But it's all right, Sam. No fooling. There are plenty of other tankers around. Plenty. Down towards the Amboys, maybe moored out in the channel. There must be. We'll find them."

'No,' I said. '*You* will.'

And that was all I said, because I am forgiving by nature; but I thought a great deal more.

Surprisingly, though, he did find a tanker with a full load, the very next day.

It became a question of getting the tanker to the *Queen*. I left that part up to Vern, since he claimed to be able to handle it.

It took him two weeks. First it was finding the tanker, then it was locating a tug in shape to move, then it was finding someone

to pilot the tug. Then it was waiting for a clear and windless day
– because the pilot he had found had got all his experience sailing Star boats on Long Island Sound – and then it was easing
the tanker out of Newark Bay, into the channel, down to the pier
in the North River –

Oh, it was work and no fooling. I enjoyed it very much, because I didn't have to do it.

But I had enough to keep me busy at that. I found a man who
claimed he used to be a radio engineer. And if he was an engineer, I was Albert Einstein's mother, but at least he knew which
end of a soldering iron was hot. There was no need for any great
skill, since there weren't going to be very many vessels to com-
municate with.

Things began to move.

The advantage of a ship like the *Queen*, for our purposes, was
that the thing was pretty well automated to start out with. I
mean never mind what the seafaring unions required in the way
of flesh-and-blood personnel. What it came down to was that
one man in the bridge or wheelhouse could pretty well make
any part of the ship go or not go.

The engine-room telegraph wasn't hooked up to control the
engines, no. But the wiring diagram needed only a few little
changes to get the same effect, because where in the original
concept a human being would take a look at the repeater down
in the engine room, nod wisely, and push a button that would
make the engines stop, start, or whatever – why, all we had to
do was cut out the middleman, so to speak.

Our genius of the soldering iron replaced flesh and blood
with some wiring and, presto, we had centralized engine control.

The steering was even easier. Steering was a matter of electronic control and servomotors to begin with. Windjammers in
the old movies might have a man lashed to the wheel whose
muscle power turned the rudder, but, believe me, a big superliner doesn't. The rudders weigh as much as any old windjam-
mer ever did from stem to stern; you have to have motors to
turn them; and it was only a matter of getting out the old soldering iron again.

By the time we were through, we had every operational facil-
ity of the *Queen* hooked up to a single panel on the bridge.

Engdahl showed up with the oil tanker just about the time we got the wiring complete. We rigged up a pump and filled the bunkers till they were topped off full. We guessed, out of hope and ignorance, that there was enough in there to take us half a dozen times around the world at normal cruising speed, and maybe there was. Anyway, it didn't matter, for surely we had enough to take us anywhere we wanted to go, and then there would be more.

We crossed our fingers, turned our ex-ferry-stoker loose, pushed a button —

Smoke came out of the stacks.

The antique screws began to turn over. Astern, a sort of hump of muddy water appeared. The *Queen* quivered underfoot. The mooring hawsers creaked and sang.

'Turn her off!' screamed Engdahl. 'She's headed for Times Square!'

Well, that was an exaggeration, but not much of one; and there wasn't any sense in stirring up the bottom mud. I pushed buttons and the screws stopped. I pushed another button, and the big engines quietly shut themselves off, and in a few moments the stacks stopped puffing their black smoke.

The ship was alive.

Solemnly Engdahl and I shook hands. We had the thing licked. All, that is, except for the one small problem of Arthur.

The thing about Arthur was they had put him to work.

It was in the power station, just as Amy had said, and Arthur didn't like it. The fact that he didn't like it was a splendid reason for staying away from there, but I let my kind heart overrule my good sense and paid him a visit.

It was way over on the East Side, miles and miles from any civilized area. I borrowed Amy's MG, and borrowed Amy to go with it, and the two of us packed a picnic lunch and set out. There were reports of deer on Avenue A, so I brought a rifle, but we never saw one; and if you want my opinion, those reports were nothing but wishful thinking. I mean if people couldn't survive, how could deer?

We finally threaded our way through the clogged streets and parked in front of the power station.

'There's supposed to be a guard,' Amy said doubtfully.

I looked. I looked pretty carefully, because if there was a

guard I wanted to see him. The Major's orders were that vital defence installations – such as the power station, the PX and his own barracks building – were to be guarded against trespassers on a shoot-on-sight basis and I wanted to make sure that the guard knew we were privileged persons, with passes signed by the Major's own hand. But we couldn't find him. So we walked in through the big door, peered around, listened for the sounds of machinery and walked in that direction.

And then we found him; he was sound asleep. Amy, looking indignant, shook him awake.

'Is that how you guard military property?' she scolded. 'Don't you know the penalty for sleeping at your post?'

The guard said something irritable and unhappy. I got her off his back with some difficulty, and we located Arthur.

Picture a shiny four-gallon tomato can, with the label stripped off, hanging by wire from the flashing-light panels of an electric computer. That was Arthur. The shiny metal cylinder was his prosthetic tank; the wires were the leads that served him for fingers, ears and mouth; the glittering panel was the control centre for the Consolidated Edison Eastside Power Plant No. 1.

'Hi, Arthur,' I said, and a sudden ear-splitting thunderous hiss was his way of telling me that he knew I was there.

I didn't know exactly what it was he was trying to say and I didn't want to; fortune spares me few painful moments, and I accept with gratitude the ones it does. The Major's boys hadn't bothered to bring Arthur's typewriter along – I mean who cares what a generator-governor had to offer in the way of conversation? – so all he could do was blow off steam from the distant boilers.

Well, not quite all. Light flashed; a bucket conveyor began crashingly to dump loads of coal; and an alarm gong began to pound.

'Please, Arthur,' I begged. 'Shut up a minute and listen, will you?'

More lights. The gong rapped half a dozen times sharply, and stopped.

I said: 'Arthur, you've got to trust Vern and me. We have this thing figured out now. We've got the *Queen Elizabeth* –'

A shattering hiss of steam – meaning delight this time, I thought. Or anyway hoped.

'– and it's only a question of time until we can carry out the

plan. Vern says to apologize for not looking in on you –' *hiss* –
'but he's been busy. And after all, you know it's more important
to get everything ready so you can get out of this place, right?'

'Psst,' said Amy.

She nodded briefly past my shoulder. I looked, and there was
the guard, looking sleepy and surly and definitely suspicious.

I said heartily: 'So as soon as I fix it up with the Major, we'll
arrange for something better for you. Meanwhile, Arthur, you're
doing a capital job and I want you to know that all of us loyal
New York citizens and public servants deeply appreciate –'

Thundering crashes, bangs, gongs, hisses, and the scream of
a steam whistle he'd found somewhere.

Arthur was mad.

'So long, Arthur,' I said, and we got out of there – just
barely in time. At the door, we found that Arthur had reversed
the coal scoops and a growing mound of it was pouring into the
street where we'd left the MG parked. We got the car started
just as the heap was beginning to reach the bumpers, and at that
the paint would never again be the same.

Oh, yes, he was mad. I could only hope that in the long run
he would forgive us, since we were acting for this best interests,
after all.

Anyway, I *thought* we were.

Still, things worked out pretty well – especially between Amy
and me. Engdahl had the theory that she had been dodging the
Major so long that *anybody* looked good to her, which was
hardly flattering. But she and I were getting along right well.

She said worriedly: 'The only thing, Sam, is that, frankly, the
Major has just about made up his mind that he wants to marry
me –'

'He *is* married!' I yelped.

'Naturally he's married. He's married to – so far – one hundred and nine women. He's been hitting off a marriage a month
for a good many years now and, to tell you the truth, I think he's
got the habit. Anyway, he's got his eye on me.'

I demanded jealously: 'Has he said anything?'

She picked a sheet of onionskin paper out of her bag and
handed it to me. It was marked *Top Secret*, and it really was,
because it hadn't gone through his regular office – I knew that

because I *was* his regular office. It was only two lines of text and sloppily typed at that:

> Lt. Amy Bankhead will report to HQ at 1700 hours
> 1 July to carry out orders of the Commanding Officer.

The first of July was only a week away. I handed the orders back to her.

'And the orders of the Commanding Officer will be –' I wanted to know.

She nodded. 'You guessed it.'

I said: 'We'll have to work fast.'

On the thirtieth of June, we invited the Major to come aboard his palatial new yacht.

'Ah, thank you,' he said gratefully. 'A surprise? For my birthday? Ah, you loyal members of my command make up for all that I've lost – all of it!' He nearly wept.

I said: 'Sir, the pleasure is all ours,' and backed out of his presence. What's more, I meant every word.

It was a select party of slightly over a hundred. All of the wives were there, barring twenty or thirty who were in disfavour – still, that left over eighty. The Major brought half a dozen of his favourite officers. His bodyguard and our crew added up to a total of thirty men.

We were set up to feed a hundred and fifty, and to provide liquor for twice that many so it looked like a nice friendly brawl. I mean we had our radio operator handing out high-balls as the guests stepped on board. The Major was touched and delighted; it was exactly the kind of party he liked.

He came up the gangplank with his face one great beaming smile. 'Eat! Drink!' he cried. 'Ah, and be merry!' He stretched out his hands to Amy, standing by behind the radio op. 'For tomorrow we wed,' he added, and sentimentally kissed his proposed bride.

I cleared my throat. 'How about inspecting the ship, Major?' I interrupted.

'Plenty of time for that, my boy,' he said. 'Plenty of time for that.' But he let go of Amy and looked around him. Well, it was worth looking at. These Englishmen really knew how to build a luxury liner. God rest them.

The girls began roaming around.

It was a hot day and late afternoon, and the girls began discarding jackets and boleros, and that began to annoy the Major.

'Ah, cover up there!' he ordered one of his wives. 'You too there, what's-your-name. Put that blouse back on!'

It gave him something to think about. He was a very jealous man, Amy had said, and when you stop to think about it, a jealous man with a hundred and nine wives to be jealous of really has a job. Anyway, he was busy watching his wives and keeping his military cabinet and his bodyguard busy too, and that made him too busy to notice when I tipped the high sign to Vern and took off.

In Consolidated Edison's big power plant, the guard was friendly. 'I hear the Major's over on your boat, pal. Big doings. Got a lot of the girls there, hey?'

He bent, sniggering, to look at my pass.

'That's right, pal,' I said, and slugged him.

Arthur screamed at me with a shrill blast of steam as I came in. But only once. I wasn't there for conversation. I began ripping apart his comfy little home of steel braces and copper wires, and it didn't take much more than a minute before I had him free. And that was very fortunate because, although I had tied up the guard, I hadn't done it very well, and it was just about the time I had Arthur's steel case tucked under my arm that I heard a yelling and bellowing from down the stairs.

The guard had got free.

'Keep calm, Arthur!' I ordered sharply. 'We'll get out of this, don't you worry!'

But he wasn't worried, or anyway didn't show it, since he couldn't. I was the one who was worried. I was up on the second floor of the plant, in the control centre, with only one stairway going down that I knew about, and that one thoroughly guarded by a man with a grudge against me. Me, I had Arthur, and no weapon, and I hadn't a doubt in the world that there were other guards around and that my friend would have them after me before long.

Problem. I took a deep breath and swallowed and considered jumping out the window. But it wasn't far enough to the ground.

Feet pounded up the stairs, more than two of them. With Arthur dragging me down on one side, I hurried, fast as I could, along the steel galleries that surrounded the biggest boiler. It was a nice choice of alternatives – if I stayed quiet, they would find me; if I ran, they would hear me, and then find me.

But ahead there was – what? Something. A flight of stairs, it looked like, going out and, yes, *up*. Up? But I was already on the second floor.

'Hey, you!' somebody bellowed from behind me.

I didn't stop to consider. I ran. It wasn't steps, not exactly; it was a chain of coal scoops on a long derrick arm, a moving bucket arrangement for unloading fuel from barges. It did go up, though, and more important it went *out*. The bucket arm was stretched across the clogged roadway below to a loading tower that hung over the water.

If I could get there, I might be able to get down. If I could get down – yes, I could see it; there were three or four mahogany motor launches tied to the foot of the tower.

And nobody around.

I looked over my shoulder, and didn't like what I saw, and scuttled up that chain of enormous buckets like a roach on a wash-board, one hand for me and one hand for Arthur.

Thank heaven, I had a good lead on my pursuers – I needed it. I was on the bucket chain while they were still almost a city block behind me, along the galleries. I was halfway across the roadway, afraid to look down, before they reached the butt end of the chain.

Clash-clatter. *Clank!* The bucket under me jerked and clattered and nearly threw me into the street. One of those jokers had turned on the conveyer! It was a good trick, all right, but not quite in time. I made a flying jump and I was on the tower.

I didn't stop to thumb my nose at them, but I thought of it.

I was down those steel steps, breathing like a spouting whale, in a minute flat, and jumping out across the concrete, coal-smeared yard towards the moored launches. Quickly enough, I guess, but with nothing at all to spare, because although I hadn't seen anyone there, there was a guard.

He popped out of a doorway, blinking foolishly; and over-heard the guards at the conveyer belt were screaming at him. It took him a second to figure out what was going on, and by that time I was in a launch, cast off the rope, kicked it free, and fumbled for the starting button.

It took me several seconds to realize that a rope was required, that in fact there was no button; and by then I was floating yards away, but the pudgy pop-eyed guard was also in a launch, and he didn't have to fumble. He knew. He got his motor started a fraction of a second before me, and there he was, coming at me, set to ram. Or so it looked.

I wrenched at the wheel and brought the boat hard over; but he swerved too, at the last moment, and brought up something that looked a little like a spear and a little like a sickle and turned out to be a boathook. I ducked, just in time. It sizzled over my head as he swung and crashed against the windshield. Hunks of safety glass splashed out over the forward deck, but better that than my head.

Boathooks, hey? I had a boathook too! If he didn't have another weapon, I was perfectly willing to play; I'd been sitting and taking it long enough and I was very much attracted by the idea of fighting back. The guard recovered his balance, swore at me, fought the wheel around and came back.

We both curved out towards the centre of the East River in intersecting arcs. We closed. He swung first. I ducked –

And from a crouch, while he was off balance, I caught him in the shoulder with the hook.

He made a mighty splash.

I throttled down the motor long enough to see that he was still conscious.

'*Touché,* buster,' I said, and set course for the return trip down around the foot of Manhattan, back towards the *Queen*.

It took a while, but that was all right; it gave everybody a nice long time to get plastered. I sneaked aboard, carrying Arthur, and turned him over to Vern. Then I rejoined the Major. He was making an inspection tour of the ship – what he called an inspection, after his fashion.

He peered into the engine rooms and said: 'Ah, fine.'

He stared at the generators that were turning over and nodded when I explained we needed them for power for lights and everything and said: 'Ah, of course.'

He opened a couple of stateroom doors at random and said: 'Ah, nice.'

And he went up on the flying bridge with me and such of his officers as still could walk and said: 'Ah.'

Then he said in a totally different tone: 'What the devil's the matter over there?'

He was staring east through the muggy haze. I saw right away what it was that was bothering him – easy, because I knew where to look. The power plant way over on the East Side was billowing smoke.

'Where's Vern Engdahl? That gadget of his isn't working right!'

'You mean Arthur?'

'I mean that brain in a bottle. It's Engdahl's responsibility, you know!'

Vern came up out of the wheelhouse and cleared his throat. 'Major,' he said earnestly, 'I think there's some trouble over there. Maybe you ought to go look for yourself.'

'Trouble?'

'I, uh, hear there've been power failures,' Vern said lamely. 'Don't you think you ought to inspect it? I mean just in case there's something serious?'

The Major stared at him frostily, and then his mood changed. He took a drink from the glass in his hand, quickly finishing it off.

'Ah,' he said, 'hell with it. Why spoil a good party? If there are going to be power failures, why, let them be. That's my motto!'

Vern and I looked at each other. He shrugged slightly, meaning, well, we tried. And I shrugged slightly, meaning, what did you expect? And then he glanced upwards, meaning, take a look at what's there.

But I didn't really have to look because I heard what it was. In fact, I'd been hearing it for some time. It was the Major's entire air force – two helicopters, swirling around us at an average altitude of a hundred feet or so. They showed up bright against the gathering clouds overhead, and I looked at them with considerable interest – partly because I considered it an even-money bet that one of them would be playing crumplefender with our stacks, partly because I had an idea that they were not there solely for show.

I said to the Major: 'Chief, aren't they coming a little close? I mean it's *your* ship and all, but what if one of them takes a spill into the bridge while you're here?'

He grinned. 'They know better,' he bragged. 'Ah, besides, I want them close. I mean if anything went wrong.'

I said, in a tone that showed as much deep hurt as I could manage: 'Sir, what could go wrong?'

'Oh, you know.' He patted my shoulder limply. 'Ah, no offence?' he asked.

I shook my head. 'Well,' I said, 'let's go below.'

All of it was done carefully, carefully as could be. The only thing was, we forgot about the typewriters. We got everybody, or as near as we could, into the Grand Salon where the food was, and right there on a table at the end of the hall was one of the typewriters clacking away. Vern had rigged them up with rolls of paper instead of sheets, and maybe that was ingenious, but it was also a headache just then. Because the typewriter was banging out:

LEFT FOUR THIRTEEN FOURTEEN AND TWENTY-ONE BOILERS WITH A FULL HEAD OF STEAM AND THE SAFETY VALVES LOCKED BOY I TELL YOU WHEN THOSE THINGS LET GO YOURE GOING TO HEAR A NOISE THATLL KNOCK YOUR HAT OFF.

The Major inquired politely: 'Something to do with the ship?'

'Oh, *that*,' said Vern. 'Yeah. Just a little, uh, something to do with the ship. Say, Major, here's the bar. Real scotch, see? Look at the label!'

The Major glanced at him with faint contempt – well, he'd had the pick of the greatest collection of high-priced liquor stores in the world for ten years, so no wonder. But he allowed Vern to press a drink on him.

And the typewriter kept rattling:

LOOKS LIKE RAIN ANY MINUTE NOW HOO BOY IM GLAD I WONT BE IN THOSE WHIRLYBIRDS WHEN THE STORM STARTS SAY VERN WHY DONT YOU EVER ANSWER ME QQ ISNT IT ABOUT TIME TO TAKE OFF XXX I MEAN GET UNDER WEIGH QQ

Some of the 'clerks, typists, domestic personnel and others' – that was the way they were listed on the T/O; it was only co-incidence that the Major had married them all – were staring at the typewriter.

'Drinks!' Vern called nervously. 'Come on, girls! Drinks!'

The Major poured himself a stiff shot and asked: 'What *is* that thing? A teletype or something?'

'That's right,' Vern said, trailing after him as the Major wandered over to inspect it.

I GIVE THOSE BOILERS ABOUT TEN MORE MINUTES SAM WELL
WHAT ABOUT IT Q Q READY TO SHOVE OFF Q Q

The Major said, frowning faintly: 'Ah, that reminds me of
something. Now what is it?'

'More scotch?' Vern cried. 'Major, a little more scotch?'

The Major ignored him, scowling. One of the 'clerks, typists'
said: 'Honey, you know what it is? It's like that pross you had,
remember? It was on our wedding night, and you'd just got it,
and you kept asking it to tell you limericks.'

The Major snapped his fingers. 'Knew I'd get it,' he glowed.
Then abruptly he scowled again and turned to face Vern and
me. 'Say –' he began.

I said weakly: 'The boilers.'

The Major stared at me, then glanced out of the window.
'What boilers?' he demanded. 'It just a thunderstorm. Been
building up all day. Now what about this? Is that thing –'

But Vern was paying him no attention. 'Thunderstorm?' he
yelled. 'Arthur, you listening? Are the helicopters gone?'

YESYESYES

'Then shove off, Arthur! Shove off!'

The typewriter rattled and slammed madly.

The Major yelled angrily: 'Now listen to me, you! I'm asking
you a question!'

But we didn't have to answer, because there was a thrum-
ming and a throbbing underfoot, and then one of the 'clerks,
typists' screamed: 'The dock!' She pointed at a porthole. 'It's
moving!'

Well, we got out of there – barely in time. And then it was up
to Arthur. We had the whole ship to roam around in and there
were plenty of places to hide. They had the whole ship to search.
And Arthur *was* the whole ship.

Because it was Arthur, all right, brought in and hooked up by
Vern, attained to his greatest dream and ambition. He was skipper of a superliner, and more than any skipper had ever been –
the ship was his body, as the prosthetic tank had never been; the
keel his belly, the screws his feet, the engines his heart and lungs,
and every moving part that could be hooked into central control his many, many hands.

Search for us? They were lucky they could move at all! Fire
Control washed them with salt water hoses, directed by Arthur's

brain. Watertight doors, proof against sinking, locked them away from us at Arthur's whim.

The big bull whistle overhead brayed like a clamouring Gabriel, and the ship's bells tinkled and clanged. Arthur backed that enormous ship out of its berth like a racing scull on the Schuylkill. The four giant screws lashed the water into white foam, and then the thin mud they sucked up into tan; and the ship backed, swerved, lashed the water, stopped, and staggered crazily forward.

Arthur brayed at the Statue of Liberty, tooted good-bye to Staten Island, feinted a charge at Sandy Hook and really laid back his ears and raced once he got to deep water past the moored lightship.

We were off!

Well, from there on, it was easy. We let Arthur have his fun with the Major and the bodyguards – and by the sodden, whimpering shape they were in when they came out, it must really have been fun for him. There were just the three of us and only Vern and I had guns – but Arthur had the *Queen Elizabeth*, and that put the odds on our side.

We gave the Major a choice: row back to Coney Island – we offered him a boat, free of charge – or come along with us as cabin boy. He cast one dim-eyed look at the eighty or so 'clerks, typists' and at Amy, who would never be the hundred and tenth.

And then he shrugged and, game loser, said: 'Ah, why not? I'll come along.'

And why not, when you come to think of it? I mean ruling a city is nice and all that, but a sea voyage is a refreshing change. And while a hundred and nine to one is a respectable female-male ratio, still it must be wearing; and eighty to thirty isn't so bad, either. At least, I guess that was what was in the Major's mind. I know it was what was in mine.

And I discovered that it was in Amy's, for the first thing she did was to march me over to the typewriter and say: 'You've had it, Sam. We'll dispose with the wedding march – just get your friend Arthur here to marry us.'

'Arthur?'

'The captain,' she said. 'We're on the high seas and he's empowered to perform marriages.'

Vern looked at me and shrugged, meaning, you asked for this

one, boy. And I looked at him and shrugged, meaning, it could be worse.

And indeed it could. We'd got our ship; we'd got our ship's company — because, naturally, there wasn't any use stealing a big ship for just a couple of us. We'd had to manage to get a sizeable colony aboard. That was the whole idea.

The world, in fact, was ours. It could have been very much worse indeed, even though Arthur was laughing so hard as he performed the ceremony that he jammed up all his keys.

1

Hardee parked his jeep across the street from the Administration Building, opened the hatch and got out, gasping.

It was cold midnight, better than the heat of the day, but he shivered and his breath made a white mist in the thin air.

Mars – curse the place! Too hot by day, too cold by night, the air too thin all the time.

He looked up. The stars were densely drifted in the sky overhead. Both moons were out of sight; the stars made a white light, not bright enough to be obtrusive but enough, after he had turned out the lights of the jeep, to pick out details of the street, the kerbs, the sidewalks, the low buildings. The little town did not possess street lights and, on nights like this, few persons bothered to turn on the outer lights of their homes; it wasn't necessary.

Around the corner there was a glow of red. Hardee took his sack out of the back of the jeep, grunted as he threw it over his shoulder and headed for the welcome glow.

It came from a sign that read:

BUNNIE'S PLACE
Liveliest Night Spot on Mars

In the doorway, Hardee stood blinking.

It was only a matter of fifty yards or so from the jeep, but he was sweating like a hog because of the weight of the sack. There was no dampness from the sweat – sweat was sucked greedily away into the thin dry air as soon as it was formed. But it was wearing on the muscles and the skin; it was like pounding a treadmill. He was panting, and noise and light beat out at him.

'Hardee!' yelled somebody. He nodded and waved, not troubling to identify whoever it was. Squinting, he moved inside and found a table.

Bunnie's Place. The Liveliest Night Spot on Mars. That was a flat lie – probably. There might be other places, but no one in Bunnie's Place had ever seen them; and if there were, they were bound to be livelier. What Bunnie's Place had to offer was:

A piano, dried from the desert air and in sad disrepair, on which, at the present moment, someone was trying to play a medley of familiar tunes, handicapped by the fact that all the B-flat keys in the middle octaves were broken.

A bar stocked with ceaselessly replenished cases of blended whiskey, gin and brandy, but with very little else.

A dozen tables surrounding a cleared space suitable for dancing, now in use.

A record player with several hundred L.P. records, mostly rock-and-roll, all well worn.

Two pool tables, the felts of which were held together with sticking plaster.

Two ping-pong tables.

A 'library'. It contained twenty-six books, all novels, dating from the years 1950-1955.

Nearly one hundred persons, about a dozen of them women, the youngest of them thirty years old.

That was Bunnie's Place. As a night club, it was a failure. As the recreation room for a penal colony, however, it was not so bad; and that was what it was.

Old Man Tavares came over to take Hardee's order.

'You're late,' he wheezed. He claimed to have had lung trouble once, back on Earth in that former life that each of them talked of endlessly. 'The Probation Officer was looking for you.'

'I'll see him later,' said Hardee. 'Get me a highball first.'

Tavares nodded and limped heavily away. The room was crowded. It was the dark of the moon, or nearly – moonrise would precede the morning sun by only an hour or so – so that practically all the trappers, like Hardee, tried to concentrate their monthly probation reports into this short period of three or four days.

If a trapper made his report on a full-moon night, it meant losing a night's work. A trapper couldn't afford that. He was on his own, despite being a prisoner. He needed every skitterbug he could catch to pay his bills and provide his stake for the next month.

The alternative was to make your report during daylight hours. But that was bad if you had more than ten or fifteen miles to travel – Hardee had fifty – because at this time of year the desert by day was just plain too hot. Besides, the Probation Officer didn't like having his day's sleep interrupted. And he was a prissy, querulous old man who had little real power – he was as much a felon as any of his charges (there was no one in the whole colony who hadn't been sentenced there) – and so he threw his weight around.

'Hello, Hardee.'

Hardee looked up, and for the first time smiled.

'Hello, Joan.'

Joan Bunnell, the 'Bunnie' of Bunnie's Place, was short, warm-faced, honey-haired. Hardee was fond of her; they had slept together several times; they had even talked of getting married. But this was not a place for getting married. There was no rule against it – there were very few rules, everything considered, only the Big Rule against travelling more than a hundred miles from the little town, and a few lesser ones. But how could they talk seriously of getting married when either or both of them might still be married to someone back on Earth?

She had two drinks on a tray, his and one for herself. She sat down, fanning herself. It wasn't very hot, but the room's bright colours and loud voices and the juke-box crashing against the sound of the battered piano gave the impression of a cauldron.

'Drink up,' said Joan Bunnell, toasting him. 'You've got to keep your liquids up.'

'You gotta keep *something* up,' bawled an ape's voice from behind Hardee. It laughed raucously.

Hardee turned, frowning. He recognized the voice. The man's name was Wakulla.

There, thought Hardee irritably, was the kind of man this place was made for. You knew just by looking at him that this was no bank embezzler or forger; this was knock-them-dead and loot-their-pockets. There was no finesse or cunning to those sloping shoulders and the curled black body hair that held his thin shirt cushioned an inch from his chest. The man was an ape.

He boomed with an ape's bellow: 'Hardee, you dumb chump, how many skits did you bring in this time?'

His shout didn't exactly silence the room, but it did create a small oasis of quiet – an area roughly equal to the reach of his enormous fists. He was not liked. But he was feared; in a little world without law, he was feared very much.

Hardee said clearly: 'A hundred and fourteen.'

'In there?' Wakulla kicked the sack beside Hardee's chair.

'Only about a dozen. The rest are outside in the jeep.'

Wakulla nodded, then grinned an ape's grin. 'Good for you, Hardee! You won the pool this month. You know what you won?'

Hardee waited.

'You won the privilege of buying drinks for the house!' Wakulla yelled. 'Come on, boys. Line up!'

Hardee glanced at Joan Bunnell and pressed his shoulders against the back of his chair.

There was a chance, he thought judiciously, that he could take Wakulla. The ape was inches shorter than himself, and that might make a difference. Everything else was going for Wakulla – reach, weight and the indestructible animal combat urge that made all other considerations unimportant. Still, there was that chance.

But it was better to avoid a fight.

Hardee took a deep breath and managed a grin. 'Fair enough,' he said.

Wakulla scowled, waiting.

'Why not?' said Hardee reasonably. 'But if I win that for bringing in a few lousy skitterbugs, what do I win for this?'

He hefted the sack to the top of the table and opened the draw-strings.

There were a couple of skitterbugs on top. He pulled them out and laid them on the table, where their long jointed legs began to twine feebly under the room lights. Then, beneath them, was what he was looking for.

He took it out, stood up and shook it loose.

It hung from his hand limply. It was a grey canvas coverall, filthy, sweat-stained, spotted with what looked like blood.

Wakulla demanded: 'What the hell is that?'

'What does it look like? It's a coverall. I took it off a man I found out in the desert three days ago. On foot.'

It created a sensation.

Old man Tavares limped up, pushing his way through the men around Hardee's table, and clutched the filthy garment. 'The man who was wearing it. He was dead?'

'What do you think?'

It went without saying. It was possible to walk around the desert for short distances, but not for anything like the distance from one prospector's prefab to another. For that you needed a jeep. 'I buried him out in the desert. He was a stranger.'

'A stranger!'

Tavares let go of the garment and stared at it.

Hardee dropped the skitterbugs back into the sack and closed it; as the light was cut off, the stirring stopped. He downed his drink.

'You know that old mine, Wakulla – out between your place and mine? I was out there at daybreak and I found this fellow. He wasn't dead then.'

Wakulla growled: 'But you just said –'

'He was close enough to it. He was face-down on the sand and not moving. I stopped and went over.'

Nearly everybody in the room was clustered around, listening. The penal colony had been in existence for five years now – Hardee himself had been there for nearly three – and this was the first time a stranger had ever appeared. It was an event of the first magnitude, almost as though someone had finally completed his term, or as though, somehow, radio contact had been established with Earth.

Hardee's hand closed over the girl's.

'I tried to lift him up,' he said. 'He was still breathing, but not too well – you know, gasping. Panting. You know how it was when you first got here? Only it seemed even worse with him. He was on his way out. And then he opened his eyes and looked at me.'

Hardee paused, remembering the dry, opaque eyes in the tortured face.

'It wasn't just thirst and exposure,' he said, 'because the man was pretty well scarred up. One of his arms was broken, I think. And – well, look at the coverall. You can see the blood. That's how he was. He raised his head and he said something. I could hardly understand him. And then he sat up and began to choke. And he died. He was pretty far gone, as I say.'

Joan Bunnell demanded: 'Hardee! What did he say?'

Hardee put down his glass and touched the coverall thoughtfully.

'He said: "Thank God. A man!"'

2

Four hours later, Hardee was driving up to the shelter of his own prefab.

The moon was peeping over the eastern horizon in a wash of white light that picked out the mountains around them. Hardee opened the door and looked up, gasping – that was the way it always was when you had been sitting for a while. In this thin air, when you began to lift yourself, the lungs strained for oxygen and found it only with difficulty.

Let's see, thought Hardee, staring at the broad white moon. That would be Deimos. Oh Phobos. Some said the big one was Deimos, some the little. Nobody knew for sure, or nobody had yet convinced the rest of the colony. Old man Tavares was the only one who was really likely to know, and he only laughed when he was asked.

Hardee thought the big one was Deimos. That was the one that was bright and useful, and for weeks on end you didn't see it at all. The other one – what was the use of it? It was a rapid little comet, steel-blue and brighter than a star, yes, but not bright enough. It moved fast, fast; every night it soared across the sky two or three times. But it was no good for hunting.

He got out of the jeep, wheezing. He left it with its motor going – he would be right back – and twisted the combination that unlocked the door of his home, his and the boy's.

Not everyone bothered locking the doors when they went out, but it was habit with Hardee. That was the way he was and, besides, he had something more precious than most to protect.

Inside, he dumped his supplies on the floor and quickly looked into the boy's room. That was all quiet. He closed the door gently and returned to the larger room, stowed the perishables in the freezer, leaving everything else where it lay. He pulled out of his pocket the little sheaf of vouchers that represented the surplus skitterbugs – those whose profits had not been used up in paying for the supplies, for the instalments on the jeep, the prefab itself and all of its furnishings.

He locked the door behind him and rode out into the desert.

There was still an hour of moonlight before the rising of the sun. It didn't do to waste hours; there were just so many hours in the month when the skitterbugs could be caught.

Old man Tavares said that the skitterbugs weren't animals — they were machines.

Tavares might know. He had been in the colony longer than most, and although his mind was wandering and he somtimes thought there was a war going on and all of them were in a concentration camp, he had once been an electronics engineer. Or so he claimed.

Tavares rambled about mussels filtering iodine out of sea water and plants splitting oxygen out of CO_2. Maybe it made sense and maybe not, but what he said was that the skitterbugs all came from one master skitterbug that had been made in a laboratory back on old Earth. There was iron in the sand, said old Tavares, and other elements, and so somebody had invented a sort of basic reproducible pattern for a simple machine operated by sunlight which could extract from sand and rock the ingredients necessary to produce other machines just like itself.

Maybe so. Maybe not. It was true that the skitterbugs *looked* like machines; they were metal. And yet they grew. The theory was simple. Maybe so. Even Hardee could see that, and *he* had been only a traffic policeman in the old days on Earth. Or thought he had.

It didn't matter much, one way or the other, to Hardee. What mattered to him was that during the hours of moonlight it was possible to capture the skits and that if you captured a hundred of them, you kept even with the necessary payments for supplies and instalments to the Probation Officer; if you captured more than that you could even afford luxuries. And that mattered. Not so much for Hardee — he had too much self-punishment yet to inflict on himself for that — but for the boy.

The boy deserved a few luxuries. For he had nothing else.

A mile from the prefab, Hardee switched on the RDF unit.

The radio antenna that sprouted from the tail end of the jeep began to circle slowly, feeling for broadcast radio energy. That was the important thing about moonlit nights.

The skitterbugs, whatever they were, operated on light energy. When light hit their domed, absorbent carapaces, the tiny circuits inside them busily converted the light into heat and kinetic energy. But not quite all of it. There was a certain amount of waste in the form of free radio impulses. This the RDF scanner was designed to locate.

Come to think of it, Hardee pondered, maybe that certain

amount of waste was no waste at all. If it was true that the skitterbugs were artificial, it might perfectly well be that the waste was designed into them, for exactly the purpose for which it was used – to locate and harvest them.

But there had to be light to make them radiate and thus be found.

By day, the blinding sunlight made them radiate like mad, of course, but that was no good. In daylight, the skitterbugs could outrun a man and even a jeep; they produced strong signals, but what was the use of that when you couldn't catch them?

Starlight wasn't very satisfactory either. On a particularly bright night, you might, if you were very, very lucky, pick up a few stray wisps of signal, but only provided you happened to blunder within fifty yards or so of a skit and then the impulses were too weak to be much help for direction finding. No, it had to be moonlight – the big moon – energy enough to make them radiate, but not so much that they could get away.

Hardee checked the little blips of light on his cathode screen and marked a concentration of a dozen or more. Undoubtedly half of them would be under the legal limit. Half a kilogram was the minimum; you could be fined the vouchers for a dozen full-sized skits for bringing in one under the limit. But with any luck at all, he should be able to bag one or two of the fullgrown ones before the others succeeded in tunnelling into the sand and out of sight.

Hardee hunted until the broad red rising sun began to heat the desert and then raced back towards the prefab with four skitterbugs in the shielded locker. He circled the area where a long-abandoned shack marked the old mine, then took his foot off the gas, paused and looked back.

Under the faded board sign that said almost illegibly 'Joe's Last Hope Shaft No. 1' was the shallow grave Hardee had dug out for the stranger. There had been no name, no papers, nothing in the pockets that told him anything, and accordingly, there was no inscription on the little wooden headboard Hardee had hacked out in the growing heat of the morning sun.

Hardee sat there for a moment, his mind vacant, vaguely wondering about the man he had found. But it was growing hot. He put the jeep in gear and headed again for home.

The boy was awake and waiting for him at the door.

'Daddy, Daddy!' he chanted, looking grave and sleepy. 'Did you get it?'

'Hi,' said Hardee inadequately. He bent over to pick the child up.

Chuck was small for his age, a serious-faced, brown-eyed, dark-haired little five-year-old. He said immediately, throwing his arms around Hardee's neck: 'Daddy, did you get the tractor? I've been thinking about it! I woke up three times all night while you were gone.'

'I'll bet you did,' said Hardee. He tousled the boy's hair. 'Well, I got it. It's in the sack.'

'Oh, *Daddy!*' crowed the child. He wriggled frantically to be put down.

As soon as he was on his feet, he raced into the house, through the little foyer where the foot-scrapers waited to get sand off the feet of visitors, and the hooks lined the wall for their clothes. He made a beeline for the pile of supplies. By the time Hardee got rid of his sand boots and sweat-jacket, the boy was making a horrible scraping sound, tugging crates of canned goods out of his way; by the time Hardee reached the door of the room, Chuck had already opened the sack and was feeling inside.

'Oh, *Daddy!*' he cried again, taking the tractor out. It was an exact model of a jeep with a bulldozer blade mounted before it for sand moving; it was battery operated and controlled through a little hand-plate connected to the tractor with a long, thin wire.

'I've only got one battery,' Hardee warned. 'Make it last. I don't know when I can get another one.'

'Oh, that's all right, Daddy. I don't mind *that.*'

Experimentally, the boy turned on the power. The tractor lurched, whined, began pushing its blade across the linoleum floor.

The boy chortled: 'Wait till I get outside! I'll stay near the house, Daddy, I promise. I'm going to make a fort and a castle! I'm going to dig a long canal all the way from the house to the trash burner! I'm going to get the soldier and my red truck and I'm going to make an Army camp that –'

'Sure you are,' said Hardee, patting the boy on the head. 'But first you're going to have breakfast. Right?'

Hardee managed to keep himself awake while the child and

he had breakfast. He even managed to stay awake for nearly an hour afterward, but that was the limit.

He stripped off his clothes, hung them neatly and fell into his bed. Outside, the boy was whooping at his new tractor.

It wasn't, Hardee admitted to himself, the best possible arrangement for him and the boy. But it was important that he be awake nights. And the boy was still too young to be trusted to roam around by himself while Hardee was out hunting.

This way, they didn't see as much of each other as Hardee would have liked – and, heaven knew, it was tough on Chuck to have to find his amusement for eight hours every day, to take his own meals at least twice a day and even to put himself in for a nap when the big hand and the little hand on the clock met at 12. Children are most marvellously adaptable organisms, but it was too bad, all the same.

But what else was there to do?

This way, the child was completely alone only at night – when Hardee was out hunting, and Chuck himself was asleep. True, that wasn't entirely safe. Something could happen – a fire, a sudden sickness, even a fall out of bed. It was better being close at hand, even if asleep, by day, when the child was up and about and thus more likely to run into trouble. Chuck could be trusted to wake him up.

Hardee sighed and turned over. Overhead, he heard the engines of a transport plane and, outside, excited shouts from Chuck. Hardee could imagine him cavorting and waving at the plane.

No, thought Hardee, covering himself lightly and closing his eyes, it wasn't a perfect existence for either of them; but what else could you expect in a penal colony?

3

In the light of the morning, Joan Bunnell closed the door of her room and began to take off her clothes.

She put on light sleeping shorts and a short-sleeved top, patched and faded, but the best she had been able to buy, and stood at the window, looking out at the desert. She was facing west, away from the sunrise. She could see the black shadows streaming away from the sun-touched tops of the buttes and dunes. It was going to be a hot day.

This time of year, you could say that it was going to be a hot day every morning and never be wrong. Funny, she thought, she'd never had any idea that Mars was as hot as this. Back in the old days – before – she hadn't, in fact, thought about Mars much at all.

There was a lot of talk, she remembered cloudily, about rockets and satellites, and even some dreamers who ventured the hope that men would some day touch the surface of the Moon. But Mars? That was for the Sunday comics. She'd paid no attention to that sort of nonsense. She most especially never had dreamed that some day she herself would be a prisoner on Mars, stripped of her freedom and her memories.

Neither had any of the others – no freedom, no memories.

She cranked down the filter panels that would keep out nearly all of the heat, and went over to her little dressing table to complete her going-to-bed ritual. Cleansing cream. Skin cream. Fifty strokes of the brush on each side of her part. Carefully rubbing in the cream below the eyes, behind the jaws, along the line of the throat – the places where wrinkles and sagging would start first.

No, she told herself brutally, *had* started. This hot, dry air was devastating on a girl's skin and hair; it was impossible to let things go for a single day.

She was sleepy, but she sat on the edge of the bed before lying down.

It was impossible for her to go to bed without performing, once again, another and different sort of daily ritual.

She looked across the room at her reflection in the mirror, wondering. Then, hopelessly, automatically, she pushed back the short sleeves of her jacket and examined the skin of her inner arm, pulled back the hem of her shorts and examined the flesh of the thigh.

There were no needle marks.

'Dear God,' whispered Joan wretchedly. She had looked a thousand times before and there had been none. Well, maybe she ought to accept the evidence of her eyes as definite; whatever it was that she had been sentenced to this place for, narcotics addiction was not the answer.

It was the most severe portion of the punishment that not one of the prisoners knew what they were being punished for.

Framed on the wall, over the head of her brass bedstead, was an excerpt from *Martian Penal Colony Rules and General Information*. She had never seen the manual itself, though it was generally understood that the Probation Officer had a copy. But the excerpt she knew by heart. Everyone did. Nearly every room in the colony had it framed and hung:

You are here because you have been tried, convicted and sentenced for a felony.

In former times, felonies were punished by prison sentences. This ordinarily failed of its purpose, in that it did not act as a deterrent to repetitions of the same offence.

In recent years, a technique has been developed of erasing memories after a certain date – usually, for technical reasons, 16 October 1959. By virtue of the XXVth Amendment, provision for the use of this technique has been incorporated in the Uniform Penal Code of the United States, and under it you have been sentenced to rehabilitation and to transportation to the Martian Penal Colony for an indefinite period.

You will be observed from time to time, and the degree of your rehabilitation evaluated. When you are ready to return to normal life, you will be paroled.

It is not in the interests of your best efforts towards rehabilitation that you be advised of the crime of which you were convicted. However, the categories covered by the Uniform Penal Code include:

Murder, first degree.
Murder, second degree.
Manslaughter, in connection with a felony.
Grand larceny, grand fraud and embezzlement – but only after the third offence in each case.
Habitual use of drugs, without voluntary rehabilitation.
Habitual prostitution.

That was the list. Joan knew it well.

It was a choice selection, and she had to be guilty of one of them. But which one?

Joan Bunnell stared long at her own face, wondering if those eyes were the eyes of a murderess. Had she killed a husband, a lover? Perhaps her parents, seeking to inherit their wealth? Perhaps even a child – had she *had* a child? Could she have given birth to a baby, perhaps a boy small and grave-faced like Hardee's youngster – and could she, in madness or in hate, have killed the child?

It was not fair to carve out a piece of her mind and cast it away.

Joan lay back on the pillow, her closed eyes cushioned on her own long hair against her forearm. It was the cruellest of all punishments, this mind-washing they called rehabilitation.

The Arabs chopped off a hand, the ancient English lopped off a finger or an ear, the Indians gouged out an eye . . . and those were kinder things, much kinder; for at least the victim knew exactly what he had lost.

But here was Joan Bunnell, thirty-one years old, according to the records in the Probation Office. She remembered her childhood in a monotonous brownstone two-family house on a monotonously uniform block in Philadelphia very well. She remembered going to school and she remembered her first job. She remembered a birthday party, and, closing her eyese, was able to count the candles – twenty-one.

She remembered years after that; loves and partings. She remembered yearning after the man she worked for and that he married someone else. (Had she killed him?) She remembered that life coursed full and complete through days compact with trivia and detail, up until a certain day – yes, the sixteenth day of October, in that year of 1959 – when she got up in the morning, dressed herself, ate breakfast at a corner drugstore, got into a subway train to go to work –

And woke up in a place where she had never been.

What had happened?

There was no clue, except the framed excerpt over her bed, and the gossip of the other prisoners.

Like her, they had awakened; like her, they had been questioned endlessly; like her, they had been confined. And, like her, they had been put, blindfold, into an airplane, flown for some hours – and released here.

They knew that they had committed a crime. Of course. That was why they were here.

But what crime?

How many years had been lopped off their minds?

Joan lay against the pillow too tired to weep; wept out.

After a while, and just as she might have slept, she heard a distant roar of engines growing closer.

She got up and looked out the window, pulling back the screens that cut down the light and heat.

A silvery plane was limping in low over the sand hills, from the west. It didn't circle or seek a traffic pattern; it came in and down, dumping its landing flaps, along the level sand that was kept bulldozed flat for it.

Joan, no longer sleepy, got up and began getting dressed again. The plane meant supplies – perhaps new clothes, and she could use them; perhaps some toys that she might be able to get for Hardee's son. Most of all, the plane might mean a few new inmates for the colony.

In slacks, blouse and a broad-brimmed sun hat, she hurried out after the growing crowd around the rickety old plane.

Wakulla had stayed over – not even the son of Polish miners wakes up and crosses the desert after drinking a bottle and a half of rye.

'I got to see these guys,' he said thickly with a painful grin. 'I got to see what a free man looks like in case they ever let me out of here.'

'They never will,' muttered someone, and Joan edged away as Wakulla lifted his squat head and looked around to see who it was. She wasn't looking for trouble.

The Probation Officer came up hastily, eagerly panting for the big moment of his being.

'Out of the way!' he quavered. 'Here there, please! Out of the way, Saunders! Here, let me through, Tavares! Come on. Please!'

'Let the keeper through!' bawled Wakulla, forgetting about the man who had muttered. 'Hurry up, Tavares, you old bag of bones!'

The three sputtering propellers of the aircraft coughed and choked and then stopped. Tavares and two other men hurried to push a metal ladder on wheels – with great difficulty – through the clinging sand up to the side of the plane, as the door jerked and then flew open.

Even Joan Bunnell, who was far from a mechanic, had not grown accustomed to the sight of a Ford tri-motor lumbering around in the thin air of Mars. That washboard fuselage, those ancient woodbladed props, they were period accessories from an old movie, not anything you ever expected to see in the air – anywhere. True, some of the men talked wisely about how the old Ford was a great plane for its time and a record-breaker; and they maintained that in all sorts of out-of-the-way places little out-of-the-way airlines had for decades kept up a sort of service using the Fords . . . but on *Mars*?

But there it was, as it had always been for all of them – it was the ship each of them had arrived in. And by and by the wonder had grown duller, submerged in the greater, special wonderment that each of them had, that went incessantly: *What was it that I did that got me sent here*?

The door of the plane swung rasping on its hinges, catching the bright hour-high sun and sending blinding rays into the faces of the colonists. Behind the glare, a man poked his head out – an old, haggard head.

'Hello, Mr. Griswold!' cried the Probation Officer in a thin high voice, greeting him. He waved violently. 'Here I am, Mr. Griswold!'

This was the Probation Officer's *time*. Barring this time, he was nobody – not even in the penal colony of brain-blotted felons, not anywhere. All his days and nights at the penal colony were alike; they were partly bookkeeper's routine and partly file-clerk's duties, and partly they were without any shape at all. They deserved little respect from anyone and they got none – all those days. But on the few, the very occasional days when the Ford transport waddled in – then he, the Probation Officer, he was the one that Mr. Griswold spoke to.

Mr. Griswold came with the plane, always. Mr. Griswold was the only man they ever saw who went back to freedom. And the Probation Officer was the link between the colony and Mr. Griswold – and, through him the rest of Mars and, more remotely, that unimaginably most distant of dreams, Earth and home.

'Hello,' murmured Griswold in a faded, wispy sort of voice. He stood there, haggard and blinking in the sunlight, nodding to the Probation Officer. 'I've got some new mouths to feed,' said Griswold – and, through him, the rest of Mars and, more remotely, that a joke but could never laugh again.

Joan Bunnell pressed closer, though she disliked Griswold and usually, instinctively, stayed well clear of him. Each time Joan saw him, he appeared decades older, degrees more demon-haunted than the time before. She knew his age well enough, because she remembered him from her own trip to the colony, three years before. He had been about fifty then . . . could hardly be fifty-five now . . . but he looked seventy at the least, or perhaps some remote and meaningless age past a hundred.

His hands shook, his voice shook, his face was a working collision of jumpy muscles and fast-blinking eyes. Drugs? Drink? A terminal disease? It could hardly be any of those things, Joan thought; but if it was his job that made him so decrepit and so weak, then working conditions outside the penal colony must be even worse than within it.

And there was one other thing about Mr. Griswold. He never left the old plane.

In the three years of Joan's experience, he had yet to climb down that metal ladder to stand on the ground.

Since Griswold would not come down the ladder, the Probation Officer eagerly and importantly puffed up it.

There was a moment while he and Griswold talked to each other, low-voiced, at the door to the cabin of the old tri-motor plane.

Then the Probation Officer stepped aside. 'Let 'em out, please,' he ordered. 'Let the new fish come down the ladder!'

Five men and women began to file out of the plane, squinting in dazed unbelief at the sunwashed scene around them.

Wakulla caught sight of one of the women and yelled an animal's cry of glee. 'That's for me!' He meant it for a playful aside, but that voice was not meant for stage whispers. He grinned at the woman; then his expression changed to astonishment.

He wasn't alone. There was a gasp. 'She's got a kid with her!' cried one of the women beside Joan Bunnell. Joan caught her breath. That was very odd – and very rare and very precious. There were four babies in the colony, born there, three of them in wedlock and one in doubt. But this was a girl of five or six, not a newborn. That was almost without precedent – the only other child who had been *brought* to the colony was Hardee's boy.

A dozen hands helped the woman with the child down the ladder. They led her, with the others, across the hot sands towards the shelter.

Joan cast one glance at the plane. Already Tavares's crew was beginning to unload crates of supplies. Already the tied sacks of skitterbugs, feebly stirring in the light that filtered through the burlap, were being trundled out on wheelbarrows to be loaded into the plane for return to – where? No one had ever said. Back to Earth, perhaps. Perhaps not.

The glass windscreens of the tri-motor's battered old nose glittered opaquely.

Joan glanced at them and then away – there was nothing there; she never could see inside the cockpit; no one ever had. Behind those glittering windshields were, undoubtedly, the pilot and co-pilot – for surely Griswold was no aviator, not with that tic and those eyes. But she had never seen the pilots, not even when she herself was part of the plane's cargo, coming here. And she didn't expect to see them now.

But something was nagging at her.

She looked again, and her eye was caught by old Dom Tavares, who should have been helping to load the plane, and who instead was standing in a queerly tense attitude, staring at the open door.

Joan tried to peer past the door, but it was hard to see from the bright sun outside into the black shadows within. There was Griswold, and there was the Probation Officer, surely – at least there were two shadows. And the taller, fatter shadow was handing something to the lean, bent one – something that looked like a rag, or an old garment; they were talking about it.

Joan hesitated, wondered if it was worth thinking about.

But there were the newcomers – new faces, when all the old faces were worn so familiar.

And Tavares was, it was perfectly true, getting a little odd in his ways anyhow. Everyone knew that.

She turned, dismissing whatever it was that disturbed Tavares, and hurried after the newcomers as they were shepherded into the recreation room.

By day, the 'Liveliest Night Spot on Mars' was even less attractive than by night.

The night before had been a big one; the signs of it were all over the room, overturned chairs, spilled drinks, the grime of a couple of dozen men in town. No one had taken the time to tidy up – that was done later, usually in the waning heat of the afternoon – and the new arrivals stared around them with revulsion in their eyes.

'They're very young,' someone whispered to Joan. She nodded. One of the women was middle-aged, but the one with the
child was just into her twenties. And of the men, one was little
more than a boy.

He was a blond-haired youngster, his eyes violet and inno-
cent, his face far from the time of shaving. What, Joan wondered, had brought *him* here? For that matter, what was the
crime of the dowdy-looking, plump little woman who was staring around in such panic?

The colonists were all over the new women – particularly
Wakulla, gallant with an ape's clumsy politeness. 'A chair!' he
bawled. 'A chair for the lady!' And he wrenched one from Joan's
hand. 'I'll take the calf to get the heifer,' he whispered hoarsely,
with an exaggerated wink, and slid the chair clattering to the girl
with the child. The girl only stared at him fearfully.

Joan tried to stay back and give the newcomers room.

She had a vivid sense of what they must be feeling; she remembered; she could read their eyes and know what they must
be thinking:

The strangeness of their surroundings.

The sudden shock. (For it was always a shock, everyone
agreed on it; one minute you were going about your business, a
minute later you woke up somewhere else. A strange somewhere,
and removed in time – in a white-walled room, with a couple of
tense and worried-looking doctors and nurses around you, with
television scanner lenses in the walls ... and, very quickly, a
tense and worried-looking man in uniform coming in to talk to
you, to tell you that you had become a criminal, in a life that
was now wiped out of your mind, and that you were on Mars,
headed for a penal colony. Shock? It was a wonder that it didn't
prove fatal. And perhaps for some it had; they had no way of
knowing.)

But more than these things – after that first shock wore off
and you had become reconciled to the fact that your whole life
had somehow been perverted into that of a criminal – after you
had been bundled, blindfolded, into that rattling old three-
motored plane and flown for windowless hours across the unseen Martian deserts – then you arrived.

And that was bad.

For there was always the uneasy, shamefaced question in the
crowd: *Does this one know who I am? And that other one – why*

*is he grinning like that? Does he know what I did? And what did
he himself do, to be in this place?*

Nobody ever got it.

But the early days were worst of all, before the pain became
an accustomed one.

The heat was beating in on them. The woman with the child,
half afraid, half contemptuous of Wakulla's gallantry, leaned
white-faced against the back of her chair. The little girl, a thumb
in her mouth and the other hand clutching her mother's skirt
beside her, watched silently.

The boy was talking – his name was Tommy and he had told
them he was seventeen years old. 'That's what they *tell* me,' he
said, with a painful effort to be adult and sure of himself. His
voice was a soft high mumble, hardly the voice of even a seven-
teen-year-old. 'But – I don't remember that. Really, I don't. The
last thing I remember, I was twelve!'

Twelve! Joan made a faint sound; almost she patted him on
the head, though he was taller than she. Twelve! What sort of
criminal could have hatched at twelve? Even at seventeen, the
thing was ridiculous! But somewhere, this child had lost five
years.

She tried to explain it to him: 'You must have done something, Tommy. Maybe you got involved with the wrong bunch
at school – who knows? But somehow, you went wrong. That's
why they send people here, you know. It's the new law. Instead
of putting someone in jail and keeping them there – that would
be a waste, you see, and cruel – they wipe out the part of the
minds that has the criminal pattern in it. They go back erasing
memory, until they come to a part that is clean and unaffected,
not only before the crime was committed but before, even, the
first seed of the crime was planted. That's why none of us know
what it was we did. It's been taken away from us. We've been
given a second chance. We should be grateful.'

But should they? It was the old question; she cast it off.

'Then,' she said, 'after they're cleaned out our memories and
taken us back to the right path, they send us up here. To Mars.
This is a colony where we can try to get reoriented and –' She
hesitated. And what? 'And go back to normal life,' she finished
strongly, though there was still the relentless reminder of her
memory that *no one* had ever gone back. 'It isn't so bad, Tommy,' she promised.

He didn't look convinced.

Someone was calling her name: 'Joan! Joan, come here, please!'

It was old man Tavares. He was standing in the door, his face blenched a muddy mottled colour in spite of the dark the sun had given it.

She turned and hurried to him. Heat-stroke, she thought at once. It was far from uncommon, especially when a man as old as Tavares had to work in the blinding sun helping to lift boxes and bales.

But he caught her feverishly by the hand and drew her outside into the sunwashed street.

'Joan,' he whispered raggedly, terror peeping out of his eyes. 'Joan, can you borrow a jeep?'

'Why – I suppose so. But –'

'Take me to Hardee,' he begged. His lined old face was quivering with senile worry and fear; his dry, hot hand was crushing hers. 'Quickly! It will take hours for us to drive there. And we may not have hours, because they can fly in the plane! Quickly, for his sake and your own!'

Joan said reasonably: 'Now hold on, Dom. You're excited. Sit down for a minute.' She tried to lead him back into the recreation room. She'd seen the signs coming on, she reproached herself, when he behaved so queerly at the plane; she should have done something about it at the time. Poor old man! 'Come on, Dom,' she coaxed. 'I'll get you a nice cool drink of water and –'

'Quickly!' He planted his feet firmly, surprisingly strong, and halted her. His eyes were terrified; they flicked past her, out towards the plane. 'You don't understand, Joan! The Probation Officer, he has told Griswold about the stranger Hardee found. It is a terrible thing, do you not realize?'

'Stranger?' she repeated.

'The dead man, Joan! I saw them with the coverall, and then I knew. So I came close and listened and, yes, he was telling Griswold. And Griswold was frantic! Of course. Hurry, Joan!'

Doubtfully, she said: 'Well, let's see. You want to go out to Hardee's place? Wakulla's not far from here. I suppose I can persuade him to take us out, though he's got that new woman on his mind. It's a bad time of day, but –'

'Hurry!'

The panic in his voice finally reached her. All right, she thought, why not? She could handle Wakulla – even in the face of the constant threat of a boiled-out motor and trouble, the natural risk you took in driving across the sand by summer daylight. But Tavares gave her no choice.

Still she protested, half-resisting: 'Can't it wait until night, Dom? Surely it can't be as serious as all that. After all, what's so dangerous about a stranger? I suppose he's merely a man who got lost in the desert – at most, perhaps he escaped from another prison camp, somewhere else on Mars, but certainly that doesn't –'

'Mars!' Tavares hissed in a terrible whisper. Convulsively he squeezed her arm. 'Joan, do you not understand? All these years – and you still think that this is *Mars*?'

4

Hardee woke groggily to the sound of the boy's voice calling: 'Daddy! Somebody's coming!'

It was only about noon.

Hardee swung himself out of bed, half asleep, his eyes aching. He stumbled over to the window and pushed back the shutters.

Fierce light beat in. He blinked, dazzled. The sun was directly overhead. The boy had been right; there was a jeep coming, still a long way off, but he could hear the faint whine and echo of its motor as the driver shifted gears, coaxing it around the worst of the bumps, trying to keep it from overheating. Someone driving at this time of day!

It must be an urgent errand, he thought, and began to clamber into his clothes. He couldn't make out who was in it, in the blinding light; but by the time he was into his shirt and pants and ready to come downstairs, he could hear voices. Tavares and Joan Bunnell – and his son, crying out to greet them.

'Aunt Joan!' Chuck was babbling excitedly – it was a great day for him when there were visitors. 'Look at what Daddy got me, Aunt Joan! A *tractor*. And see, I can make a farm with Alice and Alfie – see? This is my tractor, and Alice and Alfie are the cows!' Alice and Alfie were his pet skitterbugs Hardee had captured them with the regular bag; but they were undersized, not of legal limit to bring in, so he had given them to the boy to play with for lack of a kitten or a pup.

Hardee nodded without speaking and started down the stairs. The child was pushing the quiescent skitterbugs around on the floor with the tractor, whooping with joy. In the filtered, screened-down light that came inside the prefab, they had just enough energy to try to creep out of its way.

Joan stared up at Hardee, began to speak, then caught herself. She took the boy's arm lightly. 'Chuck,' she said, 'listen to me. We have to talk to your father. Go outside and play, please.'

He stood up, his eyes wide and disturbed. 'Oh, let me stay, Aunt Joan! My tractor's —'

'Please, Chuck.'

He looked up at his father, hesitated, and started towards the door. Then he paused, looking at Wakulla and Tavares; even in his child's mind, he knew that it was not usual to see them there.

With a child's response, an incantation against evil, he summoned up politeness: 'Hello, Mr. Tavares. Hello, Mr. Wakulla.' He hesitated, then remembered one more cantrip. 'Don't worry, Daddy,' he piped. 'I'll be careful to stay in the shade.'

Joan Bunnell, torn, said:

'There isn't any shade. I tell you what.' She glanced at Wakulla. 'You'd better play in Mr. Wakulla's jeep. Make believe you're driving it all by yourself.'

'Whee!' The boy shouted gleefully. He dropped tractor and skitterbugs, flung the door open and leaped out into the sand.

Sunlight flared in.

One of the bugs — it was impossible to tell which; only the boy could tell them apart — lay squarely in the path of the sun's rays. There was a sudden crinkling *snap* of sparking energy as the light it fed on struck it; like a released spring, the little spidery metal thing spun around, leaped out the door and was gone.

It was like a meteorite flung up into space, so quick and glittering.

Hardee closed the door behind it and turned to face the others. 'What's the matter?' he demanded.

Old man Tavares sank into a chair. 'That stranger,' he croaked. 'The Probation Officer told Griswold about him, and now there will be trouble. For there is a lie here, Hardee. This is not the sort of place we are told it is. It is not on Mars; we are not criminals. And there must be a reason for this lie. What reason? I do not know, but whoever is telling the lie will protect it.'

He leaned forward. 'It may cost your lift to protect it, Hardee! Others have died, and I think for the same reason – you are in danger, and, with you, all of us because of the fact that you told us!'

Hardee shook his head. He was still more than half drowsy. The world had not yet come into focus; he was drugged from heat and sleep and none of this was making sense.

He said thickly: 'What the hell are you talking about, Tavares?'

'I am talking about death!' said the old man. And then he stopped, and there was sudden fear on his face. 'Listen!'

Outside, a noise. An engine. No – more than one.

'Someone coming?' guessed Hardee. 'A jeep?'

'It is death that is coming,' sobbed Tavares. 'That's no jeep, Hardee. It is the plane, coming for you!'

They ran to the door and flung it open.

It came from the east, like a faint angry snarl of bees, the sound of the Ford tri-motor's three labouring engines.

'There it is!' cried the girl. 'Look, over the dunes!'

Sunlight glinted off a wing. It was the plane, all right, hardly five hundred feet up. It was heading off to one side, more in the direction of Wakulla's hut than Hardee's; clearly whoever was flying it was unfamiliar with the exact locations of the prefabs.

But clearly also, it would not take long to straighten them out.

'Come on!' said Hardee, and flung out the door. Whatever it was that Tavares was talking about, something of the old man's panic and desperation had reached him. 'We'll have to hide! Wakulla, you know the old mining shack? Let's go!'

Hardee caught his son up and raced for his own jeep, leaving the others to follow in Wakulla's.

The heat was murderous. Before they had gone a hundred yards, the radiator needle was climbing; in a hundred more, it was pressing perilously against the backstop. But Hardee couldn't wait to baby the motor now, not when the plane had begun to wheel around towards them. Already it might be too late; it was quite possible that the plane had spotted them. But it was at least a chance that the plane had not. A desert drenched in a vertical sun is not easy to scan, and there was a lot of it.

Next to him, on the seat, the little boy looked up wonderingly at his father, and was silent.

'It's all right, Chucky,' Hardee said, the automatic lie coming to his lips. It *wasn't* all right. There was nothing all right. There was nothing all right about it.

But it satisfied the boy. He squirmed around and knelt backward on the seat, peering out the rear mirror. 'They're catching up, Daddy!' he yelped cheerfully. 'Step on it! We'll beat them!'

Even through heat and worry and overpowering weariness, Hardee had enough left to feel fondness and pride for his child.

At the abandoned old mine site, Hardee spun the jeep in towards the shed. He parked it under the overhang of the dangling board sign marked *Joe's Last Chance No. 1,* crowding over as far as he could to make room for the other. In a moment, Wakulla drove up beside him and squeezed in.

Climbing out, they stared at the hostile bright sky. 'Stay under the shed!' Hardee said. 'If they've seen us –'

But apparently the plane had not.

They could see it clearly, dropping down over the dunes. It picked out Hardee's prefab, banked and swung around it twice; then levelled off, headed out across the desert, banked again, came in and landed bruisingly on the uneven sand.

It was a rotten landing, but as good as could be expected for drifted sand. A tyre might have blown or a wheel collapsed, but did not. The plane was lucky and the hidden fugitives were not; they would not be saved by a crash that would destroy their pursuers.

The plane stopped perhaps a quarter of a mile from the prefab but well out of their sight. The motors died.

They waited.

'Now what?' demanded Wakulla angrily. He had been dragged away from a woman, and made to drive bouncingly across the hot sand with a hangover, and there was talk he hardly understood of danger that was never quite clear, and he was irritable.

Hardee climbed to the top of the old shed wordlessly. He stretched tall and peered towards his home.

'Can't see,' he called down to the others. 'I can't even see the house. I wonder what they're doing.'

'Come down,' said old man Tavares in a tired voice.

He sat on the sand with his back against the weathered boards, his eyes half closing, but not with drowsiness. The heat was very great, especially for a man near seventy, and especially for a man who had lived with outrageous fear for four years and now found his fears exploding in his face.

'Doing?' Tavares repeated wearily. 'I shall tell you what they are doing. They are searching.' His voice was hardly louder than a whisper, in the perfect quiet of the hot desert air. 'They see that your jeep is not there, but they search your house. They observe that you are not in it. It takes very little time to do this; there is not much to search.'

'Right,' said Hardee roughly, dropping to the sand beside him. 'Then what will they do next?'

Old man Tavares opened his eyes. He looked out across the sand. 'Then I think they will take off again in the plane and look all through the desert for you. They will figure to find you easily from the air. But –' He paused, thinking. 'Yes,' he said. 'It is not a good plane for the purpose and in any case they will want more, for they do not wish to miss you. So more will be summoned.'

'More planes?' repeated Joan. 'I never saw any other planes.'

'You will,' said Tavares sadly. 'In an hour, perhaps, or two hours, there will be many planes flying overhead. But in much less time than that, this one that is by Hardee's home will search for us.'

Out behind the shed was the blank headboard and the shallow grave where Hardee had buried the stranger. Tavares looked at it longingly.

'If he were alive,' he whispered, 'then perhaps we could learn something.'

'We could dig him up,' Wakulla rumbled.

The girl made a faint sound. 'In this heat? After nearly a week?'

Hardee shook his head. 'No, we won't dig him up. Not because of the heat – it's dry, Joan; he'll be half a mummy by now. But I put him there and I know what I buried. There's nothing on him but ragged shorts and a pair of shoes. Nothing that would tell us anything.' He gestured back towards the ringing hills. 'That's where his trail came from. I didn't follow it, and now the wind has wiped it out, but that's where it was.'

'No matter,' said Tavares with the calm of resignation. 'It is too late for any of those things.' He nodded towards where the plane had landed.

'You think they mean trouble?' Wakulla demanded.

'Think?' Tavares glanced at him opaquely, then once again out across the hot, dry sand. 'I do not think. I know. Look.'

A flare of flame, almost invisible against the bright sky, fringed with bits of metal and sand and unidentifiable debris, leaped up over the dunes. Smoke followed.

'They are taking no chances,' said Tavares slowly. 'They looked for you, and when you were not to be found, they destroyed your home – perhaps you had hidden, you see. But now they will look some more.'

In a moment, the sound of the explosion reached them.

The boy began to cry.

5

The sky was full of aircraft, high-winged light planes that chopped the desert into sector strips and patrolled them, seeking, seeking; helicopters that darted from place to place.

'I never saw so many planes,' breathed Joan Bunnell, one arm around the boy. He was thrilled, so excited that he forgot to be afraid; he had never seen so many planes either, had hardly believed that so many planes existed.

All through the afternoon, they lay there in the waning heat, while the searching planes crisscrossed the sky. Wakulla looked angry, then puzzled, then contemptuous. He said: 'Stupid! Why don't they follow our tracks? If it was me up there, I'd find the jeeps in ten minutes!'

Tavares shrugged. He was very silent; he didn't want to talk, it seemed. Hardee and the others kept probing at him with questions, but he only shook his head. The heat was wearing. Even under the strain of the time, it lulled them, drugged them . . .

Hardee woke up, and it was a cold, bright night.

The sun had set.

Overhead, the stars washed across the sky. While he watched, one larger star – no, not a star; the second moon – soared in a great wide arc down towards the eastern horizon, steel-blue and familiar. Hardee squinted up wonderingly. If this was not Mars, then what was this lesser moon in the sky?

He woke the others.

The planes were gone and the desert was silent. They crept out and got into their jeeps and headed back towards the demolished prefab.

They stopped a couple of hundred yards away.

Still in the night, a faint red glow and ruddy smoke showed where part of the destroyed house still smouldered. Hardee caught his breath and touched Tavares on the shoulder.

'Look,' he whispered.

In the starlight, metal glinted. It was a wing of the old Ford tri-motor.

The plane was still there!

For an instant, panic filled them all. But there was no sound, only their own breathing and the metallic pinging from the smouldering ruin of the house.

The boy, silent and sleepy, stirred restlessly next to his father. 'My tractor,' he mumbled, and was silent. There was no toy tractor any more. There was no house. Only the smouldering metal and plastic were left.

Tavares said quaveringly: 'I think perhaps they could not get the plane off the ground. There were helicopters, and it may be that they took the crew off with them. It is bad sand here for a plane.'

'And maybe it's a trap!' rumbled Wakulla.

Tavares said softly: 'Yes. Maybe it is.'

Hardee said: 'We don't have any choice. Let's take a look.'

Cautiously they moved up with the jeeps. Hardee backed his near the open door in the washboard fuselage; Wakulla rolled to a stop a dozen yards away and turned his headlights on the plane. They climbed onto the hood of Hardee's jeep and peered inside.

Tinkling crystal bells whispered in their ears.

Under the lights from Wakulla's jeep, a metallic scurry of wavy jointed legs and of sliding, clicking bodies: the hold of the plane was full of skitterbugs.

Hardee took a deep breath.

'Come on,' he said. 'Let's look around.'

They clambered into the plane.

The skitterbugs clicked and pinged protestingly underfoot. Chuck dove for a pair of them and came up with them proudly.

'Daddy, can I keep them? I mean now that Alfie and Alice are gone?'

'Sure,' said Hardee gently, and set the boy out of the way. To Wakulla, he said: 'You come with me. If there's anybody left in the plane, they'll probably be up front, by the controls –'

Screech of metal, and a tinny crash.

The door slammed shut. Lights blazed on inside the plane. The elliptical door at the forward end of the ship opened and Griswold, his haunted eyes staring, peered out.

'There is,' he said. 'Welcome aboard, all of you.'

Hardee tensed to jump him, and felt Wakulla gathering his muscles beside him – but it was too late, too late! There was a choking sputtering roar from outside – another, and a third; the three engines were spinning, warming up. Griswold stepped back a second before their leap and the door slammed in their faces.

As Hardee and Wakulla piled up against the elliptical door that led to the pilot's cabin, the engines shrilled louder and louder. The vibrations evened, smoothed, were synchronized.

Then – crash, crash! Two thundering blows smote them. The plane was a croquet ball, and a mallet huger than Thor's slammed it forward – bump and bump – across the uneven sands. Through the one small window left unblocked, they could see the trail of exhaust flame from the engines; and then, beside that flame and below it, a huger, brighter torch – a JATO unit, hurling the tired old transport up and out and into the thin air.

The JATO rockets flared twenty yards of heaving flame and then they were dark, but by then their work was completely done.

The plane sagged for a second. Waddling in the thin cold air, it began lumpishly to climb and gain altitude.

They were trapped.

A while later, the elliptical door opened again briefly – long enough for Griswold, carrying a gun, to come back to join them.

He said heavily: 'I was afraid we would catch you.'

He stood regarding them. Queerly, he seemed more afraid than they. 'Don't try anything,' he told them, shouting over the racket of the motors. 'It's a waste of time. You see?'

And he held open the elliptical door for them to look. Through it they saw the bucket seats for pilot and co-pilot, and what was in those seats. And then the door was closed again, and Griswold was gone.

Hardee felt a sudden sharp convulsion in his stomach. He heard Wakulla swear and the girl cry out and knew that they had seen what he had seen: In the seats, clinging to a metal grid, a pair of skitterbugs.

And riding on them, like a jockey on a horse: Bright bronze death's heads with beady black eyes.

Wakulla rumbled: 'What – what the hell was *that*?'

'Martians?' whispered the girl. 'But, Dom, you said we weren't on Mars!'

Tavares shrugged. His face was quiet and resigned now; he had given up. 'I didn't say where we were,' he pointed out. 'Nor did I say what manner of creature might be with us.'

Hardee shook his head to clear it.

His arm was tight around the shoulders of the boy. Having him there was a help; it made it necessary for Hardee to think. He couldn't merely give up, for the boy's life was dependent on what he did now.

He tried to reason it out.

'We are not on Mars,' he said, testing the truth of the statement. 'You're sure of that, Dom?'

'Sure?' Tavares laughed. 'Can you lift three hundred pounds?' he asked queerly, his eyes watering. 'Do you see two tiny moons he asked queerly, his eyes watering. 'Do you see two tiny moons in the sky? No, not the big moon. That is too big, too bright; that might be Earth's moon, but not one of those of Mars!'

'There *are* two moons,' Joan said reasonably.

'No.' Tavares shook his head. 'A moon and a satellite. An orbiting spaceship. I believe. It is a hoax. We were never on Mars.'

'But what's the *purpose* of it?' demanded Hardee.

Tavares shook his head. 'Don't you think I've wondered, for five years? But I haven't been able to guess. All that I know is that they told us this was Mars, but it is not. Mars is a red star in the sky. I have seen it myself. This I know. I know nothing else.'

'And all these years you haven't said anything?' asked Hardee roughly.

'I have not. Why? For the reason that I did not dare, Hardee. Yes, I, Tavares, who was once a fighter in France, in the war that happened before you were born – I did not dare. You recall when you woke up, eh?'

'Woke up? You mean the first time, before I came to the colony?' Hardee nodded. 'I remember. I was in a room –'

'Yes,' said Tavares. 'That room. And you were asked many questions, were you not, like the rest of us?'

'I was. Crazy ones.'

'No, Hardee! Not crazy. They were for a purpose. Consider. You were asked what you knew about Mars – they said it was because you were being sent there, eh? And you told them, very truly, that you knew nothing. I do not know what would have happened if, by chance, you had been an astronomer, or perhaps a journalist, and had answered that question differently. But I know that you would never have come to the colony.'

Hardee, frowning, ground out: 'Go on!'

'And then they began to describe the planet Mars to you – to get you ready for your experience, they said. Right? They described it just as it turned out – in fine, *not like Mars itself!* And they watched you. And you showed no signs of doubting them.

'I know that this is so. For, at the time when I awoke, there was another with me, also awakened; and this one doubted, and let them see that he doubted. 'Mars has a light gravity,' he told them. 'And almost no air! And –' Oh, he went on and on.

'It was a mistake.'

'They took him away.'

Hardee said reasonably: 'But that doesn't prove anything, Tavares. There could have been some perfectly simple reason.'

'*I heard him scream!*' Tavares plunged his face into his hands, rocking slowly. 'And so all these years, I have said nothing, I have questioned nothing, for I did not dare. But now it is too late to be afraid. For that stranger you found, Hardee, he proved that all of this is a lie.

'And now the liars must come out into the open – at least for us here, who know of this lie. And the liars – we have seen them.'

He flung his arm out, pointing towards the elliptical door to the pilot's chamber – where they had seen the skitterbugs poised calmly on their metalic webs, with the bronze death's-head riders perched on their shining carapaces.

The flying antique thumped and pounded in strong air

currents. But it was not air-sickness that made them feel sick and faint.

The elliptical door opened. Griswold came back, carrying the gun. Behind him they caught another glimpse of the skitterbugs and their bronze inhuman riders.

Griswold closed the door and called: 'Sit down, all of you. We're coming down!'

'Thanks,' said Hardee shortly. 'I didn't expected this much consideration.'

Griswold measured him with the eyes of a man who knew demons. 'You blame me,' he said. 'Of course you do. What can I do about it?'

He motioned Hardee to the tiny window. 'Look down there,' he ordered. 'See that city? It's full of skitterbugs – hundreds of thousands of them! There's hardly a human being alive in it, though it used to be full of them. The skitterbugs have taken over!'

'Taken over?' Hardee echoed, puzzled. 'Then – are we –'

'On Earth, yes.' Griswold nodded. 'But it doesn't belong to the human race any more. You'll find out.' He stared at Hardee with pity and fright. 'You could have lived out your life in the colony,' he said sombrely, 'but you had to find that man. Now God knows what the bugs will do to you. But you'll never see the colony again.'

'And neither will you!' bawled an enormous voice behind them.

Griswold spun, trying to bring the gun up, but there was no time, and the shifting footing of crawling bugs beneath them tripped him, caught him off balance. Wakulla, grinning like a maddened gorilla, caught the old man with one square hand. The gun fell one way and Griswold fell the other – out cold.

'Come on!' shouted Wakulla, and dived for the gun. He stumbled knee deep through the crawling little monsters up towards the elliptical door. Hardee followed, almost without thought. They burst through the door –

Twin bronze creatures turned to regard them out of black and hollow eyes. They were small by human standards, built like huge metallic frogs, golden bronze, with tiny limbs and huge faces. They rode the skitterbugs, but they were not joined to them. One of them made a harsh metallic whistling sound and flopped off its mount, towards something that glittered on the floor – a weapon, perhaps.

Whatever it was, the bronze creature never reached it. Wakulla, bellowing madly, lunged into the cabin and brought his heavy foot down on the creature. There was a screech and a thin crackling sound; and that was the end of that one.

The other was getting into motion by now. But it never had a chance. Wakulla steadied himself, took aim and fired – again and again, pumping bullets at the thing, and though his aim was none too good, enough of them connected to splatter the creature against the control panels.

The ancient plane wobbled and begun to fall off on one wing.

'Hold on!' bawled Wakulla, and grabbed for the control wheel.

Hardee, panting, fought his way into the seat beside him. 'Can you fly one of these things?'

'I can try!' said Wakulla, grinning. Straight ahead of them, through the glass, Hardee could see a patchwork of trees and houses, roads and open land. 'I'll land it there!' Wakulla yelled, horsing the stick back.

They hit the ground hard at more than a hundred miles an hour, bounced, came down on one wheel, blew a tyre and slid crab-wise across an open meadow. If there were brakes, Wakulla didn't know where to find them; if there was a way to stop the plane before it reached the fence at the edge of the field, he didn't know it. It hit the brush fence, still going fast.

Hardee felt the windshield fly up and smack him in the face. The last thought he had was: *Fire.*

6

It was full morning; he had been unconscious for at least an hour.

Over against the trees, an enormous smoke plume showed where the tri-motor was giving up the ghost. Joan Bunnell was leaning over him, her cheek bloody, her clothing torn. 'Hardee, you're all right?' she breathed.

He pushed himself up. 'I guess so.' He looked around. 'Wakulla –?'

'His neck was broken.' The girl rocked back on her heels. Tavares was sitting on the damp grass nearby, cradling the boy in his lap. Beside him, Griswold lay face down, unmoving. 'The rest of us are all right,' Joan said. 'Griswold has a bad arm. That's all.'

Hardee shook his head and began to rub his ears. It felt like golf-tees driven into his eardrums; the old crate had come down fast and the change in pressure was bad. He could hardly hear what Joan was saying.

'Poor Wakulla,' she murmured. 'Maybe he saved our lives.'

'And maybe he killed us all,' said Griswold, painfully turning on one side to face them. His face was perspiring, and he clutched one arm with the other hand. 'They'll never let this go by,' he warned.

Hardee got up dizzily and strode over to the old man. 'Talk!' he said. 'What are the bugs? Where are they from?'

Griswold said wretchedly: 'I don't know. The bugs don't matter – it's the skulls that are important. They're smart. And they aren't from Earth.'

He sat up, holding his twisted arm. In the hot sunlight, the field they were in was alive with skitterbugs, flashing and leaping, loosed from the wrecked plane.

Griswold said: 'The bugs are only brainless machines. They are seeded and grow, and when they are large enough, the skulls harvest them. Sometimes they use human beings for the job of harvesting – like you.'

Hardee walked over to the burning plane. The heat kept him yards away. Wakulla was in there, probably hardly more than a cinder by now, but he couldn't be seen. Just as well, thought Hardee. A few skitterbugs, damaged in the crash, limped brokenly around on the grass, excited by the floods of radiant energy from the sun and the fire, but unable to move very fast.

And something else metallic lay in the grass.

Hardee bent for it; his head thundered, but he kept his balance and picked it up. It was the gun Wakulla had taken from Griswold. Hardee opened it, looked inside and swore.

Only one bullet left.

But it was better than nothing.

Back where the others were waiting, Tavares was relentlessly questioning Griswold. 'These creatures, you say they came from space, in that great ship that now orbits around the Earth?'

'Five years ago,' said Griswold, nodding. 'They have a ray –

I don't know how it works. But they sprayed the world with it, and every living thing went to sleep. Some are sleeping yet – those that haven't starved to death, though metabolism is slowed considerably.'

Hardee looked at Joan Bunnell and put his arm protectingly around the boy. 'Would that be October, 1959?' he asked.

'It would,' said Griswold heavily. 'You begin to understand, I see. That's what happened to all of you at the colony. You weren't criminals – except that, in the eyes of the skulls, it's a crime to be human at all.'

Not criminals! No forgotten crime to expiate! Hardee could scarcely believe it. But Griswold was still talking:

'They want our planet,' he explained. 'One shipload came, to get things ready, an advance party. I don't know when the rest of them will be here – but they're on their way. Perhaps a year or two. And they need to have the human race under control by then.'

He rubbed his arm and stared up at the sky. 'So some of us are helping them,' he said flatly. 'Call us traitors – we are! But what else is there to do? The skulls gave us a very simple alternative. Either we help them study us so that they can learn to rule the human race . . . or they go back out into their ship and spray the Earth with another ray. Not a sleep ray, but one that will wipe out all life entirely.'

Griswold spread his hands. 'It's a choice that isn't any choice,' he said. 'What else was there? So when they woke me – I was one of the first few hundred; now there must be tens of thousands – they learned, after we established communication, that I was a psychologist. It was exactly what they needed. They set me the problem of contriving an experimental colony – a test farm, if you like, where the human animal could be kept in conditions as close to natural as possible.

'It was their ship, orbiting out there, that made me think of Mars – it does look like a second moon. Luna was no real problem. A simple post-hypnotic command and none of you could focus on it enough to recognize the features. But I couldn't erase knowledge of Mars, if it existed in any of you. There is no invention, of course, that causes partial – and selective – amnesia in criminals. That was a lie to make you accept this plateau as a penal colony on Mars.'

'But what in hell *for*?' Hardee asked angrily.

'So nobody would try to escape. Thinking you were on Mars, you wouldn't hope to get to Earth. Knowing you were on Earth, you'd do anything to reach civilization — not realizing there wasn't any left. Skitterbugs wouldn't get harvested. Skulls would be killed. The colony would be trouble instead of useful — and it would then be wiped out.

'I wanted to keep as many people alive for as long as I could.' said Griswold. 'There was no other chance for humanity.'

'What do we do now?' Hardee grimly demanded.

Griswold hesitated. 'There are a few free humans,' he said reluctantly. 'Not many. They live in the woods in hiding, some of them in the cities themselves. Mostly they are ignored by the skulls — because there are so few. If there weren't, the skulls would take the easy way out. The Earth is their new home, you see, and they regard it as you would your house. You might tolerate a few vermin — but if there are too many, you'll call in the exterminators. But there are these few, and if we can somehow make our way to them, we might have a chance to —'

'Hush!' breathed Joan Bunnell.

She caught the boy to her, pointing. Out of the woods at the side of the field raced a posse of skitterbugs, each with its bronze death's-head rider.

Hardee tried to fight, though there were hundreds of the creatures. If Wakulla had not been so profligate with his bullets —

But he had been; and the single bullet in the gun was more frustrating than none at all.

'Too late,' groaned Griswold, his tortured face sagging with fear. 'Give up, Hardee! Otherwise they'll kill us right here!'

They were marched down a road and into the environs of a city, the skitterbugs with their bright bronze riders a disorderly rabble around them.

None of them recognized the city; it might have been anywhere. It was a silent city, a city of death. Even from the streets, they could see men and women who had been struck down in the middle of life. A mother with three children around her sprawled in a Laocöon down porch steps; a postman with his two-wheeled cart beside him, his letters long since blown away.

And there were living, waking humans too. Chuck shivered and caught his father's arm as they rounded a corner and saw a work gang – ten or twelve men, in rags of clothing, clearing rubble from a tumbled house that lay across a side street; they looked up as Hardee and the rest passed, but there was no emotion in their eyes, only weariness.

'Those others,' whispered Joan. 'Are they dead?'

'No,' said Tavares heavily, 'not if what Griswold tells us is true. But they might as well be. Unless –'

'Don't even think it!' begged Griswold. 'Some of the skulls can understand English!'

'Let them understand!' cried Hardee. He stopped and faced them. 'We'll fight you!' he shouted. 'You can't have our planet – not now or ever! The human race isn't going to be taken over by a bunch of bugs from another planet!'

Incuriously, the blank-eyed bronze skulls stared at him; almost as incuriously, the ragged men looked on.

The skulls prodded Hardee on, and the ragged men went back to their work.

The prisoners were taken to a big building that bore on it a sign, *Hotel Winchester*. Once it had been a commercial hotel; now it seemed to be headquarters for the skitterbugs and the skulls that rode them.

Without a word, they were put in a room on a gallery that overlooked the lobby. The floor of the lobby was a seething mass of skitterbugs with their riders – and some skulls which had found a different sort of mount, for they perched on the shoulders of ragged men.

The door was closed, and they were left alone.

It was a partly glass door; Hardee peered out. 'They must have come from a light-gravity planet,' he guessed. 'They move badly without the skitterbugs. They can't be very strong.'

'They don't need to be,' said Griswold sombrely. 'Not with their weapons.'

'What about at night?' asked Hardee. 'Surely the skitterbugs can't operate very well without light. Can't we –'

But Griswold was shaking his head. 'They keep all the areas of the city where they move about well lighted. No, Hardee. The skulls are way ahead of you.' He sat down and sighed. 'I think they'll kill us,' he said without emotion. 'It's either that or the labour gangs.'

Old man Tavares said something incandescent in Spanish. 'You may die, Griswold, but I'll fight. Look, why can we not get away? Soon it will be dark, as Hardee says, and it is then only a matter of getting away from the lighted areas. Why not?'

'Wait,' Hardee interrupted, staring out the glass of the door. 'Someone's coming.'

They crowded around.

Down the long gallery that surrounded the lobby, a tall man with angry eyes approached.

Hope surged – a human, and free!

But then they saw that on his shoulder rode one of the bronze skulls, motionless, the hollow eyes emptily staring.

'He is probably our executioner,' said Griswold, as though announcing the time of day.

'Not without a fight,' said Hardee tensely. 'Tavares, you stand over here. I'll wait on the other side. Joan, you take Chuck to the far side of the room. See if you can make the skull look at you! And Griswold –'

'It won't work,' said Griswold stubbornly, but he went with Joan and the boy.

The door opened.

As soon as the man and his rider were inside, Hardee lunged against the door, slammed it shut. 'Now!' he shouted, and leaped towards the pair.

The angry eyes of the man opened wide in astonishment. Hastily he stepped back. 'Wait!' he cried, stumbling –

And the bronze skull toppled from his shoulder.

It rolled across the room and lay motionless on the floor.

Hardee jumped for it as though it were a hand grenade, fallen back into his own rifle pit; but the new man with the angry eyes yelled: 'Don't waste your time! That one's dead – I killed it myself!'

Hardee stopped short, gaping.

The man grinned tightly. 'It keeps the others from bothering me,' he explained. 'Don't mess it up – we'll need it to get out of here. Come on!'

'Where?' asked Hardee, trying to take it in. It was hope, it was rescue – when they had expected it least.

'Down the end of the gallery,' said the man, 'there's a linen closet. In it is a laundry chute. It goes down to the cellar. The skulls don't go there much – the lights are bad; we keep them that way. And there are sewers and passages. If we reach the chute, we're safe.'

He opened the door, peered out. 'You go ahead, all of you. I'll follow, as though I'm taking you somewhere.' He closed the door and bent down to recover his skull. 'Mustn't forget Oscar,' he said. 'He's our passport.'

He opened a leather strap that passed around his neck and shoulder, bound it around the dead skull, buckled it again. Experimentally he bowed slightly from the waist. The skull wobbled but stayed on.

'Don't jar me,' he said, and crossed his fingers. He opened the door a crack, looked down the corridor and nodded.

'Let's go!' he said, and flung it wide.

The procession moved down the gallery. Dust was thick on the leather settees that lined it; the skulls had no need for them, and no human without a skull possessing it had passed that way in five years. There were skitterbugs with skulls upon them at the end of the gallery, but they didn't seem to notice anything. Down in the lobby, a few of the men with skull riders glanced up, but no one challenged.

It was twenty yards to the door of the linen closet.

Fifteen yards were easy.

Then, out of a ballroom that was now a pen for the human slaves of the skulls, two skitterbugs with skulls upon them came out. They paused and then one of them opened its queerly articulated transverse mouth and made a sound, a chanting metallic whine – speaking to the skull on the shoulder of their rescuer.

Hardee caught Joan's arm, took a tighter grip on the hand of the boy by his side, lengthening his stride. So near! And then –

Quick as lightning, the skitterbug with the skull on it leaped forward and clutched at the legs of the man who was shepherding them.

He kicked it away. 'Run!' he yelled.

The skull on his shoulder fell free and bumped lifelessly away. Three more skulls, riding skitterbugs, popped out of the ballroom. Down on the lobby floor there was a stirring and a whining commotion.

'Run!' he yelled again, and shoved them powerfully forward to the linen closet.

They made the door, just in time. It was the size of a small room, and they all crammed inside.

Hardee slammed the door and held it. 'Jump! I'll stay here and keep them out.'

The boy cried out once, then was silent. He glanced at his father as Tavares and the other man lifted him into the chute; but he didn't say a word when they let go and he slid out of sight.

'Go ahead, Joan!' barked Hardee.

Restless scratchings outside told him the skitterbugs were there. Then he could feel the door pressing against him. He cursed the clever, economical designers of the building, who had known better than to put a lock on the inside of a linen closet. If there had been one, they could all escape. But since there was not –

Griswold glanced at the chute, looked at Hardee, and nervously tongued his dry lips.

Tavares was in the chute now; he waved, and dropped out of sight.

Griswold turned his back on the chute.

He walked over to Hardee. 'I've got a broken arm,' he said, 'and, you know, I'm not sure the free humans would welcome me. You go, Hardee.'

'But –'

'Go ahead!' Griswold thrust him away. There was more strength than Hardee had expected in the worn, injured body. 'I doubt I could make it anyway, with this arm – but I can hold *them* for a minute!'

Already the other man was gone; it was only Griswold and Hardee there, and the scratching and shoving were growing more insistent.

'All right,' said Hardee at last. 'Griswold –'

But he didn't know what it was, exactly, that he wanted to say; and besides, there was no time.

Griswold, sweat pouring into his eyes, chuckled faintly for the first time since Hardee had known him.

'Hurry!' he said, and looked embarrassed as he held up two fingers in a shaky V. But he looked embarrassed only for an instant. The fingers firmed into a spiky, humanly stubborn, defiant sign of victory. 'Save the children,' Griswold said. 'I couldn't get the skulls to let many into the colony – a waste, they told me, because kids can't work. Save the children!'

Hardee turned away – towards the laundry chute, and towards a new life.

Well, we moved in pretty promptly. This Van Pelt turned up at the Pentagon on a Thursday, and by the following Monday I had a task force of a hundred and thirty-five men with full supply bivouacked around the old man's establishment.

He didn't like it. I rather expected he wouldn't. He came storming out of the big house as the trucks came in. 'Get out of here! Go on, get out! This is a private property and you're trespassing. I won't have it, do you hear me? Get out!'

I stepped out of the jeep and gave him a soft salute. 'Colonel Windermere, sir. My orders are to establish a security cordon around your laboratories. Here you are, sir, your copy of the orders.'

He scowled and fussed and finally snatched the orders out of my hand. Well, they were signed by General Follansbee himself, so there wasn't much argument. I stood by politely, prepared to make matters as painless for him as I could. I don't hold with antagonizing civilians unnecessarily. But he evidently didn't want it to be painless. 'Van Pelt!' he bellowed. 'Why, that rotten, decrepit, back-stabbing monster of a –'

I listened attentively. He was very good. What he was saying, in essence, was that he felt his former associate, Van Pelt, had had no right to report to the Pentagon that there was potential military applicability in the Horn Effect. Of course, it was the trimmings with which he stated his case that made it so effective.

I finally interrupted him. 'Dr. Horn,' I said, 'the general asked me to give you his personal assurance that we will not in any way interfere with your work here. It is only a matter of security. I'm sure you'll understand the importance of security, sir.'

'Security! Now listen here, Lieutenant, I –'

'Colonel, sir. Lieutenant Colonel Windermere.'

'Colonel, General, Lieutenant, what the hell do I care? Listen to me! The Horn Effect is my personal property, not yours, not Van Pelt's, and not the government's. I was working in personality dissociation before you were born, and –'

'*Security, sir!*' I made it crackle. He looked at me pop-eyed and I nodded to my driver. 'He isn't cleared, Dr. Horn,' I explained. 'All right, O'Hare. You're dismissed.' Sergeant O'Hare saluted from behind the wheel and took off.

I said soothingly, 'Now, Dr. Horn, I want you to know that I'm here to help you. If there's anything you want, just ask; I'll get it. Even if you want to go into town, that can be arranged – of course, you'd better give us twenty-four hours notice so we can arrange a route and –'

He said briefly, 'Young man, go to the devil.' And he turned and stalked into the big house. I watched him, and I remember thinking that for a lean old goat of eighty or eighty-five he had a lot of spirit.

I went about my business, and Dr. Horn picked up the phone in his house and demanded the Pentagon, to complain about our being there. When he finally realized he was talking to our intercept monitor, and that no calls would go out on his line without authorization from me, he yelled up another storm.

But that wasn't going to get him anywhere, of course. Not when General Follansbee himself had signed the orders.

About oh-eight-hundred the next morning I ran a surprise fullscale inspection and simulated infiltration to keep the detachment on its toes. It all checked out perfectly. I had detailed Sergeant O'Hare to try to sneak in from the marshland south of the old man's place, and he was spotted fifty yards from the perimeter. When he reported to me he was covered with mud and shaking. 'Those trigger-happy ba – Those guards, sir, nearly blew my head off. If the officer of the day hadn't happened by I think they would have done it, only he recognized me.'

'All right, Sergeant.' I dismissed him and went in to breakfast. The wire-stringing detail had worked all night, and we were now surrounded with triple-strand electrified barbwire, with an outer line of barbwire chevaux-de-frise. There were guard-towers every fifty yards and at the corners, and a construction detail was clearing the brush for an additional twenty yards outside the wire. I thought briefly of bulldozing a jeep path in the cleared area for permanent rotating patrols, but it didn't really seem necessary.

I was rather hungry, and a little sleepy – that wire-stringing detail had made quite a lot of noise. But on the whole I was pleased, if a little irritable.

The O.D. phoned in for instructions while I was breakfasting; Van Pelt had arrived from town and the O.D. wouldn't let him in without my approval. I authorized it, and in a moment Van Pelt turned up in my private mess, looking simultaneously worried and jubilant. 'How'd he take it, Colonel?' he asked. 'Is he – I mean, is he sore?'

'Very.'

'Oh.' Van Pelt shook slightly, then shrugged. 'Well, you're here. I guess he won't try anything.' He looked hungrily at my buckwheat cakes and sausages. 'I, uh, I didn't get a chance to have breakfast on the way down –'

'Be my guest, Dr. Van Pelt.' I ordered another place set, and extra portions of everything. He ate it all, God knows how. Looking at him, you'd think he could march two hundred miles on the stored fat he already had. He wasn't much over five-six, perhaps five-seven, and I'd guess two hundred and eighty pounds at the least. He was about as unlike Dr. Horn as you could imagine. I wondered how they had got along, working together – but of course I knew the answer. They got along badly. Else Van Pelt never would have gone running to the Pentagon. I tried to keep an open mind about that, of course. I mean, General Follansbee thought it was important to national defence, and so on – But I couldn't help thinking how I would feel if some junior went over my head in that way. Of course, military discipline is one thing, and civilian affairs, as I understand it, are something else. But all the same . . .

Anyway, he had done it; and here we were. Not much like a fighting command for me. But orders are orders.

At fourteen hundred I paid a call on Dr. Horn.

He looked up as the clerk-typist corporal and I came in. He didn't say anything, just stood up and pointed to the door.

I said, 'Good afternoon, Dr. Horn. If this is an inconvenient time for you to make your daily progress report, just say the word. I'm here to help you, you know. Would from twelve to thirteen hundred hours every day be more satisfactory? Or in the morning? Or –'

'Every *day*?'

'That's right, sir. Perhaps you didn't notice Paragraph Eight of my orders. General Follansbee's orders were to –'

He interrupted me with an irrelevant comment on General Folansbee, but I pretended not to hear. Besides, he might have been right. I said, 'As a starter, sir, perhaps you'll be good enough to show us around the laboratories. I think that you'll find that Corporal McCabe will be able to take your words down at normal speed.'

'Take *what* words down?'

'Your progress report, sir. What you've accomplished in the past twenty-four hours. Only this time, of course, we'd better have a fill-in on everything to date.'

He roared: '*No.* I won't –'

I was prepared for that. I let him roar. When he was through roaring I put it to him very simply. I said, 'That's the way it's going to be.'

He stuttered and gagged. 'Why, you stinking little two-bit Army – Listen, what's the idea –'

He stopped and looked at me, frowning. I was glad that he stopped, since in the confidential section of my orders – the paragraphs I didn't show Dr. Horn, as he was not cleared for access to that material – there had been a paragraph which was relevant here. Van Pelt had told the General that Horn's health was not good. Apoplexy, I believe – perhaps cancer, I am not very familiar with medical terms. At any rate, Van Pelt, while being debriefed by the General's intelligence section, had reported that the old man might drop dead at any minute. Well, he looked it, when he was mad at least. I certainly didn't want him to drop dead before I had made a proper Situation Analysis, for which I needed his report.

Horn sat down. He said, with rusty craft: 'You're going to stick to what you say?'

'Yes, sir.'

'Then,' he said, with a pathetic, senile cunning, 'I suppose I must reconcile myself to the situation. Exactly what is it you want, Lieutenant?'

'The report, sir.'

He nodded briefly. 'Just so.'

Ah-ha, I thought – to myself, of course – this will prove interesting. Do you suppose he will try to win my confidence so that he can phone his congressman? Or merely get me to turn my back so he can clobber me over the head?

'Yes, yes, the report. Just so,' he said, staring thoughtfully at a machine of some kind – it rather resembled an SCR-784, the Mark XII model; the one that has something to do with radar, or radio, or something or other. I leave that sort of thing to the Signal Corpsmen, naturally. Anyway, it was something electrical. 'Just so,' he repeated. 'Well, Captain, I shall have to do as you wish. Observe,' he said, rising, 'My polycloid quasitron. As you see –'

There was a strangling noise from Corporal McCabe. I looked at him; he was in difficulties.

'Sir,' I interrupted the doctor, 'will you spell that, please?'

He chuckled, rather grimly. 'Just so. P-O-L-Y-C-L-O-I-D Q-U-A-S-I-T-R-O-N. Well, Lieutenant, you're familiar with the various potentiometric studies of the brain which – Perhaps I should begin farther back. The brain, you must realize, is essentially an electrical device. Potentiometer studies have shown –'

He went on. Every thirty to fifty seconds he glanced at me, and turned his head half to one side, and waited. And I said, 'I see,' and he said, 'Just so,' and he went on. Corporal McCabe was in acute distress, of course, but I rather enjoyed the exposition; it was restful. One learns to make these things restful, you see. One doesn't spend much time in staff meetings without learning a few lessons in survival tactics.

When he had entirely finished (McCabe was sobbing softly to himself), I summed it all up for him.

'In other words, sir, you've perfected a method of electronically killing a man without touching him.'

For some reason that rocked him.

He stared at me. 'Electronically,' he said after a moment. 'Killing. A man. Without. Touching. Him.'

'That's what I said, sir,' I agreed.

'Just so, just so.' He cleared his throat and took a deep breath. 'Lieutenant,' he said, 'will you tell me one thing? What in the sweet name of heaven did I say that gave you that particular stupid notion?'

I could hardly believe my ears. 'Why – why – That's what the General said, Dr. Horn! And he talked to Van Pelt, you realize.'

I wondered: Was that his little trick? Was he trying to pretend the weapon wouldn't work?

He raved for twenty-five seconds about Van Pelt. Then he checked himself and looked thoughtful again.

'No,' he said. 'No, it can't be Van Pelt. That idiot general of yours must be off his rocker.'

I said formally: 'Dr. Horn, do you state that your, ah –' I glanced at McCabe. He whispered the name. 'Your polycloid quasitron does not, through electronic means, remove a person's life at a distance?'

He scowled like a maniac. It was almost as if something were physically hurting him. With an effort he conceded: 'Oh – yes, yes, perhaps. Would you say a locomotive oxidizes coal into impure silicaceous aggregates? It does, you know – they call them ashes. Well, then you could say that's what the quasitron does.'

'Well, then!'

He said, still painfully: 'All right. Just so. Yes, I see what you mean. No doubt that explains why you're here – I had wondered, I confess. You feel this is a weapon.'

'Of course, sir.'

'Ah.'

He sat down and took out a fat, stickily black pipe and began to fill it. He said cheerfully: 'We understand each other then. My machine renders humans into corpses. A chipped flint will also do that – pithecanthropus discovered that quite independently some time ago – but no matter, that is the aspect which interests you. Very good.' He lit the pipe. 'I mention,' he added, puffing, 'that my quasitron does something no chipped flint can do. It removes that thing which possesses only a negative definition from the human body, that quantity, which we will term "x", which added to the body produces a man, subtracted from it leaves a corpse. You don't care about this.'

He had me going for a moment, I admit. I said briskly: 'Sir, I'm afraid I don't understand you.'

'You're bloody well told you don't understand me!' he howled. 'We're all corpses, don't you understand? Corpses inhabited by ghosts! And there's only one man in the world who can separate the two without destroying them, and that's me; and there's only one way in the world to do it, and that's with my quasitron! Lieutenant, you're a stupid, pig-headed man! I –'

Well, enough was enough.

'Good afternoon, sir,' I said politely, though I knew he couldn't hear what I said with his own voice drowning me out. I nodded to Corporal McCabe. He closed his notebook with a snap, jumped to open the door for me; and the two of us left.

There was no reason to stay, do you see? I already had all the material for my Situation Analysis.

All the same I got Van Pelt into my private quarters that evening; I wanted to see if I could make an assessment of the old man's sanity.

'He's perfectly sane, Colonel Windermere. Perfectly!' Van Pelt's jowls were shaking. 'He's dangerous – oh, yes. Very dangerous. Particularly dangerous to me – I mean, of course, if I hadn't had your promise of complete protection. Of course. But dangerous. I –'

He paused, glancing at the sideboard where the bowl of fruit (I always take fruit after the evening meal) still reposed. 'I –' He coughed. 'Colonel,' he said, 'I wonder if –'

'Help yourself,' I told him.

'Thank you, thank you! My, but that looks good! Honestly, Colonel Windermere, I feel that an apple is almost Nature's rarest treat. Well, pears, yes. I must say that pears –'

I said, 'Mr. Van Pelt, excuse me. I want the straight dope on Horn. What's this ghost business?'

He looked at me blankly, crunching. 'Ghost business?' He took another bite. Crunch, crunch. 'My goodness, Colonel –' crunch, crunch – 'Colonel Windermere, I don't know – Oh, the *ghost* business!' Crunch. 'Oh, that. Why, that's just Dr. Horn's way of putting it. You know his manner, of course. You see, there is a difference between a living man and a dead man, and that difference is what Dr. Horn whimsically terms a "ghost".' He chuckled, tossed the apple core into my wastebasket and took another. 'Call it life, plus intelligence, plus soul, if there is such a word in your lexicon, Colonel – Dr. Horn merely sums them up. And terms the total "ghost".'

I pressed him closely. 'This machine is a – a ghost conjurer?'

'No, no!' he cried, quite losing his temper. 'Colonel, don't permit yourself to be fooled, Dr. Horn is an arrogant, unprincipled man, but he is not an idiot! Forget the term ghost, since it distresses you. Think of – think of –'

He stared about wildly, shrugged. 'Think merely of the difference between being alive and being dead. It is that difference that Dr. Horn's machine works on! Life, intelligence – electrical phenomena, you understand? And Dr. Horn drains them from the body, stores them – can, if he wishes, replace them, or even put them in another body.' He nodded, beamed at me, bit into the second apple. Crunch, crunch, crunch.

Well, sir!

When I had got rid of him, I sat, trying to control my temper, for some time.

This strange old man had a machine that could take a mind right out of a body – yes, and put it in another body!

Confound them, why hadn't they said so instead of beating around the bush?

Naturally, I didn't believe it until I saw it – and then I saw it. The next morning, at my request, Dr. Horn put a hen and a cocker spaniel into what he called his polycloid quasitron, and exchanged them.

Then I believed. I saw the hen trying to wag its tail and the spaniel, whimpering, bruised, endeavouring to peck corn.

Corporal McCabe's eyes were popping out of his head. He started to write something, glanced at me, shook his head slowly and sat staring into space.

Well, time for him later. I said: 'You can do it. You can take a hen and put it into a cocker spaniel.'

He nodded, too stiff-necked to show his gratification. 'Just so, Lieutenant.'

'And – and you can do it with people, too?'

'Oh, indeed I can, Major. Indeed I can!' He scowled. 'These ridiculous laws,' he complained, 'governing the conduct of institutions! I've tried, I swear I've tried, to be permitted to conduct a simple exchange. A man dying of terminal cancer, you see, and a feeble-minded youth. Why not? Put the sound mind in the sound body, let the decayed parts rot together! But will they let me?'

I said, 'I see. Then you've never done it.'

'Never.' He looked at me, his old eyes gleaming. 'But now you're here, Lieutenant. A military man. Very brave, eh? All I've needed is a volunteer – that coward Van Pelt refused, my gardener refused, everyone has refused! But you –'

'Negative, sir!' I was shaking – confound the man's arrogance! 'I am not a lieutenant, I am a field grade officer! I don't imagine you appreciate the investment our service has in me!'

'But, Lieutenant, the importance –'

'No, no! Never!' The man's stupidity amazed me. Me, a lieutenant colonel! What would it do to my 201 file? What about my time in grade? The Pentagon would rock, literally rock! I said, trying to be calm: 'You don't understand military matters, Dr. Horn. I assure you, if there is a need for volunteers we will find them for you. Believe me, sir, we are here to help! Why, one of our enlisted men will be pleased – proud, sir! – to offer his services in this – Corporal McCabe! Come back here!' But it was too late. Moaning, he had fled the room.

I turned to Dr. Horn, a little embarrassed. 'Well, sir, we understand these things – a shock to the boy, of course. But I'll find you a volunteer. Trust me.'

The man was as pleased as a fourth-year cadet in June Week, but he still wouldn't show it. Stiffly he said: 'Just so, Lieutenant – Major, I mean. Or Captain. Tomorrow will do splendidly.'

Tomorrow! Oh, that wonderful day! For I saw Dr. Horn do just as he had promised ... and I, I alone among them all, I saw what it meant. A weapon? Nonsense, it was much, much more than that!

There was the matter of finding volunteers. Trust me for that, as I had told Dr. Horn. There was the latrine orderly in Able Company – AWOL, he was; and when I explained to him what a court-martial would do, he volunteered with blinding speed. Didn't even ask what he was volunteering for. We needed two; my executive officer, I am proud to say, volunteered to be the second. A courageous man, typical of the very best leadership type.

We arrived in Dr. Horn's laboratory; the men were strapped in place and anesthetized – at my request; I wanted to maintain security, so naturally I couldn't let them know what was happening. Just before he went under the exec whispered, 'Sir – no Korea?'

'I promise, Captain,' I said solemnly, and before his eyes I ripped up the transfer recommendation I had written the night before. He went to sleep a happy man.

Biz, buzz, crackle – I don't understand these scientific things. But when the electric sparks had stopped flashing and the whiney, droney sounds had died away, Dr. Horn gave them each a shot of something, one at a time.

The latrine orderly opened his eyes. I stepped before him. 'Name, rank and serial number!'

'Sir,' he said crisply, 'Lefferts, Robert T., Captain, A.U.S., Serial Number 0–3339615!'

Good heavens! But I made sure, with a test question: 'Where is it you don't want to be transferred?'

'Why – why, Korea, sir. Please, sir! Not there! I'll volunteer for your test, I'll –'

I nodded to Dr. Horn, and another needle put him back to sleep.

Then – the body that was my exec. The body opened its eyes. 'Cunnel, suh! I changin' my mind. I'll take the guard-house, suh, only –'

'At ease!' I commanded, and nodded to Dr. Horn.

There was no doubt about it. 'You really did it.'

He nodded. 'Just so, Lieutenant. I really did.'

As he switched them back again, I began to realize what it all meant.

In my office I got on the phone. 'Crash priority!' I ordered. 'The Pentagon! General Follansbee, priority and classified; ask him to stand by for scrambler!'

I slapped the field phone into its case. A weapon? Oh, we had the world by the tail, a weapon was nothing by comparison. I confess I was floating on a cloud of pure joy. I saw my eagles within my grasp, perhaps in a year or less my first star – there was nothing the Army would deny the officer who could give them what I had to give!

A rattle and a crash, and Van Pelt thumped into my room, his face smeared, one hand clutching a melting chocolate bar. 'Colonel Windermere!' he gasped. 'You let Horn make his test! But that's all he's been waiting for! He –'

It was unbearable. 'O'Hare!' I roared. Sergeant O'Hare appeared, looking uncomfortable. 'How dare you let this man in here without my permission? Don't you realize I'm making a classified scrambler call to the *Pentagon*?'

O'Hare said weakly, 'Sir, he –'

'Get him out of here!'

'Yessir!' The fat little man kicked up a fuss, but O'Hare was much bigger than he. All the same, Van Pelt gave him a tussle. He was yelling something, all upset; but my call to the Pentagon came through, and I frankly didn't listen.

'General Follansbee here, sir. Please scramble!' I slapped the button that scrambled the call from my end. In a moment I heard the General's voice come through in clear; but anyone tapping in on the scrambled circuit would hear nothing but electronic garbage.

I gave him a quick, concise account of what I had seen. He was irritated at first – disappointed. As I thought he would be.

'Change them around, Windermere?' he complained in a high-pitched voice. 'Why, what's the use of changing them around? Do you see any strategic value in that? Might confuse them a little, I suppose – if we could get a couple of the enemy commanders. Good God, is that all there is to it? I was looking for something bigger, Windermere, something of more immediate tactical advantage. That Van Pelt must learn not to waste the time of high Army officers!'

'Sir,' I said. 'General Follansbee, may I point out something? Suppose – suppose, sir, that Khrushchev or someone should visit the States. Suppose, for instance, that we surrounded him, him and his whole entourage. Switched them all. Put our own men in their bodies, you see?'

'*What*?' He was thinking I was insane, you could· tell it. 'Colonel Windermere, what are you talking about?'

'It would work, sir,' I said persuasively. 'Believe me, I've seen it. But suppose we couldn't do that. What about a Polish U.N. envoy, eh? Get him, put one of G-2's operatives inside his body. Do you follow me, sir? No question about whose Intelligence would get the facts in a case like that, is there, sir? Or – maybe we wouldn't want to do anything like that in peacetime; but what about in war? Take a couple of their prisoners, sir, put our own men in their bodies. Exchange the prisoners!'

Well, I went on; and I won't say I convinced him of anything. But by the time he hung up, he was thinking pretty hard.

And I had an appointment to see him in the Pentagon the following day. Once I was on the spot, I knew I was in; for he wouldn't take the responsibility of passing up a thing like this alone, he'd call a staff meeting; and somewhere on the staff somebody would understand.

I could feel the stars on my shoulders already. . . .

'What is it, O'Hare?' I demanded.

I was becoming very irritated with the man; he was sticking his head in the door, looking very worried. Well, that was reasonable; I was quite close to giving him something to worry about.

'Sir – it's that Van Pelt.' He swallowed, and looked a little foolish. 'I – I don't know if he's nuts or what, sir, but he says. . . . He says that Dr. Horn wants to live forever! He says all Horn was waiting for was to make a test on a human being. I don't know what he's talking about, but he says that now that you've given Horn his test, sir, Horn's going to grab the first man he sees and, uh, steal his body. Does that make sense, sir?'

Did it make sense?

I shoved him out of the way, stopping only to grab my side-arm.

It made all the sense in the world. It was just what you'd expect of a man like Horn, he'd take an invention like this and use it to steal other people's bodies, to prolong his own worthless, nearly senile existence in a younger body!

And if that happened, what would become of my general's star?

Oh, I knew just the way Horn's mind would work. Steal a body; smash the machine; get away. Could we trace him? Impossible; there was no test in the world, no fingerprints, no eye-retina charts, no blood-type classifications that could distinguish John Smith from Horn inhabiting John Smith. It was the obvious thing to do; it had occurred to me at once.

Van Pelt had gone blundering in, conquering his cowardice. His objective was to try to stop Horn, I supposed, but what was the effect of his mad rush into the laboratory? Why, to furnish Horn with a body! And if one was not enough, there would be others; for there were the men of my own detachment, standing guard, going about their duties; it would not be impossible for Horn to lure one inside. He would not wait. No, for the chance that his own body would wear out on him in a moment, any moment, was very great – old, worn, and now subject to the pounding of a new hope and excitement, it might collapse like the bombed-out hulk of a barracks, at the lightest touch.

So I hurried – Into the building, through the long dark halls, into the room where the big polycloid quasitron stood –

And I was too late.

I tripped over a human body, stumbled, fell, the gun spinning out of my hand. I scrambled to my hands and knees, touching the body – still warm, but not very warm. Dr. Horn! His castoff cocoon, abandoned!

And before me capered and screeched the figure that once had been Van Pelt, holding a weapon. 'Too late!' he cried. 'Too late, Colonel Windermere!' Van Pelt! But it was not Van Pelt that lived in that fat soft corpse today, I knew; for the Horn-in-Van Pelt held a gun of his own in one hand, and in the other a bar of metal. And with it he was bashing, bashing the polycloid quasitron! Bam, and showers of sparks flew from it; crash, and it began to glow, sag, melt.

And he had the gun. It was a very difficult situation.

But not hopeless! For we were not alone.

Next to my fallen gun lay another body. Not dead, this one; unconscious. It was Corporal McCabe, struck down with a blow to the head.

But he was quivering slightly. Consciousness was not far away.

'Stop!' I cried strongly, getting to my knees. The Horn Van Pelt turned to stare at me. 'Stop, don't wreck the machine! More depends on it than you can possibly realize, Dr. Horn. It isn't only a matter of your life – trust me for that, Dr. Horn, I shall see that you have bodies, fine bodies, to hold your mind as long as you want it. But think of national defence! Think of the safety of our country! And think of your sacred duty to science!' I cried, thinking of my general's stars.

And Corporal McCabe twitched and stirred.

I stood up. Horn's carrier, Van Pelt, dropped his iron bar in alarm, switched the gun to his right hand, stared at me. Good! Better at me than at McCabe. I said: 'You must not destroy the machine, Dr. Horn! We need it.'

'But it is destroyed already,' the little fat figure said stupidly, gesturing. 'And I am not –'

Splat.

McCabe's bullet caught him at the base of the skull. The brain that had evicted Van Pelt to house a Horn now housed no one; the blubbery little figure was dead.

And I was raging!

'You fool, you idiot, you unutterable ass!' I screamed at McCabe. 'You killed him! Why did you kill him? Wing him, yes; injure him, break his leg, shoot the gun out of his hand. Any of those things, and still we could make him rebuild the machine! But now he's dead, and the machine is gone!'

And so, sadly, were my general's stars.

The Corporal was looking at me with a most peculiar expression.

I got hold of myself. A life's dream was gone, but there was no help for it now. Maybe the engineers could tinker and discover and rebuild – but, glancing at the wreck of the polycloid quasitron, I knew that was a dream.

I took a deep breath.

'All right, McCabe,' I said crisply. 'Report to your quarters. I'll talk to you later on. Right now I must phone the Pentagon and try to account for your blundering in this matter!'

McCabe patted the gun fondly, put it on the floor and turned to go.

'Just so, Lieutenant,' said Corporal McCabe.

Just ahead of us we saw a cluster of smoke trees suddenly quiver, though there wasn't a whisper of a breeze, and begin to emit their clouds of dense yellow vapour from their branch-tips.

'Let's get a move on, Will,' said Jack Demaree. His voice was thin and piercing, like the thin air all about us. 'It's going to get really hot here in the next twenty minutes.'

The steel and glass town of Niobe was in sight, a quarter mile ahead, 'Sure,' I said, and changed pace. We had been shambling along, as lazily as we could, in the effort-saving walk you learn in your first week on Mars. I stepped it up to the distance-devouring loose run that is only possible on a light-gravity planet like Mars.

It is tough to have to run in a thin atmosphere. Your lungs work too hard; you feel as though every step is going to be your last. Hillary and Tensing found no harder going on Everest than the friendliest spot on the surface of Mars – except, of course, that by day the temperature is high, and the light gravity lets you stand effort that would otherwise kill you. But we hadn't much choice but to run. The smoke trees had passed their critical point, and the curious gelatinous sulphur compounds that served them for sap had passed into gas with the heat. When that happened, it meant that the sun was nearly overhead; and with only Mars's thin blanket of air to shield you, you do not stay out in the open at high noon.

Not that we needed to see the smoke trees to know it was getting hot. A hundred and twenty in the shade it was, at least. If there had been any shade.

Demaree passed me with a spurt just as we reached the outskirts of Niobe, and I followed him into the pressure chamber of the General Mercantile office. We use helium in our synthetic atmosphere instead of Earth's nitrogen. So they gave us the pressure in one big ear-popping dose, without any danger of the bends we might have got from nitrogen. I swallowed and rubbed my ears; then we shed our sandcapes and respirators and walked into the anteroom.

Keever looked out of his private office, his lean horse face sagging with curiosity.

'Demaree and Wilson reporting,' I said. 'No sign of natives. No hostile action. No anything, in fact, except it's hot.'

Keever nodded and pulled his head back in. 'Make out a slip,' his voice floated out. 'And you go out again in two hours. Better eat.'

Demaree finished shaking the loose sand out of his cape into a refuse shaft and made a face. 'Two hours. Oh, lord.' But he followed me to the Company cafeteria without argument.

The first thing we both did was make a dash for the drinking fountain. I won, and sopped up my fill while Demaree's dry and covetous breath seared the back of my neck. Sand patrol can dehydrate a man to the point of shock in three hours; we had been out for four. You see why we were taking it easy?

We sat down in the little booth where we had put aside our card game with Bolt and Farragut a few hours before, and Marianna, without waiting for our order, brought coffee and sandwiches. Her eyes were hooded and unhappy; nerves, I thought, and tried to catch Demaree's eye. But it didn't work. He said in his customary slow and biting drawl, 'Why, Mary, you're getting stupider than ever. You took away our cards. I swear, girl, I don't know why the Company keeps you –'

He trailed off, as she looked straight at him, and then away.

'You won't need them,' she said after a moment. 'Farragut's patrol got it this morning.'

Farragut and Bolt, Cortland and VanCaster. Four good men, and it was the same old story. They were a four man patrol, ranging far beyond the defence perimeter of Niobe; they had got caught too far from town before it got really hot, and it was a choice between using their cached sand cars or getting stuck in the noonday sun. They had elected to try the sand car; and something bright and hot had come flashing over a sand dune and incinerated men and car alike.

The hell of it all was we never saw the Martians.

The earliest expeditions had reported that there wasn't any life on Mars at all, barring the tiny ratlike forms that haunted the sparse forests of the North. Then air reconnaissance had reported what turned out to be the Martians – creatures about the size of a man, more or less, that stood up like a man, that built villages of shacks like men. But air reconnaissance was severely limited by the thinness of Mars' air; helicopters and

winged aircraft simply did not work, except at speeds so high
that it was nearly impossible to make out details. It wasn't until
one of the orbiting mother spacecraft, after launching its space-
to-ground shuttle rockets and standing by for the return, spent
a dozen revolutions mapping Mars' surface that the first really
good look at Martians and their works was available. Really
good? Well, let's say as good as you could expect, considering the
mother ship was five hundred miles up.

It was easy enough to send a surface party to investigate the
Martian villages; but they were empty by the time Earthmen
got there. Our sand cars could move faster than a Martian afoot,
but it wasn't healthy to use a sand car. Somehow, what weapons
the Martians found to use against us (and nothing resembling a
weapon had ever been found in the deserted villages) seemed
most effective against machines. It was flatly impossible that they
should have electronic aimers to zero in on the radio-static from
the machines; but if it had been possible, it would have been
certain – for that was the effect.

I had plenty of time to think about all this as Demarée and I
ate our glum and silent meal. There just wasn't anything much
for us to say. Farragut and Bolt had been friends of ours.

Demarée sighed and put down his coffee. Without looking at
me he said, 'Maybe I ought to quit this job, Will.'

I didn't answer, and he let it go. I didn't think he meant it
but I knew how he felt.

General Mercantile was a good enough outfit to work for, and
its minerals franchise on Mars meant a terrific future for any
young fellow who got in on the ground floor. That's what everybody said, back on earth, and that's what kept us all there: the
brilliant future.

That – and the adventure of developing a whole new world.
Suppose those old Englishmen who went out for the Hudson
Bay Company and the East India Company and the other
Middle Ages monopolies must have had the same feeling.

And the same dangers. Except that they dealt with an enemy
they could see and understand; an enemy that, regardless of
skin colour or tongue, was human. And we were fighting
shadows.

I tasted my coffee, and it was terrible. 'Hey, Mary –' I started,
but I never finished.

The alarm klaxon squawked horrifyingly in the cafeteria; we

could hear it bellowing all over the GM building. We didn't wait
to ask questions; we jumped up and raced for the door, Demaree
colliding with me as we tried to beat each other through. He
clutched at me and looked at me blankly, then elbowed me aside.
Over his shoulder he said, 'Hey, Will – I don't *really* want to
quit. . . .'

The news was: Kelcy.

Kelcy was our nearest village, and the Martians had schlagged
it. Demaree and I were the first in the Ready Room, and Keever
snapped that much information at us while we were waiting the
few seconds for the rest of the patrols to come racing in. They
had been in other buildings and came leaping in still wearing
their sand capes; they had had to race across the blindingly hot
streets in the midday Martian glare. There were twelve of us
altogether – the whole station complement, less the four who
had been lost that morning. We were on the books as 'personnel
assistants'; but what we really were was guards, the entire
trouble-shooting force and peace-and-order officers for the town
of Niobe.

Keever repeated it for the others: 'They attacked Kelcy thirty
minutes ago. It was a hit-and-run raid; they fired on all but one
of the buildings, and every building was demolished. So far,
they report twenty-six survivors. There might be a couple more –
out in the open – that's all that are in the one building.' Out in
the open – that meant no other survivors at all; it was just past
high noon.

Big, fair-haired Tom van der Gelt unsteadily shredded the
plastic from a fresh pack of cigarettes and lit one. 'I had a
brother in Kelcy,' he remarked to no one.

'We don't have a list of survivors yet,' Keever said quickly.
'Maybe your brother's all right. But we'll find out before anybody else, because we're going to send a relief expedition.'

We all sat up at that. Relief expedition? But Kelcy was forty
miles away. We could never hope to walk it, or even run it, between the end of the hot-period and dark; and it made no sense
for us to be out in the open at the dusk sandstorm. But Keever
was saying:

'This is the first time they've attacked a town. I don't have to
tell you how serious it is. Niobe may be next. So – we're going to
go there, and get the survivors back here; and see if we can

find out anything from them. And because we won't have much time, we're going to travel by sand car.'

There was a thoroughgoing silence in that room for a moment after that, while the echoes of the words 'sand car' bounced around. Only the echoes made it sound like 'suicide'.

Keever coughed. 'It's a calculated risk,' he went on doggedly. 'I've gone over every skirmish report since the first landings, and never – well, almost never – have the Martians done more than hit and run. Now, it's true that once they hit a settlement the usual custom is to lay low for a while; and it's true that this is the first time they've come out against a town, and maybe they're changing their tactics. I won't try to tell you that this is safe. It isn't. But there's at least a chance that we'll get through – more of a chance, say, than the twenty-six survivors in Kelcy have if we don't try it.' He hesitated for a second. Then, slowly: 'I won't order any man to do it. But I'll call for volunteers. Anybody who wants to give it a try, front and centre.'

Nobody made a mad rush to get up there – it still sounded like suicide to all of us.

But nobody stayed behind. In under a minute, we were all standing huddled around Keever, listening to orders.

We had to wait another forty minutes – it took time for the maintenance crew to get the sand cars out of their hideaway, where they'd been silently standing, not even rusting in the dry Martian air, since the first Earthman drew the connection between sand cars and Martian attack. Besides, it was still hot; and even in the sand cars it would help for the sun to be a few degrees past the meridian.

There were fourteen of us in three cars – the patrols, Keever and Dr. Solveig. Solveig's the only doctor in Niobe, but Keever requisitioned him – we didn't know what we might find in Kelcy. Keever's car led the party; Demaree, Solveig and I were in the last, the smallest of the lot and the slowest.

Still, we clipped off fifteen miles of the forty-mile trip in eight minutes by the clock. The cats were flapping until I was sure they would fly off the drive wheels, but somehow they held on as we roared over the rolling sand. It sounded as though the car was coming to pieces at every bump – a worrisome sound but not, I think, the sound that any of us was really worrying about. *That* sound was the rushing, roaring thunder of a Martian missile leaping at us over a dune; and none of us expected to hear it more than once. . . ,

The way to Kelcy skirts what we call the 'Split Cliffs', which all of us regarded as a prime suspect for a Martian hangout. There had been expeditions into the Split Cliffs because of that suspicion; but most of them came back empty-handed, having found nothing but an incredible tangle. However, the ones that didn't come back empty-handed didn't come back at all; it was, as I say, a prime suspect. And so we watched it warily until it was almost out of sight behind us.

Martians or no, the Split Cliffs is a treacherous place, with nothing worth an Earthman's time inside. Before Mars's internal fires died completely, there were centuries of fierce earthquakes. The sections we called the Split Cliffs must have been right over a major fault. The place is cataclysmic; it looks as though some artist from the Crazy Years, Dali or Archipenko, had designed it, in a rage. Sharp upcroppings of naked, metallic rock; deep gashes with perfectly straight hundred-foot sides. And because there happens to be a certain amount of poisonously foul water deep underground there, the place is as heavily vegetated as any-thing on Mars. Some of the twisted trees reach as high as thirty feet above the ground – by Martian standards, huge!

Even Demaree, at the wheel of the sand car, kept glancing over his shoulder at the Split Cliffs until we were well past them. 'I can't help it,' he said half-apologetically to me, catching my eyes on him. 'Those lousy trees could hide anything.'

'Sure,' I said shortly. 'Watch what you're doing.' I wasn't in a mood for conversation – not only because of the circumstances, but because my nose was getting sore. Even in the car we wore respirators, on Keever's orders – I think he had an idea that a Martian attack might blow out our pressure before we could put them on. And three hours that morning, plus five hours each of the several days before, had left my nose pretty tender where the respirator plugs fit in.

Dr. Solveig said worriedly, 'I agree with William, please. You have come very close to the other cars many times. If we should hit –'

'We won't hit,' said Demaree. But he did concentrate on his driving; he maintained his forty metres behind the second car, following their lead as they sought the path of least ups-and-downs through the sand dunes towards Kelcy. It began to look,

I thought as I watched the reddish sand streaming by, as though Keever's 'calculated risk' was paying off. Certainly we had come nearly twenty miles without trouble, and past the worst spot on the trip, the Split Cliffs. If our luck held for ten minutes more –

It didn't.

'God almighty!' yelled Demaree, jolting me out of my thoughts. I looked where he was looking, just in time to see flame coursing flat along the ground. It snaked in a quivering course right at the middle sand car of our three; and when the snaking light and the jolting car intersected –

Catastrophe. Even in the thin air, the sound was like an atomic bomb. The spurt of flame leaped forty yards into the air.

We were out of the car in seconds, and the men from Keever's car joined us. But there was nothing to do for the seven men in the second car.

'They went after the biggest,' Keever said bitterly. 'Now –' He shrugged. One thing was sure, and he didn't have to say it. None of us wanted to be in a sand car with the motor going right there and then.

There was no sign of the enemy. Around us were empty sand dunes – but not empty, because out of them had come the missile. The only break was the fringe of the Split Cliffs behind us.

Keever methodically zipped up his sand cape and went through the routine of tucking in flaps at the neck and arms without speaking. None of us had anything to say either. Demaree, with a stronger stomach than mine, took another look inside the blackened frame of the second sand car, and came back looking as though his stomach wasn't so strong after all.

We scattered away from the parked sand cars and the wreck of the one that would never move again, and held a council of war. By Keever's watch, we had time to get to Kelcy or go back to Niobe – at a half trot in either case. We were exactly at midpoint between the two towns. No one even suggested using the sand cars again, though there wasn't a flicker of a threat from the dunes.

But we knew by experience how abruptly they could explode.

The decision was for Kelcy.

But the Martians took the decision out of our hands.

We trotted along for nearly an hour, on the move for twenty minutes, resting for five, and it began to look as if we'd make it to Kelcy without any more trouble – though, in truth, we had

had trouble enough; because it would be enough of a job to try to get ourselves back to Niobe without the strong probability of carrying injured survivors from Kelcy. The remorseless noonday deadline would apply the next day; and travel on Mars by night was nearly out of the question. It is a thin-aired planet, so the sun beats down fiercely; it is a thin-aired planet, so the heat is gone minutes after sundown. I suppose all of us were thinking those thoughts, though we hadn't the breath to speak them, when the Martians struck again, this time with something new. There was a golden glow from a sand dune ahead of us to the right, and one from a dune ahead of us to the left. Keever, in the lead, hesitated for a second; but he didn't hesitate enough. He plunged on, and when he and two of the others were between the two dunes, golden lightning flashed. It was like the spray of a fiery hose, from one dune top to the other; and where it passed, three man lay dead.

It wasn't fire; there wasn't a mark on the bodies; but they were dead. We instinctively all of us blasted the tops of the glowing dunes with our flame rifles, but of course it was a little late for that. Demaree and I broke for the dune to the right, rifles at the ready. We scrambled up the sides and spread out halfway up to circle it – it was slagged from our own rifles at the top, and certainly nothing could be alive up there. But nothing was alive behind it, either – nothing we could see. The sands were empty.

Demaree swore lividly all the way back to where the bodies of the three men lay. Dr. Solveig, bending over them, said sharply, 'That is enough, Demaree! Think what we must do!'

'But those filthy –'

'Demaree!' Solveig stood up straight and beckoned to the only other survivor – who had raced to explore the dune to the left, with the same results. He was a man named Garcia; he and I had come out together, but I didn't know him very well. 'Have you seen anything?' Solveig demanded.

Garcia said bitterly, 'More of that fire, Doc! From that hill I could see two or three others shining, down along the way to Kelcy.'

'I had thought so,' Solveig said sombrely. 'The Martians were of course aware of what we proposed. Kelcy is booby-trapped; we cannot expect to get there.'

'So where does that leave us?' demanded Demaree. 'We can't stay here! We can't even make it back to Niobe – we'll get caught

in the sandstorm. Maybe you'd like that, Doc – but I saw a man
after the sandstorm got him a year ago!' And so had I; patrolman like ourselves, who incautiously found himself out in the
middle of nowhere at dusk, when the twilight sandstorm rages
from East to West and no human can live for an hour, until the
gale passes and the tiny, lethal sand grains subside to the surface
of the planet-wide desert again. His own respirators had killed
him; the tiny whirl-pumps were clogged solid with sand grains
packed against the filters, and he had died of suffocation.

Solveig said, 'We go back. Believe me, it is the only way.'

'Back where? It's twenty-five miles to –'

'To Niobe, yes. But we shall not go that far. I have two proposals. One, the sand cars; at least inside them you will not
suffocate. Two – the Split cliffs.'

We all looked at him as though he had gone insane. But in
the end he talked us around – all but Garcia, who clung ob-
stinately to the cars.

We got back to the Split Cliffs, leaving Garcia huddled inside the first car with something of the feelings of the worship-
pers leaving Andromeda chained to the rock. Not that we were
much better off – but at least there were three of us.

Solveig had pointed out, persuasively, that inside the growth
of the Split Cliffs the sandstorm couldn't touch us; that there
were caves and tunnels where the three of us, huddled together,
might keep each other alive till morning. He admitted that the
probability that we would find Martians there before us was
high – but we *knew* the Martians had spotted the cars. And at
least inside the jungle-like Split Cliffs, they would be at as grave
a disadvantage as we; unless they could overpower us by num-
bers, we should be able to fight them off if they discovered us.
And even if they did outnumber us, we might be able to kill a
few – and on the sand dunes, as we had discovered, they would
strike and be gone.

Dr. Solveig, in the lead, hesitated and then slipped into the
dense yellowish vegetation. Demaree looked at me, and we followed.

There were no trails inside, nothing but a mad tangle of
twisty, feather-leaved vines. I heard dry vine-pods rattling ahead
as Solveig spearheaded our group, and in a moment we saw him
again.

The ground was covered with the fine red sand that overlies all of Mars, but it was only an inch or two deep. Beneath was raw rock, split and fissured with hairline cracks into which the water-seeking tendrils of the vegetation disappeared.

Demaree said softly, 'Dr. Solveig. Up ahead there, by the little yellow bush. Doesn't that look like a path?'

It wasn't much, just a few branches bent back and a couple broken off; a certain amount of extra bare rock showing where feet might have scuffed the surface sand off.

'Perhaps so,' said Solveig. 'Let us look.'

We bent under the long, sweeping branches of a smoke tree – too cool now to give off its misty yellow gases. We found ourselves looking down an almost straight lane, too straight to be natural.

'It is a path,' said Dr. Solveig. 'Ah, so. Let us investigate it.'

I started to follow him, but Demaree's hand was on my shoulder, his other hand pointing. I looked, off to one side, and saw nothing but the tangle of growth.

Solveig turned inquiringly. Demaree frowned. 'I thought I heard something.'

'Oh,' said Solveig, and unlimbered his flame rifle. All three of us stood frozen for a moment, listening and watching; but if there had been anything, it was quiet and invisible now.

Demaree said, 'Let me go first, Doc. I'm a little younger than you.' And faster on the draw, he meant. Solveig nodded.

'Of course.' He stepped aside, and Demaree moved silently along the trail, looking into the underbrush from side to side. Solveig waited a moment, then followed; and a few yards behind I brought up the rear. I could just see Demaree's body flickering between the gnarled tree trunks and vines up ahead. He hesitated, then stepped over something, a vine or dead tree, that lay snaked across the path. He half turned as if to gesture –

Snap!

The vine whipped up and twisted about his leg, clung and dragged him ten feet into the air, hanging head down, as a long straight tree beside the path snapped erect.

A deadfall – the oldest snare in the book!

'Jack!' I yelled, forgetting about being quiet – and half-forgetting, too, that I was on Mars. I leaped towards him, and blundered against the trees as my legs carried me farther than I thought. Solveig and I scrambled to him, rifles ready, staring around for a sight of whatever it was that had set the trap. But again – nothing.

Demaree wasn't hurt, just tangled and helpless. A flood of livid curses floated down from him as he got his wind back and began struggling against the vine loop around his legs. 'Take it easy!' I called. 'I'll get you down!' And while Solveig stood guard I scrambled up the tree and cut him loose. I tried to hold the vine but I slipped, and he plunged sprawling to the ground – still unhurt, but angry.

And the three of us stood there for a moment, waiting for the attack. And it didn't come.

For a moment the Martians had had us; while Demaree was in the tree and Solveig and I racing towards him, they could have cut us down. And they hadn't. They had set the trap – and passed up its fruits.

We looked at each other wonderingly.

We found a cave just off the trail, narrow and high, but the best protection in sight against the dusk sandstorm and the night's cold. The three of us huddled inside – and waited. Demaree suggested making a fire; but, although the wood on the ground was dry enough to burn even in Mars's thin air, we decided against it. Maybe, later on, if we couldn't stand the cold, we'd have no choice; but meanwhile there was no sense attracting attention.

We asked Solveig, who seemed to be in command of our party, if he thought there was any objection to talking, and he shrugged. 'How can one tell? Perhaps they hear, perhaps they do not. Air is thin and sounds do not carry far – to our ears. To Martian ears? I don't know.'

So we talked – not loud, and not much, because there wasn't, after all, much to say. We were preoccupied with the contradictions and puzzlements the Martians presented. Fantastic weapons that struck from nowhere or shimmered into being between sand dunes – and a culture little beyond the neolithic. Even Earth's best guided missiles could have been no more accurate and little more deadly, considering the nature of the target, than the one that obliterated car number two. And the golden glow that killed Keever was out of our experience altogether. And yet – villages of sticks! There had been no trace in any Martian dwelling of anything so complicated as a flame-rifle, much less these others. . . .

It grew very slightly darker, bit by bit; and then it was black. Even in our cave we could hear the screaming of the twilight wind. We were in a little slit in the raw rock, halfway down one of the crevasses that gave the Split Cliffs area its name. Craggy, tumbled, bare rocks a hundred feet below us, and the other wall of the crevasse barely jumping distance away. We had come to it along an irregular sloping ledge, and to reach us at all the wind had to pass through a series of natural baffles. And even so, we saw the scant shrubbery at the cave mouth whipped and scoured by the dusk-wind.

Demaree shivered and attempted to light a cigarette. On the fourth try he got it burning, but it went out almost at once – it is possible to smoke in Mars's air, but not easy, because of the pressure. The tobacco burns poorly, and tastes worse. He grunted, 'Damn the stuff. You think we'll be all right here?'

'From the wind?' asked Solveig. 'Oh, certainly. You have seen how little sand was carried in here. It is the cold that follows that I am thinking of . . .'

We could feel the cold settling in the air, even while the twilight wind was blowing. In half an hour the wind was gone, but the cold remained, deeper and more intense than anything I had ever felt before. Our sand capes were a help, almost thermally non-conducting in either direction; we carefully tucked under all the vents designed to let perspiration escape, we folded them around us meticulously, we kept close together – and still the cold was almost unbearable. And it would grow steadily worse for hours. . . .

'We'll have to build a fire,' said Solveig reluctantly. 'Come and gather wood.' The three of us went scouring up the ledge for what we could find. We had to go all the way back to the top of the crevasse to find enough to bother carrying; we brought it back, and while Demaree and I worked to set it afire Solveig went back for more. It wasn't easy, trying to make that thin and brittle stuff burn. Demaree's pocket lighter wore itself out without success. Then he swore and motioned me back, levelling his flame rifle at the sticks. *That* worked beautifully – every last stick was ablaze in the wash of fire from his gun. But the blast scattered them over yards, half of them going over the side of the ledge; and we charred our fingers and wore ourselves out picking up the burning brands and hurling them back into the little hollow where we'd started the fire. We dumped the remaining armload on the little blaze, and watched it grow. It helped – helped very much. It was all radiant heat, and our backs were freezing while we toasted in front; but it helped. Then Demaree had an idea, and he slipped a cartridge out of his rifle and stripped it. The combustible material inside came in a little powder, safe enough to handle as long as no spark touched it. He tossed the detonator cap in the fire, where it exploded with a tiny snap and puff of flame, and carefully measured out the powder from the cartridge in little mounds, only a few grams in each, wrapping each one in a twist of dried vine-leaves.

'In case it goes out,' he explained. 'If there's any life in the embers at all, it'll set one of these off, and we won't have to blow up the whole bed of ashes to get it started again.'

'Fine,' I said. 'Now we'd better build up a woodpile –'

We looked at each other, suddenly brought back to reality.

Astonishing how the mind can put aside what it does not wish to consider; amazing how we could have forgotten what we didn't want to know. Our woodpile reminded us both: Dr. Solveig had gone for more, nearly three quarters of an hour before.

And it was only a five-minute climb to the top of the crevasse.

The answer was obvious: The Martians. But, of course, we had to prove it for ourselves.

And prove it we did: at the expense of our weapons, our safe cave and fire, and very nearly our lives. We went plunging up the ledge like twin whirligigs, bouncing in the light Martian gravity and nearly tumbling into the chasm at every step. I suppose that if we thought at all, we were thinking that the more commotion we made the more likely we were to scare the Martians off before they killed Dr. Solveig. We were yelling and kicking stones into the gorge with a bounce and clatter; and we were up at the top of the crevasse in a matter of seconds, up at the top – and smack into a trap. For they were waiting for us up there, our first face-to-face Martians.

We could see them only as you might see ghosts in a sewer; the night was black, even the starlight half drowned by the branches overhead, but they seemed to gleam, phosphorescently, like decaying vegetation. And decay was a word that fitted the picture, for they looked like nothing so much as corpses. They had no hands or arms, but their faces were vaguely human – or so they seemed. What passed for ears were large and hung like a spaniel's; but there were eyes, sunken but bright, and there was a mouth; and they were human in size, human in the way they came threateningly towards us, carrying what must have been weapons.

Demaree's flame rifle flooded the woods with fire. He must have incinerated some of them, but the light was too blinding, we couldn't see. I fired close on the heels of Demaree's shot, and again the wood was swept with flame; and the two of us charged blindly into the dark. There was light now, from the blazes we had started, but the fires were Mars-fires, fitful and weak, and casting shadows that moved and disguised movement. We beat about the brush uselessly for a moment, then retreated and regrouped at the lip of the crevasse. And that was our mistake. 'What about Solveig?' Demaree demanded. 'Did you see anything –'

But he never got a chance to finish the sentence. On a higher cliff than ours there were scrabblings of motion, and boulders fell around us. We dodged back down the ledge, but we couldn't hope to get clear that way. Demaree bellowed:

'Come on, Will!' And he started up the ledge again; but the boulder shower doubled and redoubled. We had no choice. We trotted, gasping and frozen, back down to our cave, and ran in. And waited. It was not pleasant waiting; when the Martians showed up at the cave mouth, we were done. Because, you see, in our potshotting at the golden glow on the dunes and our starting a fire in the cave and salvoing the woods up above, we had been a little careless.

Our flame rifles were empty.

We kept warm and worried all of this night, and in the light from our dwindling fire, only a couple of branches at a time, we could see a figure across the crevasse from us.

It was doing something complex with objects we could not recognize. Demaree, over my objections, insisted we investigate; and so we parted with a hoarded brand. We threw the tiny piece of burning wood out across the crevasse, it struck over the figure in a shower of sparks and a pale blue flame, and in the momentary light we saw that it was, indeed, a Martian. But we still couldn't see what he was doing.

The dawn wind came, but the Martian stayed at his post; and then, at once, it was daylight.

We crept to the lip of the cave and looked out, not more than a dozen yards from the busy watching figure.

The Martian looked up once, staring whitely across the ravine at us, as a busy cobbler might glance up from his last. And just as unemotionally, the Martian returned to what he was doing. He had a curious complex construction of sticks and bits of stone, or so it seemed from our distance. He was carefully weaving bits of shiny matter into it in a regular pattern.

Demaree looked at me, licking his lips. 'Are you thinking what I'm thinking, Will?' he asked.

I nodded. It was a weapon of some sort; it couldn't be anything else. Perhaps it was a projector for the lightnings that blasted the sand cars or the golden glow that had struck down at us from the sand dunes, perhaps some even more deadly Martian device. But whatever it was it was at point-blank range; and when he was finished with it, we were dead.

Demaree said thinly, 'We've got to get out of here.'

The only question was, did we have enough time? We scrabbled together our flame rifles and packs from the back of the cave and, eyes fearfully on the busy Martian across the chasm, leaped for the cave mouth – just in time to see what seemed a procession coming down the other side. It was a scrambling, scratching tornado, and we couldn't at first tell if it was a horde of Martians or a sand car with the treads flapping. But then we got a better look.

And it was neither. It was Dr. Solveig.

The Martian across the way saw him as soon as we, and it brought that strange complex of bits and pieces slowly around to bear on him. 'Hey!' bellowed Demaree, and my yell was as loud as his. We had to warn Solveig of what he was running into – death and destruction.

But Solveig knew more than we. He came careening down the ledge across the crevasse, paused only long enough to glance at us and at the Martian, and then came on again.

'Rocks!' bellowed Demaree in my ear. 'Throw them!' And the two of us searched feverishly in the debris for rocks to hurl at the Martian, to spoil his aim.

We needn't have bothered. We could find nothing more deadly than pebbles, but we didn't need even them. The Martian made a careful, last-minute adjustment on his gadget, and poked it once, squeezed it twice and pressed what was obviously its trigger.

And nothing happened. No spark, no flame, no shot. Solveig came casually down on the Martian, unharmed.

Demaree was astonished, and so was I; but the two of us together were hardly as astonished as the Martian. He flew at his gadget like a tailgunner clearing a breach jam over hostile interceptors. But that was as far as he got with it, because Solveig had reached him and in a methodical, almost a patronizing way he kicked the Martian's gadget to pieces and called over to us:

'Don't worry, boys. They won't hurt us here. Let's get back up on top.'

It was a long walk back to Niobe, especially with the cumbersome gadgetry Solveig had found – a thing the size of a large machine gun, structurally like the bits and pieces the Martian had put together, but made of metal and crystal instead of bits of rubble.

But we made it, all four of us – we had picked up Garcia at the stalled cars, swearing lividly in relief but otherwise all right. Solveig wouldn't tell us much. He was right, of course. The important thing was to get back to Niobe as soon as we could with his gimmick. Because the gimmick was the Martian weapon that zeroed in on sand cars, and the sooner our mechanics got it taken apart, the sooner we would know how to defend ourselves against it. We were breathless on the long run home, but we were exultant. And we had reason to be, because there was no doubt in any of our minds that a week after we turned the weapon over to the researchers we would be able to run sand cars safely across the Martian plains. (Actually it wasn't a week; it was less. The aiming mechanism was nothing so complex as radio, it was a self-aiming thermocouple, homing on high temperatures. We licked it by shielding the engines and trailing smoke-pots to draw fire.)

Overconfident? No – any Earthman, of course, could have worked out a variation which would have made the weapon useful again in an hour's leisurely thought. But Earthmen are flex-

ible. And the Martians were not. Because the Martians were not-
the Martians.

That is, they were not *the* Martians.

'Successors,' Solveig explained to all of us, back in Niobe.
'Heirs, if you like. But not the inventors. Compared with whoever built those machines, the Martians we've been up against
are nothing but animals – or children. Like children, they can
pull a trigger or strike a match. But they can't design a gun – or
even build one by copying another.'

Keever shook his long, lean head. 'And the original Martians?'

Solveig said, 'That's a separate question. Perhaps they're hiding out somewhere we haven't reached – underground or at the
poles. But they're master builders, whoever and wherever they
are.' He made a wry face. 'There I was,' he said, 'hiding out in a
cleft in the rock when the dawn wind came. I thought I'd
dodged the Martians, but they knew I was there. As soon as the
sun came up I saw them dragging that thing towards me.' He
jerked a thumb at the weapon, already being checked over by our
maintenance crews. 'I thought that was the end, especially when
they pulled the trigger.'

'And it didn't go off,' said Demaree.

'It *couldn't* go off! I wasn't a machine. So I took it away from
them – they aren't any stronger than kittens – and I went back
to look for you two. And there was that Martian waiting for
you. I guess he didn't have a real gun, so he was making one –
like a kid'll make a cowboy pistol out of two sticks and a nail.
Of course, it won't shoot. Neither did the Martians, as you will
note.'

We all sat back and relaxed. 'Well,' said Keever, 'that's our
task for this week. I guess you've shown us how to clean up
what the Earthside papers call the Martian Menace, Doc. Provided, of course, that we don't run across any of the grownup
Martians, or the real Martians, or whatever it was that designed
those things.'

Solveig grinned. 'They're either dead or hiding, Keever,' he
said. 'I wouldn't worry about them.'

And unfortunately, he didn't worry about them, and neither
did any of the rest of us.

Not for nearly five years. . . .

1 : Foraminifera 9

Paptaste udderly, semped sempsemp dezhavoo, qued schmerz –
Excuse me. I mean to say that it was like an endless diet of days,
boring, tedious. . .

No, it loses too much in the translation. Explete my reasons, I
say. Do my reasons matter? No, not to you, for you are troglo-
dytes, knowing nothing of causes, understanding only acts. Acts
and facts, I will give you acts and facts.

First you must know how I am called. My 'name' is Foraminifera 9-Hart Bailey's Beam, and I am of adequate age and
size. (If you doubt this, I am prepared to fight.) Once the –
the tediety of life, as you might say, had made itself clear to
me, there were, of course, only two alternatives. I do not like
to die, so that possibility was out, and the remaining alternative
was flight.

Naturally, the necessary machinery was available to me. I arro-
gated a small viewing machine and scanned the centuries of the
past in the hope that a sanctuary might reveal itself to my aching
eyes. Kwel tediety that was! Back, back I went through the
ages. Back to the Century of the Dog, back to the Age of the
Crippled Men. I found no time better than my own. Back and
back I peered, back as far as the Numbered Years. The Twenty-
Eighth Century was boredom unendurable, the Twenty-Sixth a
morass of dullness. Twenty-Fifth, Twenty-Fourth – wherever I
looked, tediety was what I found.

I snapped off the machine and considered. Put the problem
thus: Was there in all of the pages of history no age in which a
9-Hart Bailey's Beam might find adventure and excitement?
There had to be! It was not possible, I told myself, despairing,
that from the dawn of the dreaming primates until my own
time there was no era at all in which I could be – happy? Yes,
I suppose happiness is what I was looking for. But where was
it? In my viewer I had fifty centuries or more to look back upon.
And that was, I decreed, the trouble; I could spend my life
staring into the viewer and yet never discover the time that was
right for me. There were simply too many eras to choose from.

It was like an enormous library in which there must, there had to be, contained the one fact I was looking for – that, lacking an index, I might wear my life away and never find.

'Index!'

I said the word aloud! For, to be sure, it was the answer. I had the freedom of the Learning Lodge, and the index in the reading room could easily find for me just what I wanted.

Splendid, splendid! I almost felt cheerful. I quickly returned the viewer I had been using to the keeper, and received my deposit back. I hurried to the Learning Lodge and fed my specifications into the index as follows, that is to say: Find me a time in recent past where there is adventure and excitement, where there is a secret, colourful band of desperadoes with whom I can ally myself. I then added two specifications – second, that it should be before the time of the high radiation levels, and first that it should be after the discovery of anesthesia, in case of accident – and retired to a desk in the reading room to await results.

It took only a few moments, which I occupied in making a list of the gear I wished to take with me. Then there was a hiss and a crackle, and in the receiver of the desk a book appeared. I unzipped the case, took it out, and opened it to the pages marked on the attached reading tape.

I had found my wonderland of adventure!

Ah, hours and days of exciting preparation! What a round of packing and buying, what a filling out of forms and a stamping of visas, what an orgy of injections and inoculations and preventive therapy! Merely getting ready for the trip made my pulse race faster and my adrenalin balance rise to the very point of paranoia; it was like being given a new chance to live.

At last I was ready. I stepped into the transmission capsule, set the dials, unlocked the door, stepped out, collapsed the capsule and stored it away in my carry-all, and looked about at my new home.

Pyew! Kwel smell of staleness, of sourness, above all of coldness! It was a close matter then if I would be able to keep from a violent eructative stenosis; as you say, I closed my eyes and remembered warm violets for a moment, and then it was all right.

The coldness was not merely a smell, it was a physical fact.

There was a damp greyish substance underfoot which I recognized as snow, and in a hard-surfaced roadway there were a number of wheeled vehicles moving, which caused the liquefying snow to splash about me. I adjusted my coat controls for warmth and deflection, but that was the best I could do. The reek of stale decay remained. Then there were also the buildings, painfully almost vertical. I believe it would not have disturbed me if they had been truly vertical, but many of them were minutes of arc from a true perpendicular, all of them covered with a carbonaceous material which I instantly perceived was an inadvertent deposit from the air. It was a bad beginning!

However, I was not *bored*.

I made my way down the 'street', as you say, towards where a group of young men were walking towards me, five abreast. As I came near they looked at me with interest and kwel respect, conversing with each other in whispers.

I addressed them: 'Sirs, please direct me to the nearest recruiting office, as you call it, for the dread Camorra.'

They stopped and pressed about me, looking at me intently. They were handsomely, though crudely, dressed in coats of a striking orange colour and long trousers of an extremely dark material.

I decreed that I might not have made them understand me – it is always probable, it is understood, that a quicknik course in dialects of the past may not give one instant command of spoken communication in the field. I spoke again: 'I wish to encounter a representative of the Camorra, in other words the Black Hand, in other words the cruel and sinister Sicilian terrorists named the Mafia. Do you know where these can be found?'

One of them said, 'Nay. What's that jive?'

I puzzled over what he had said for a moment, but in the end decreed that his message was sensefree. As I was about to speak, however, he said suddenly: 'Let's rove, man.' And all five of them walked quickly away a few 'yards'. It was quite disappointing. I observed them conferring among themselves, glancing at me, and for a time proposed terminating the venture, for I then believed that it would be better to return 'home', as you say, in order to more adequately research the matter.

However, the five young men came towards me again. The one who had spoken before, who I now detected was somewhat taller and fatter than the others, spoke as follows: 'You're wanting the Mafia?' I agreed. He then said, 'Are you holding?'

He was inordinately hard to understand. I said, slowly and with patience, 'Keska that "holding" say?'

'Money, man. You going to slip us something to help you find these cats?'

'Certainly, money. I have a great quantity of money instantly available,' I rejoined him. This appeared to relieve his mind. There was a short pause, directly after which this first of the young men spoke:

'You're on, man. Yeah, come with us. What's to call you?' I queried this last statement, and he expanded: 'The name. What's the name?'

'You may call me Foraminifera 9,' I directed, since I wished to be incognito, as you put it, and we proceeded along the 'street'. All five of the young men indicated a desire to serve me, offering indeed to take my carry-all. I rejected this.

I looked about me with lively interest, as you may well believe. Kwel dirt, kwel dinginess, kwel cold! And yet there was a certain charm which I can determine no way of expressing in this language. Acts and facts, of course. I shall not attempt to capture the subjectivity which is the charm, only to transcribe the physical datum – perhaps even data, who knows? My companions, for example: They were in appearance overwrought, looking about them continually, stopping entirely and drawing me with them into the shelter of the 'door' when another man, this one wearing blue clothing and a visored hat, appeared. Yet they were clearly devoted to me, at that moment, since they had put aside their own projects in order to escort me to the Mafia.

Mafia! Fortunate that I had found them to lead me to the Mafia! For it had been clear in the historical work I had consulted that it was not ultimately easy to gain access to the Mafia. Indeed, so secret were they that I had detected no trace of their existence in other histories of the period. Had I relied only on the conventional works I might never have known of their great underground struggle against what you term society. It was only in the actual contemporary volume itself, the curiously titled U.S.A. Condential by one Lait and one Mortimer, that I had described that throughout the world this great revolutionary organization flexed its tentacles, the plexus within a short distance of where I now stood, battling courageously. With me to help

them, what heights might we not attain! Kwel dramatic delight!

My meditations were interrupted. 'Boomers!' asserted one of
my five escorts in a loud, frightened tone. 'Let's cut, man!' he
continued, leading me with them into another entrance. It appeared, as well as I could decree, that the cause of his ejaculative
outcry was the discovery of perhaps three, perhaps four, other
young men, in coats of the same shiny material as my escorts,
although a different colour, being blue.

We hastened along a lengthy chamber which was quite dark,
immediately after which the large, heavy one opened a way to a
serrated incline leading downwards. It was extremely dark, I
should say. There was also an extreme smell, quite like that of
the outer air, but enormously intensified; one would suspect
that there was an incomplete combustion of, perhaps, wood or
coal, as well as a certain quantity of general decay. At any rate,
we reached the bottom of the incline, and my escort behaved
quite badly. One of them said to the other four, in these words:
'Them jumpers follow us sure. Yeah, there's much trouble.
What's to prime this guy now and split?'

Instantly they fell upon me with violence. I had fortunately
become rather alarmed at their visible emotion of fear, and
already had taken from my carry-all a Stollgratz 16, so that I
quickly turned it on them. I started to replace the Stollgratz 16
as they fell to the floor, yet I realized that there might be an
aditional element of danger. Instead of putting the Stollgratz
16 in with the other trade goods which I had brought to assist
me in negotiating with the Mafia, I transferred it to my jacket.
It had become clear to me that the five young men of my escort
had intended to abduct and rob me, indeed had intended it all
along, perhaps having never intended to convoy me to the office
of the Mafia. And the other young men, those who wore the
blue jackets in place of the orange, were already descending the
incline towards me, quite rapidly.

'Stop!' I directed them. 'I shall not entrust myself to you
until you have given me evidence that you deserve such trust.'

They halted, regarding me and the Stollgratz 16. I detected
that one of them said to another: 'That cat's got a zip.' The
other denied this, saying:

'That no zip, man. Yeah, look at them Leopards. Say, you
bust them flunkies with that thing?'

I perceived his meaning quite quickly. 'You are "correct".' I rejoined. 'Are you associated in friendship with them flunkies?'

'Hell, no. Yeah, they're Leopards and we're Boomer Dukes. You cool them, you do us much good.' I received this information as indicating that the two socio-economic units were inimical, and unfortunately lapsed into an example of the Bivalent Error. Since p implied not-q, I sloppily assumed that not-q implied r (with, you understand, r being taken as the class of phenomena pertinently favourable to me). This was a very poor construction, and of course resulted in certain difficulties. Qued, after all. I stated:

'Them flunkies offered to conduct me to a recruiting office, as you say, of the Mafia, but instead tried to take from me the much money I am holding.' I then went on to describe to them my desire to attain contact with the said Mafia, meanwhile they descended further and grouped about me in the very little light, examining curiously the motionless figures of the Leopards.

They gave every evidence of wishing to help me, but of course if I had not forgotten that one cannot assume from the statements 'Not-Leopard implies Boomer Duke' and 'not-Leopard implies Foraminifera 9' that, qued, 'Boomer Duke implies Foraminifera 9' . . . if I had not forgotten this, I say, I should not have been 'deceived'. For in practice they were as little favourable to me as the Leopards. A certain member of their party reached a position behind me.

I quickly perceived that his intention was not favourable, and attempted to turn around in order to discharge at him with the Stollgratz 16, but he was very rapid. He had a metallic cylinder, and with it he struck my head, knocking 'me' unconscious.

2: Shield 8805

This candy store is called Chris's. There must be ten thousand like it in the city. A marble counter with perhaps five stools, a display case of cigars and a bigger one of candy, a few dozen girlie magazines hanging by clothes-pin-sort of things from wire ropes along one wall. It has a couple of very small glass-topped tables under the magazines. And a juke – I can't imagine a place like Chris's without a juke.

I had been sitting around Chris's for a couple of hours, and I was beginning to get edgy. The reason I was sitting around Chris's was not that I liked Cokes particularly, but that it was one of the hanging-out places of a juvenile gang called The Leopards, with whom I had been trying to work for nearly a year; and the reason I was becoming edgy was that I didn't see any of them there.

The boy behind the counter – he had the same first name as I, Walter in both cases, though my last name is Hutner and his is, I believe, something Puerto Rican – the boy behind the counter was dummying up, too. I tried to talk to him, on and off, when he wasn't busy. He wasn't busy most of the time; it was too cold for sodas. But he just didn't want to talk. Now, these kids love to talk. A lot of what they say doesn't make sense – either bullying, or bragging, or purposeless swearing – but talk is their normal state; when they quiet down it means trouble. For instance, if you ever find yourself walking down Thirty-fifth street and a couple of kids pass you, talking, you don't have to bother looking around; but if they stop talking turn quickly. You're about to be mugged. Not that Walt was a mugger – as far as I know; but that's the pattern of the enclave.

So his being quiet was a bad sign. It might mean that a rumble was brewing – and that meant that my work so far had been pretty nearly a failure. Even worse, it might mean that somehow the Leopards had discovered that I had at last passed my examinations and been appointed to the New York City Police Force as a rookie patrolman, Shield 8805.

Trying to work with these kids is hard enough at best. They don't like outsiders. But they particularly hate cops, and I had been trying for some weeks to decide how I could break the news to them.

The door opened. Hawk stood there. He didn't look at me, which was a bad sign. Hawk was one of the youngest in the Leopards, a skinny, very dark kid who had been reasonably friendly to me. He stood in the open door, with snow blowing in past him. 'Walt. Out here, man.'

It wasn't me he meant – they call me 'Champ', I suppose because I beat them all shooting eight-ball pool. Walt put down the comic he had been reading and walked out, also without looking at me. They closed the door.

Time passed. I saw them through the window, talking to each other, looking at me. It was something, all right. They were

scared. That's bad, because these kids are like wild animals; if
you scare them, they hit first, it's the only way they know to
defend themselves. But on the other hand, a rumble wouldn't
scare them – not where they would show it; and finding out
about the shield in my pocket wouldn't scare them either. They
hated cops, as I say; but cops were a part of their environment.
It was baffling.

Walt came back in, and Hawk walked rapidly away. Walt
went behind the counter, lit a cigarette, wiped at the marble
top, picked up his comic, put it down again and finally looked
at me. He said: 'Some punk busted Fayo and a couple of the
boys. It's real trouble.'

I didn't say anything.

He took a puff on his cigarette. 'They're chilled, Champ. Five
of them.'

'Chilled? Dead?' It sounded bad; there hadn't been a real
rumble in months, not with a killing. But he shook his head.

'Not dead. You're wanting to see, you go down Gomez's cellar. Yeah, they're all stiff but they're breathing. I be along soon
as the old man comes back in the store.'

He looked pretty sick. I left it at that and hurried down the
block to the tenement where the Gomez family lived, and then
I found out why.

They were sprawled on the filthy floor of the cellar like winos
in an alley. Fayo, who ran the gang; Jap; Baker; two others I
didn't know as well. They were breathing, as Walt had said, but
you just couldn't wake them up.

Hawk and his twin brother, Yogi, were there with them, looking scared. I couldn't blame them. The kids looked perfectly all
right, but it was obvious that they weren't. I bent down and
smelled, but there was no trace of liquor or anything else on their
breath.

I stood up. 'We'd better get a doctor.'

'Nay. You call the meat wagon, and a cop comes right with
it, man,' Yogi said, and his brother nodded.

I laid off that for a moment. 'What happened?'

Hawk said, 'You know that witch Gloria, goes with one of the
Boomer Dukes? She opened her big mouth to my girl. Yeah,
opened her mouth and much bad talk came out. Said Fayo
primed some jumper with a zip and the punk cooled him, and
then a couple of the Boomers moved in real cool. Now they

got the punk with the zip and much other stuff, real stuff.'

'What kind of stuff?'

Hawk looked worried. He finally admitted that he didn't know what kind of stuff, but it was something dangerous in the way of weapons. It had been the 'zip' that had knocked out the five Leopards.

I sent Hawk out to the drugstore for smelling salts and containers of hot black coffee – not that I knew what I was doing, of course, but they were dead set against calling an ambulance. And the boys didn't seem to be in any particular danger, only sleep.

However, even then I knew that this kind of trouble was something I couldn't handle alone. It was a tossup what to do – the smart thing was to call the precinct right then and there; but I couldn't help feeling that that would make the Leopards clam up hopelessly. The six months I had spent trying to work with them had not been too successful – a lot of other neighbourhood workers had made a lot more progress than I – but at least they were willing to talk to me; and they wouldn't talk to uniformed police.

Besides, as soon as I had been sworn in the day before, I had begun the practice of carrying my .38 at all times, as the regulations say. It was in my coat. There was no reason for me to feel I needed it. But I did. If there was any truth to the story of a 'zip' knocking out the boys – and I had all five of them right there for evidence – I had the unpleasant conviction that there was real trouble circulating around East Harlem that afternoon.

'Champ. They all waking up!'

I turned around, and Hawk was right. The five Leopards, all of a sudden, were stirring and opening their eyes. Maybe the smelling salts had something to do with it, but I think not.

We fed them some of the black coffee, still reasonably hot. They were scared. They were more scared than anything I had ever seen in those kids before. They could hardly talk at first, and when finally they came around enough to tell me what had happened I could hardly believe them. This man had been small and peculiar, and he had been looking for, of all things, the 'Mafia', which he had read about in history books – *old* history books.

Well, it didn't make sense, unless you were prepared to make a certain ridiculous assumption that I refused to make. Man from Mars? Nonsense. Or from the future? Equally ridiculous. . . .

Then the five Leopards, reviving, began to walk around. The cellar was dark and dirty and packed with the accumulation of generations in the way of old furniture and rat-inhabited mattresses and piles of newspapers; and it wasn't surprising that we hadn't noticed the little gleaming thing that had apparently rolled under an abandoned potbelly stove.

It was a most peculiar object.

Jap picked it up, squalled, dropped it and yelled for me.

I touched it cautiously, and it tingled. It wasn't painful, but it was an odd, unexpected feeling – perhaps you've come across the 'buzzers' that novelty stores sell which, concealed in the palm, give a sudden surprising tingle when the owner shakes hands with an unsuspecting friend. It was like that, like a mild electric shock. I picked it up and held it. It gleamed brightly, with a light of its own; it was round; it made a faint droning sound; I turned it over, and it spoke to me. It said in a friendly, feminine whisper: *Warning, this portatron attuned only to Bailey's Beam percepts. Remain quiescent until the Adjuster comes.*

That settled it.

Any time a lit-up cue ball talks to me, I refer the matter to higher authority. I decided on the spot that I was heading for the precinct house, no matter what the Leopards thought.

But when I turned and headed for the stairs, I couldn't move. My feet simply would not lift off the ground. evidently I was remaining quiescent.

I twisted, and stumbled, and fell in a heap; I yelled for help, but it didn't do any good. The Leopards couldn't move either.

We were stuck there in Gomez's cellar, as though we had been nailed to the filthy old floor.

3: Cow

When I see what this flunky has done to them Leopards I call him a cool cat right away. But then we jump him and he ain't so cool. Angel and Tiny grab him under the arms and I'm grabbing the stuff he's carrying. Yeah, we get out of there.

There's bulls on the street, so we cut through the back and

over the fences. Tiny don't like that. He tells me, 'Cow. What's to leave this cat here? He must weigh eighteen tons.' 'You're bringing him,' I tell him, so he shuts up. That's how it is in the Boomer Dukes. When Cow talks, them other flunkies shut up fast.

We get him in the loft over the R. and I. Social Club. Damn, but it's cold up there. I can hear the pool balls clicking down below so I pass the word to keep quiet. Then I give this guy the foot and pretty soon he wakes up.

As soon as I talk to him a little bit I figure we had luck riding with us when we see them Leopards. This cat's got real bad stuff. Yeah, I never hear of anything like it. But what it takes to make a fight he's got. I take my old pistol and give it to Tiny. Hell, it makes him happy and what's it cost me? Because what this cat's got makes that pistol look like something for babies.

First he don't want to talk. 'Stomp him,' I tell Angel, but he's scared. He says, 'Nay. This is a real weird cat, Cow. I'm for cutting out of here.'

'Stomp him,' I tell him again, pretty quiet, but he does it. He don't have to tell me this cat's weird, but when he gets the foot a couple of times he's willing to talk. Yeah, he talks real funny, but that don't matter to me. We take all the loot out of his bag and I make this cat tell me what it's to do. Damn, I don't know what he's talking about one time out of six, but I know enough. Even Tiny catches on after a while, because I see him put down that funky old pistol I gave him that he's been loving up.

I'm feeling pretty good. I wish a couple of them chicken Leopards would turn up so I could show them what they missed out on. Yeah, I'll take on them and the Black Dogs and all the cops in the world all at once, that's how good I'm feeling. I feel so good that I don't even like it when Angel lets out a yell and comes up with a wad of loot. It's like I want to prime the U.S. Mint for chickenfeed, I don't want it to come so easy.

But money's on hand so I take it off Angel and count it. This cat was really loaded, there must be a thousand dollars here.

I take a handful of it and hand it over to Angel real cool. 'Get us some charge,' I tell him. 'There's much to do and I'm feeling ready for some charge to do it with.'

'How many sticks you want me to get?' he asked, holding on to that money like he never saw any before.

I tell him: 'Sticks? Nay. I'm for real stuff tonight. You find Four-Eye and get us some horse.' Yeah, he digs me then. He looks like he's pretty scared and I know he is, because this punk hasn't had anything bigger than reefers in his life. But I'm for busting a couple of caps of H, and what I do he's going to do. He takes off to find Four-Eye and the rest of us get busy on this cat with the funny artillery until he gets back.

It's like I'm a million miles down Dream Street. Hell, I don't want to wake up.

But the H is wearing off and I'm feeling mean. Damn, I'll stomp my mother if she talks big to me right then.

'I'm the first one on my feet and I'm looking for trouble. The whole place is full now. Angel must have passed the word to everybody in the Dukes, but I don't even remember them coming in. There's eight or ten cats laying around on the floor now, not even moving.

If I'm on my feet, they're all going to be on their feet, I start to give them the foot and they begin to move. Even the weirdie must've had some H. I'm guessing that somebody slipped him some to see what would happen, because he's off on Cloud Number Nine. Yeah, they're feeling real mean when they wake up, but I handle them cool. Even that little flunky Sailor starts to go up against me but I look at him cool and he chickens. Angel and Pete are real sick, with the shakes and the heaves, but I ain't waiting for them to feel good. 'Give me that loot,' I tell Tiny, and he hands over the stuff we took off the weirdie. I start to pass out the stuff.

'What's to do with this stuff?' Tiny asks me, looking at what I'm giving him.

I tell him, 'Point it and shoot it.' He isn't listening when the weirdie's telling me what the stuff is. He wants to know what it does, but I don't know that. I just tell him, 'Point it and shoot it, man.' I've sent one of the cats out for drinks and smokes and he's back by then, and we're all beginning to feel a little better, only still pretty mean. They begin to dig me.

'Yeah, it sounds like a rumble,' one of them says.

I gave him the nod, cool. 'You're calling it,' I tell him. 'There's much fighting tonight. The Boomer Dukes is taking on the world!'

4 : Sandy Van Pelt

The front office thought the radio car would give us a break in
spot news coverage, and I guessed as wrong as they did. I had
been covering City Hall long enough, and that's no place to
build a career – the Press Association is very tight there – not
much chance of getting any kind of exclusive story because of
the sharing agreements. So I put in for the radio car. It meant
taking the night shift, but I got it.

I suppose the front office got their money's worth, because
they played up every lousy auto smash the radio car covered as
though it were the story of the Second Coming of Christ, and
maybe it helped circulation. But I had been on it for four
months and, wouldn't you know it, there wasn't a decent murder or sewer explosion or running gun fight between six p.m.
and six a.m. any night I was on duty in those whole four months.
What made it worse, the kid they gave me as a photographer –
Sol Detweiler, his name was – couldn't drive worth a damn,
so I was stuck with chauffeuring us around.

We had just been out to LaGuardia to see if it was true that
a glamour doll was sneaking into town with Aly Kahn on a
night plane – it wasn't – and we were coming across the Tri-
borough Bridge, heading south towards the East River Drive,
when the office called. I pulled over and parked and answered
the radio-phone.

It was Harrison, the night City Editor. 'Listen, Sandy,
there's a gang fight in East Harlem. Where are you now?'

It didn't sound like much to me, I admit. 'There's always a
gang fight in East Harlem, Harrison. I'm cold and I'm on my
way down to Night Court, where there may or may not be a
story but at least I can get my feet warm.'

Where are you now?' Harrison wasn't fooling. I looked at
Sol, on the seat next to me; I thought I had heard him snicker.
He began to fiddle with his camera without looking at me. I
pushed the 'talk' button and told Harrison where I was. It
pleased him very much; I wasn't more than six blocks from
where this big rumble was going on, he told me, and he made it
very clear that I was to get on over there immediately.

I pulled away from the kerb, wondering why I had ever

wanted to be a newspaperman; I could have made five times as much money for half as much work in an ad agency. To make it worse, I heard Sol chuckle again. The reason he was so amused was that when we first teamed up I made the mistake of telling him what a hot reporter I was, and I had been visibly cooling off before his eyes for four straight months.

Believe me, I was at the very bottom of my career that night. For five cents cash I would have parked the car, thrown the keys in the East River and taken the first bus out of town. I was absolutely positive that the story would be a bust and all I would get out of it would be a bad cold from walking around in the snow.

And if that doesn't show you what a hot newspaperman I really am, nothing will.

Sol began to act interested as we reached the corner Harrison had told us to go to. 'That's Chris's,' he said, pointing at a little candy store. 'And that must be the pool hall where the Leopards hang out.'

'You know this place?'

He nodded. 'I know a man named Walter Hutner. He and I went to school together, until he dropped out, some weeks ago. He quit college to go to the Police Academy. He wanted to be a cop.'

I looked at him. 'You're going to college?'

'Sure, Mr. Van Pelt. Wally Hutner was a sociology major – I'm journalism – but we had a couple of classes together. He had a part-ime job with a neighbourhood council up here, acting as a sort of adult adviser for one of the gangs.'

'They need advice on how to be gangs?'

'No, that's not it, Mr. Van Pelt. The councils try to get their workers accepted enough to bring the kids in to the social centres, that's all. They try to get them off the streets. Wally was working with a bunch called the Leopards.'

I shut him up. 'Tell me about it later!' I stopped the car and rolled down a window, listening.

Yes, there was something going on all right. Not at the corner Harrison had mentioned – there wasn't a soul in sight in any direction. But I could hear what sounded like gunfire and yelling and, wow, even bombs going off! And it wasn't too far away. There were sirens, too – squad cars, no doubt.

'It's over that way!' Sol yelled, pointing. He looked as though he was having the time of his life, all keyed up and delighted. He didn't have to tell me where the noise was coming from, I could hear for myself. It sounded like D-Day at Normandy, and I didn't like the sound of it.

I made a quick decision and slammed on the brakes, then backed the car back the way we had come. Sol looked at me. 'What –'

'Local colour,' I explained quickly. 'This the place you were talking about? Chris's? Let's go in and see if we can find some of these hoodlums.'

'But, Mr. Van Pelt, all the pictures are over where the fight's going on!'

'Pictures, shmictures! Come on!' I got out in front of the candy store, and the only thing he could do was follow me.

Whatever they were doing, they were making God's own racket about it. Now that I looked a little more closely I could see that they must have come this way; the candy store's windows were broken, every other street light was smashed, and what had at first looked like a flight of steps in front of a tenement across the street wasn't anything of the kind – it was a pile of bricks and stone from the false-front cornice on the roof! How in the world they had managed to knock that down I had no idea; but it sort of convinced me that, after all, Harrison had been right about this being a *big* fight. Over where the noise was coming from there were queer flashing lights in the clouds overhead – reflecting exploding flares, I thought.

No, I didn't want to go over where the pictures were. I like living. If it had been a normal Harlem rumble with broken bottles and knives, or maybe even home-made zip guns, I might have taken a chance on it, but this was for real.

'Come on,' I yelled to Sol, and we pushed the door open to the candy store.

At first there didn't seem to be anyone in, but after we called a couple times a kid of about sixteen, coffee-coloured and scared looking, stuck his head up above the counter.

'You. What's going on here?' I demanded. He looked at me as if I was some kind of a two-headed monster. 'Come on, kid. Tell us what happened.'

'Excuse me, Mr. Van Pelt.' Sol cut in ahead of me and began talking to the kid in Spanish. It got a rise out of him; at least Sol got an answer. My Spanish is only a little bit better than my

Swahili so I missed what was going on, except for an occasional word. But Sol was getting it all. He reported: 'He knows Walt. That's what's bothering him. He says Walt and some of the Leopards are in a basement down the street, and there's something wrong with them. I can't exactly figure out what, but –'

'The hell with them. What about *that*?'

'You mean the fight? Oh, it's a big one all right, Mr. Van Pelt. It's a gang called the Boomer Dukes. They've got hold of some real guns somewhere – I can't exactly understand what kind of guns he means, but it sounds like something serious. He says they shot that parapet down across the street. Gosh, Mr. Van Pelt, you'd think it'd take a cannon for something like that. But it has something to do with Walt Hutner and the Leopards, too.'

I said enthusiastically, 'Very good, Sol. That's fine. Find out where that cellar is, and we'll go interview Hutner.'

'But Mr. Van Pelt, the pictures –'

'Sorry. I have to call the office.' I turned my back on him and headed for the car.

The noise was louder, and the flashes in the sky brighter – it looked as though they were moving this way. Well, I didn't have any money tied up in the car, so I wasn't worried about leaving it in the street. And somebody's cellar seemed like a very good place to be. I called the office and started to tell Harrison what we'd found out; but he stopped me short. 'Sandy, where've you been? I've been trying to call you for – Listen, we got a call from Fordham. They've detected radiation coming from the East Side – it's got to be what's going on up there! Radiation, do you hear me? That means atomic weapons! Now, you get th –'

Silence.

'Hello?' I cried, and then remembered to push the talk button. 'Hello? Harrison, you there?'

Silence. The two-way radio was dead.

I got out of the car, and maybe I understood what had happened to the radio and maybe I didn't. Anyway, there was something new shining in the sky. It hung below the clouds in parts, and I could see it through the bottom of the clouds in the middle; it was a silvery teacup upside down, a hemisphere over everything.

It hadn't been there two minutes before.

I heard firing coming closer and closer. Around a corner a
bunch of cops came, running, turning, firing, running, turning
and firing again. It was like the retreat from Caporetto in minia-
ture. And what was chasing them? In a minute I saw. Coming
around the corner was a kid with a lightning blue satin jacket
and two funny-looking guns in his hand; there was a silvery
aura around him, the same colour as the lights in the sky; and
I swear I saw those cops' guns hit him twenty times in twenty
seconds, but he didn't seem to notice.

Sol and the kid from the candy store were right beside me.
We took another look at the one-man army that was coming
down the street towards us, laughing and prancing and firing
those odd looking guns. And then the three of us got out of
there, heading for the cellar. Any cellar.

5: Priam's Maw

My occupation was 'short-order cook', as it is called, I practised
it in a locus entitled 'The White Heaven', established at Fifth
Avenue, Newyork, between 1949 and 1962 C.E. I had created
rapport with several of the aboriginals, who addressed me as
Bessie and presumed to approve the manner in which I heated
specimens of minced ruminant quadruped flesh (deceased, to be
sure). It was a satisfactory cover, although tiring.

Using approved techniques, I was compiling anthropometric
data while 'I' was, as they say, 'brewing coffee'. I deem the probability nearly conclusive that it was the double duty, plus the
datum that, as stated, 'I' was physically tired, which caused me
to overlook the first signal from my portatron. Indeed, I might
have overlooked the second as well except that the aboriginal
named Lester stated: 'Hey, Bessie. Ya got an alarm clock in ya
pocket-book?' He had related the annunciator signal of the portatron to the only significant datum in his own experience which
it resembled, the ringing of a bell.

I annotated his dossier to provide for his removal in case it
eventuated that he had made an undesirable intuit (this proved
unnecessary) and retired to the back of the 'store' with my carry-
all. On identifying myself to the portatron, I received information that it was attuned to a Bailey's Beam, identified as
Forminifera 9-Hart, who had refused treatment for systemic

weltschmerz and instead sought to relieve his boredom by adventuring into this era.

I thereupon compiled two recommendations which are attached: 2, a proposal for reprimand to the Keeper of the Learning Lodge for failure to properly annotate a volume entitled *U.S.A. Condential* and, 1, a proposal for reprimand to the Transport Executive, for permitting Bailey's Beam-class personnel access to temporal transport. Meanwhile, I left the 'store' by a rear exit and directed myself towards the locus of the transmitting portatron.

I had proximately left when I received an additional information, namely that developed weapons were being employed in the area towards which I was directing. This provoked that I abandon cover entirely. I went transparent and quickly examined all aboriginals within view to determine if any required removal, but none had observed this. I rose to perhaps seventy-five metres and sped at full atmospheric driving speed towards the source of the alarm. As I crossed a 'park' I detected the drive of another Adjuster whom I determined to be Alephplex Priam's Maw, that is, my father. He bespoke me as follows: 'Hurry, Besplex Priam's Maw. That crazy Foraminifera has been captured by aboriginals and they have taken his weapons away from him.' 'Weapons?' I inquired. 'Yes, weapons,' he stated, 'for Foraminifera 9-Hart brought with him more than forty-three kilograms of weapons, ranging up to and including electronic.'

I recorded this datum and we landed, went opaque in the shelter of a doorway and examined our percepts. 'Quarantine?' asked my father, and I had to agree. 'Quarantine,' I voted, and he opened his carry-all and set up a quarantine shield on the console. At once appeared the silvery quarantine dome, and the first step of our adjustment was completed. Now to isolate remove, replace.

Queried Alephplex; 'An Adjuster?' I observed the phenomenon to which he was referring. A young, dark aboriginal was coming towards us on the 'street', driving a group of police aboriginals before him. He was armed, it appeared, with a fission-throwing weapon in one hand and some sort of tranquillizer – I deem it to have been a Stollgratz 16 – in the other; moreover, he wore an invulnerability belt. The police aboriginals were attempting to strike him with missile weapons, which the belt deflected. I neutralized his shield, collapsed him and stored him in my carry-all. 'Not an Adjuster,' I asserted my father, but he had already perceived that this was so. I left him to neutralize and collapse the police aboriginals while I zeroed in on the portatron. I did not envy him his job with the police aboriginals, for many of them were 'dead', as they say.

The portatron developed to be in a 'cellar' and with it were some nine or eleven aboriginals which it had immobilized pending my arrival. One spoke to me thus: 'Young lady, please call the cops! We're stuck here and –' I did not wait to hear what he wished to say further, but neutralized and collapsed him with the other aboriginals. The portatron apologized for having caused me inconvenience, but of course it was not its fault so I did not neutralize it. Using it for d-f, I quickly located the culprit Foraminifera 9-Hart Bailey's Beam nearby. He spoke despairingly in the dialect of the locus, 'Besplex Priam's Maw, for God's sake get me out of this!' 'Out!' I spoke to him. 'You'll wish you never were "born", as they say!' I neutralized but did not collapse him, pending instructions from the Central Authority. The aboriginals who were with him, however, I did collapse.

Presently arrived Alephplex, along with four other Adjusters who had arrived before the quarantine shield made it not possible for anyone else to enter the disturbed area. Each one of us had had to abandon cover, so that this locus of Newyork 1939–1986 must require new Adjusters to replace us – a matter to be charged against the guilt of Foraminifera 9-Hart Bailey's Beam, I deem.

This concluded Steps 3 and 2 of our Adjustment, the removal and the isolation of the disturbed specimens. We are transmitting same disturbed specimens to you under separate cover herewith, in neutralized and collapsed state, for the manufacture of simulcra thereof. One regrets to say that they number three thousand eight hundred forty-six, comprising all aboriginals within the quarantined area who had first-hand knowledge of the anachronisms caused by Foraminifera's importation of contemporary weapons into this locus.

Alephplex and the four other Adjusters are at present reconstructing such physical damage as was caused by the use of said weapons. Simultaneously, while I am preparing this report, 'I' am maintaining the quarantine shield which cuts off this locus, both physically and temporally, from the remainder of its environment. I deem that if replacements for the attached aboriginals can be fabricated quickly enough, there will be no significant out side percept of the shield itself or of the happenings within it – that is, by maintaining a quasi-stasis of time while the repairs are being made, an outside aboriginal observer will see, at most, a mere flicker of silver in the sky. All Adjusters here present are working as rapidly as we can to make sure the shield can be withdrawn before so many outside aboriginals have observed it as to make it necessary to replace the entire city with simulacra. We do not wish a repetition of the California incident, after all.

Mooney looked out of his window, and the sky was white.

It was a sudden, bright, cold flare and it was gone again. It had no more features than a fog, at least not through the window that was showered with snow and patterned with spray from the windy sea.

Mooney blew on his hands and frowned at the window.

'Son of a gun,' he said, and thought for a moment about phoning the Coast Guard station. Of course, that meant going a quarter of a mile in the storm to reach the only other house nearby that was occupied; the Hansons had a phone that worked, but a quarter of a mile was a long way in the face of a December gale. And it was all dark out there now. Less than twenty miles across the bay was New York, but this Jersey shore coast was harsh as the face of the Moon.

Mooney decided it was none of his business.

He shook the kettle, holding it with an old dish towel because it was sizzling hot. It was nearly empty, so he filled it again and put it back on the stove. He had all four top burners and the oven going, which made the kitchen tolerably warm – as long as he wore the scarf and the heavy quilted jacket and kept his hands in his pockets. And there was plenty of tea.

Uncle Lester had left that much behind – plenty of tea, nearly a dozen boxes of assorted cookies and a few odds and ends of canned goods. And God's own quantity of sugar.

It wasn't exactly a balanced diet, but Mooney had lived on it for three weeks now – smoked turkey sausages for breakfast, and oatmeal cookies for lunch, and canned black olives for dinner. And always plenty of tea.

The wind screamed at him as he poured the dregs of his last cup of tea into the sink and spooned sugar into the cup for the next one. It was, he calculated, close to midnight. If the damn wind hadn't blown down the TV antenna, he could be watching the late movies now. It helped to pass the time; the last movie was off the air at two or three o'clock, and then he could go to bed and, with any luck, sleep till past noon.

And Uncle Lester had left a couple of decks of sticky,

child-handled cards behind him, too, when the family went back
to the city at the end of the summer. So what with four kinds of
solitaire, and solo bridge, and television, and a few more naps,
Mooney could get through to the next two or three a.m. again.
If only the wind hadn't blown down the antenna!

But as it was, all he could get on the cheap little set his uncle
had left behind was a faint grey herringbone pattern –

He straightened up with the kettle in his hand, listening.

It was almost as though somebody was knocking at the door.

'That's crazy,' Mooney said out loud after a moment. He
poured the water over the tea bag, tearing a little corner off the
paper tag on the end of the string to mark the fact that this was
the second cup he had made with the bag. He had found he
could get three cups out of a single bag, but even loaded with
sugar, the fourth cup was no longer very good. Still, he had
carefully saved all the used, dried-out bags against the difficult
future day when even the tea would be gone.

That was going to be one bad day for Howard Mooney.

Rap, tap. It really was someone at the door! Not knocking,
exactly, but either kicking at it or striking it with a stick.

Mooney pulled his jacket tight around him and walked out
into the frigid living room, not quite so frigid as his heart.

'Damn!' he said. 'Damn, damn!'

What Mooney knew for sure was that nothing good could be
coming in that door for him. It might be a policeman from
Sea Bright, wondering about the light in the house; it might be
a member of his uncle's family. It was even possible that one of
the stockholders who had put up the money for that unfortunate
venture into frozen-food club management had tracked him
down as far as the Jersey shore. It could be almost anything or
anybody, but it couldn't be good.

All the same, Mooney hadn't expected it to turn out to be
a tall lean man with angry pale eyes, wearing a silvery sort of
leotard.

'I come in,' said the angry man, and did.

Mooney slammed the door behind him. Too bad, but he
couldn't keep it open, even if it was conceding a sort of moral
right to enter to the stranger; he couldn't have all that cold air
coming in to dilute his little bubble of warmth.

'What the devil do you want?' Mooney demanded.

The angry man looked at him with an expression of revulsion. He pointed to the kitchen. 'It is warmer. In there?'

'I suppose so. What do –' But the stranger was already walking into the kitchen. Mooney scowled and started to follow, and stopped, and scowled even more. The stranger was leaving footprints behind him, or anyway some kind of marks that showed black on the faded summer rug. True, he was speckled with snow, but – that much snow? The man was drenched. It looked as though he had just come out of the ocean.

The stranger stood by the stove and glanced at Mooney warily. Mooney stood six feet, but this man was bigger. The silvery sort of thing he had on covered his legs as far as the feet, and he wore no shoes. It covered his body and his arms, and he had silvery gloves on his hands. It stopped at the neck, in a collar of what looked like pure silver, but could not have been because it gave with every breath the man took and every tensed muscle or tendon in his neck. His head was bare and his hair was black, cut very short.

He was carrying something flat and shiny by a moulded handle. If it had been made of pigskin, it would have resembled a junior executive's briefcase.

The man said explosively: 'You will help me.'

Mooney cleared his throat. 'Listen, I don't know what you want, but this is my house and –'

'You will help me,' the man said positively. 'I will pay you. Very well?'

He had a peculiar way of parting his sentences in the middle, but Mooney didn't care about that. He suddenly cared about one thing and that was the word 'pay'.

'What do you want me to do?'

The angry-eyed man ran his gloved hands across his head and sluiced drops of water onto the scuffed linoleum and the bedding of the cot Mooney had dragged into the kitchen. He said irritably: 'I am a wayfarer who needs a Guide? I will pay you for your assistance.'

The question that rose to Mooney's lips was 'How much?' but he fought it back. Instead, he asked, 'Where do you want to go?'

'One moment,' the stranger sat damply on the edge of Mooney's cot and, click-snap, the shiny sort of briefcase opened itself in his hands. He took out a flat round thing like a mirror and looked into it, squeezing it by the edges, and holding it this way and that.

Finally he said: 'I must go to Wednesday, the twenty-sixth of December, at –' He tilted the little round thing again. 'Brooklyn?' he finished triumphantly.

Mooney said, after a second: 'That's a funny way to put it.'

'Question?'

'I mean,' said Mooney, 'I know where Brooklyn is and I know *when* the twenty-sixth of December is – it's next week – but you have to admit that that's an odd way of putting it. I mean you don't *go* anywhere in time.'

The wet man turned his pale eyes on Mooney. 'Perhaps you are. Wrong?'

Mooney stared at his napping guest in a mood of wonder and fear and delight.

Time traveller! But it was hard to doubt the pale-eyed man. He had said he was from the future and he mentioned a date that made Mooney gasp. He had said: 'When you speak to me, you must know that my. Name? Is Harse.' And then he had curled up on the floor, surrounding his shiny briefcase like a mother cat around a kitten, and begun dozing alertly.

But not before he showed Mooney just what it was he proposed to pay him with.

Mooney sipped his cooling tea and forgot to shiver, though the draughts were fiercer and more biting than ever, now just before dawn. He was playing with what had looked at first like a string of steel ball-bearings, a child's necklace, half-inch spheres linked together in a strand a yard long.

Wampum! That was what Harse had called the spheres when he picked the string out of his little kit, and that was what they were.

Each ball bearing was hollow. Open them up and out come the treasures of the crown. Pop, and one of the spheres splits neatly in half, and out spills a star sapphire, as big as the ball of your finger, glittering like the muted lights of hell. Pop, and another sphere drops a ball of yellow gold into your palm. Pop for a narwhal's tooth, pop for a cube of sugar; pop, pop, and there on the table before Harse sparkled diamonds and lumps of coal, a packet of heroin, a sphere of silver, pearls, beads of glass, machined pellets of tungsten, lumps of saffron and lumps of salt.

'It is,' said Harse, 'for your. Pay? No, *no*!' And he headed off Mooney's greedy fingers.

Click, click, click, and the little pellets of treasure and trash were back in the steel balls.

'No, *no*!' said Harse again, grinning, snapping the balls together like poppets in a string. 'After you have guided me to Brooklyn and the December twenty-sixth. But I must say to you. This? That some of the balls contain plutonium and some radium. And I do not think that you can get them. Open? But if you did, you perhaps would die. Oh, Ho?' And, laughing, he began his taut nap.

Mooney swallowed the last of his icy tea. It was full daylight outside.

Very well, castaway, he said silently to the dozing pale-eyed man, I will guide you. Oh, there never was a guide like Mooney – not when a guide's fee can run so high. But when you are where you want to go, then we'll discuss the price . . .

A hacksaw, he schemed, and a Geiger counter. He had worn his fingers raw trying to find the little button or knob that Harse had used to open them. All right, he was licked there. But there were more ways than one to open a cat's eye.

A hacksaw. A Geiger counter. And, Mooney speculated drowsily, maybe a gun, if the pale-eyed man got tough.

Mooney fell asleep in joy and anticipation for the first time in more than a dozen years.

It was bright the next morning. Bright and very cold.

'Look alive!' Mooney said to the pale-eyed man, shivering. It had been a long walk from Uncle Lester's house to the bridge, in that ripping, shuddering wind that came in off the Atlantic.

Harse got up off his knees, from where he had been examining the asphalt pavement under the snow. He stood erect beside Mooney, while Mooney put on an egg-sucking smile and aimed his thumb down the road.

The station wagon he had spotted seemed to snarl and pick up speed as it whirled past them onto the bridge.

'I hope you skid into a ditch!' Mooney bawled into the icy air. He was in a fury. There was a bus line that went where they

wanted to go. A warm, comfortable bus that would stop for
them if they signalled, that would drop them just where they
wanted to be, to convert one of Harse's ball-bearings into money.
The gold one, Mooney planned. Not the diamond, not the pearl.
Just a few dollars was all they wanted, in this Jersey shore area
where the towns were small and the gossip big. Just the price of
fare into New York, where they could make their way to Tif-
fany's.

But the bus cost thirty-five cents apiece. Total seventy cents.
Which they didn't have.

'Here comes another. Car?'

Mooney dragged back the corners of his lips into another
smile and held out his thumb.

It was a panel truck, light blue, with the sides lettered: *Chris's
Delicatessen. Free Deliveries.* The driver slowed up, looked them
over and stopped. He leaned towards the right-hand window.

He called: 'I can take you far's Red Ba –'

He got a good look at Mooney's companion then and swallowed. Harse had put on an overcoat because Mooney insisted
on it and he wore a hat because Mooney had told him flatly
there would be trouble and questions if he didn't. But he hadn't
taken off his own silvery leotard, which peeped through between neck and hat and where the coat flapped open.

'– ank,' finished the driver thoughtfully.

Mooney didn't give him a chance to change his mind. 'Red
Bank is just where we want to go. Come on!' Already he had his
hand on the door. He jumped in, made room for Harse, reached
over him and slammed the door.

'Thank you very much,' he said chattily to the driver. 'Cold
morning, isn't it? And that was some storm last night. Say, we
really do appreciate this. Anywhere in Red Bank will be all right
to drop us, anywhere at all.'

He leaned forward slightly, just enough to keep the driver
from being able to get a really good look at his other passenger.

It would have gone all right, it really would, except that just
past Fair Haven, Harse suddenly announced: 'It is the time for
me to. Eat?'

He snip-snapped something around the edges of the gleaming
sort of dispatch case, which opened. Mooney, peering over his

shoulder, caught glimpses of shiny things and spinning things and things that seemed to glow. So did the driver.

'Hey,' he said, interested, 'what've you got there?'

'My business,' said Harse, calmly and crushingly.

The driver blinked. He opened his mouth, and then he shut it again, and his neck became rather red.

Mooney said rapidly: 'Say, isn't there – uh – isn't there a lot of snow?' He feigned fascination with the snow on the road, leaning forward until his face was nearly at the frosty windshield. 'My gosh, I've never seen the road so snowy!'

Beside him, Harse was methodically taking things out of other things. A little cylinder popped open and began to steam; he put it to his lips and drank. A cube the size of a fist opened up at one end and little pellets dropped out into a cup. Harse picked a couple up and began to chew them. A flat, round object the shape of a cafeteria pie flipped open and something grey and doughy appeared –

'Holy heaven!'

Mooney's face slammed into the windshield as the driver tramped on his brakes. Not that Mooney could really blame him. The smell from that doughy mass could hardly be believed; and what made it retchingly worse was that Harse was eating it with a pearly small spoon.

The driver said complainingly: 'Out! Out, you guys! I don't mind giving you a lift, but I've got hard rolls in the back of the truck and that smell's going to – Out! You heard me!'

'Oh,' said Harse, tasting happily. 'No.'

'*No?*' roared the driver. 'Now listen! I don't have to take any lip from hitchhikers! I don't have to –'

'One moment,' said Harse. 'Please.' Without hurry and without delay, beaming absently at the driver, he reached into the silvery case again. Snip, snippety-snap; a jointed metal thing wriggled and snicked into place. And Harse, still beaming, pointed it at the driver.

It was a good thing the truck was halted, because the whining blue light reached diffidently out and embraced the driver; and then there was no driver. There was nothing. He was gone, beyond the reach of any further lip from hitchhikers.

So there was Mooney, driving a stolen panel truck, Mooney the bankrupt, Mooney the ne'er-do-well, and now Mooney the accomplice murderer. Or so he thought, though the pale-eyed man had laughed like a panther when he'd asked.

He rehearsed little speeches all the way down U.S. One, Mooney did, and they all began: 'Your Honour, I didn't know –'

Well, he hadn't. How could a man like Mooney know that Harse was so bereft of human compassion as to snuff out a life for the sake of finishing his lunch in peace? And what could Mooney have done about it, without drawing the diffident blue glow to himself? No, Your Honour, really, Your Honour, he took me by surprise . . .

But by the time they ditched the stolen car, nearly dry of gas, at the Hoboken ferry, Mooney had begun to get his nerve back. In fact, he was beginning to perceive that in that glittering silvery dispatch case that Harse hugged to him were treasures that might do wonders for a smart man unjustly dogged by hard times. The wampum alone! But beyond the wampum, the other good things that might in time be worth more than any amount of mere money.

There was that weapon. Mooney cast a glance at Harse, blank-eyed and relaxed, very much disinterested in the crowds of commuters on the ferry.

Nobody in all that crowd would believe that Harse could pull out a little jointed metal thing and push a button and make any one of them cease to exist. Nobody would believe it – not even a jury. Corpus delicti, body of evidence – why, there would *be* no evidence! It was a simple, workable, foolproof way of getting any desired number of people out of the way without fuss, muss or bother – and couldn't a smart but misfortunate man like Mooney do wonders by selectively removing those persons who stood as obstacles in his path?

And there would be more, much, much more. The thing to do, Mooney schemed, was to find out just what Harse had in that kit and how to work it; and then – who could know, perhaps Harse would himself find the diffident blue light reaching out for him before the intersection of Brooklyn and December Twenty-sixth?

Mooney probed.

'Ah,' laughed Harse. 'Ho! I perceive what you want. You think perhaps there is something you can use in my survival kit.'

'All right, Harse,' Mooney said submissively, but he did have reservations.

First, it was important to find out just what was in the kit. After that –

Well, even a man from the future had to sleep.

Mooney was in a roaring rage. How dared the Government stick its bureaucratic nose into a simple transaction of citizens! But it turned out to be astonishingly hard to turn Harse's wampum into money. The first jeweller asked crudely threatening questions about an emerald the size of the ball of his thumb; the second quoted chapter and verse on the laws governing possession of gold. Finally they found a pawnbroker, who knowingly accepted a diamond that might have been worth a fortune; and when they took his first offer of a thousand dollars, the pawnbroker's suspicions were confirmed. Mooney dragged Harse away from there fast.

But they did have a thousand dollars.

As the cab took them across town, Mooney simmered down; and by the time they reached the other side, he was entirely content. What was a fortune more or less to a man who very nearly owned some of the secrets of the future?

He sat up, lit a cigarette, waved an arm and said expansively to Harse: 'Our new home.'

The pale-eyed man took a glowing little affair with eye-pieces away from in front of his eyes.

'Ah,' he said. 'So.'

It was quite an attractive hotel, Mooney thought judiciously. It did a lot to take away the sting of those sordidly avaricious jewellers. The lobby was an impressively close approximation of a cathedral and the bellboys looked smart and able.

Harse made an asthmatic sound. 'What is. That?' He was pointing at a group of men standing in jovial amusement around the entrance to the hotel's grand ballroom, just off the lobby. They wore purple harem pants and floppy green hats, and every one of them carried a silver-paper imitation of a scimitar.

Mooney chuckled in a superior way. 'You aren't up on our local customs, are you? That's a convention, Harse. They dress up that way because they belong to a lodge. A lodge is a kind of fraternal organization. A fraternal organization is –'

Harse said abruptly: 'I want.'

Mooney began to feel alarm. 'What?'

'I want one for a. Specimen? Wait, I think I take the big one there.'

'Harse! Wait a minute!' Mooney clutched at him. 'Hold everything, man! You can't do that.'

Harse stared at him. 'Why?'

'Because it would upset everything, that's why! You want to get to your rendezvous, don't you? Well, if you do anything like that, we'll *never* get there!'

'Why not?'

'Please,' Mooney said, 'please take my word for it. You hear me? I'll explain later!'

Harse looked by no means convinced, but he stopped opening the silvery metal case. Mooney kept an eye on him while registering. Harse continued to watch the conventioneers, but he went no further. Mooney began to breathe again.

'Thank *you*, sir,' said the desk clerk — not every guest, even in this hotel, went for a corner suite with two baths. 'Front!'

A smart-looking bellboy stepped forward, briskly took the key from the clerk, briskly nodded at Mooney and Harse. With the automatic reflex of any hotel bellhop, he reached for Harse's silvery case. Baggage was baggage, however funny it looked.

But Harse was not just any old guest. The bellboy got the bag away from him, all right, but his victory was purely transitory. He yelled, dropped the bag, grabbed his fist with the other hand.

'Hey! It shocked me! What kind of tricks are you trying to do with electric suitcases?'

Mooney moaned softly. The whole lobby was looking at them — even the conventioneers at the entrance to the ballroom; even the men in mufti mingling with the conventioneers, carrying cameras and flash guns; even the very doorman, the whole lobby away. That was bad. What was worse was that Harse was obviously getting angry.

'Wait, wait!' Mooney stepped between them in a hurry. 'I can explain everything. My friend is, uh, an inventor. There's some very important material in that briefcase, believe me!'

He winked, patted the bellhop on the shoulder, took his hand with friendly concern and left in it a folded bill.

'Now,' he said confidentially, 'We don't want any disturbance. I'm sure you understand how it is, son. Don't you? My friend can't take any chances with his, uh, confidential material, you see? Right. Well, let's say no more about it. Now if you'll show us to our room –'

The bellhop, still stiff-backed, glanced down at the bill and the stiffness disappeared as fast as any truckdriver bathed in Harse's pale blue haze. He looked up again and grinned.

'Sorry, sir –' he began.'

But he didn't finish. Mooney had let Harse get out of his sight a moment too long.

The first warning he had was when there was a sudden commotion among the lodge brothers. Mooney turned, much too late. There was Harse; he had wandered over there, curious and interested and – Harse. He had stared them up and down, but he hadn't been content to stare. He had opened the little silvery dispatch-case and taken out of it the thing that looked like a film viewer; and maybe it was a camera, too, because he was looking through it at the conventioneers. He was covering them as Dixie is covered by the dew, up and down, back and forth, heels to head.

And it was causing a certain amount of attention. Even one of the photographers thought maybe this funny-looking guy with the funny-looking opera glasses was curious enough to be worth a shot. After all, that was what the photographer was there for. He aimed and popped a flash gun.

There was an abrupt thin squeal from the box. Black fog sprayed out of it in a greasy jet. It billowed towards Harse. It collected around him, swirled high. Now all the flashguns were popping . . .

It was a clear waste of a twenty-dollar bill, Mooney told himself aggrievedly out on the sidewalk. There had been no point in buttering up the bellhop as long as Harse was going to get them thrown out anyway.

On the other side of the East River, in a hotel that fell considerably below Mooney's recent, brief standards of excellence, Mooney cautiously tipped a bellboy, ushered him out, locked the door behind him and, utterly exhausted, flopped on one of the twin beds.

Harse glanced at him briefly, then wandered over to the window and stared incuriously at the soiled snow outside.

'You were fine, Harse,' said Mooney without spirit. 'You didn't do anything wrong at all.'

'Ah,' said Harse without turning. 'So?'

Mooney sat up, reached for the phone, demanded setups and a bottle from room service and hung up.

'Oh, well,' he said, beginning to revive, 'at least we're in Brooklyn now. Maybe it's just as well.'

'As well. What?'

'I mean this is where you wanted to be. Now we just have to wait four days, until the twenty-sixth. We'll have to raise some more money, of course,' he added experimentally.

Harse turned and looked at him with the pale eyes. 'One thousand dollars you have. Is not enough?'

'Oh, no, Harse,' Mooney assured him. 'Why, that won't be nearly enough. The room rent in this hotel alone is likely to use that up. Besides all the extras, of course.'

'Ah.' Harse, looking bored, sat down in the chair near Mooney, opened his kit, took out the thing that looked like a film viewer and put it to his eyes.

'We'll have to sell some more of those things. After all –' Mooney winked and dug at the pale-eyed man's ribs with his elbow – 'we'll be needing some, well, entertainment.'

Harse took the viewer away from his eyes. He glanced thoughtfully at the elbow and then at Mooney. 'So,' he said.

Mooney coughed and changed the subject. 'One thing, though,' he begged. 'Don't get me in any more trouble like you did in that hotel lobby – or with that guy in the truck. Please? I mean, after all, you're making it hard for me to carry out my job.'

Harse was thoughtfully silent.

'Promise?' Mooney urged.

Harse said, after some more consideration: 'It is not altogether me. That is to say, it is a matter of defence. My picture should not be. Photographed? So the survival kit insures that it is not. You understand?'

Mooney leaned back. 'You mean –' The bellboy with the drinks interrupted him; he took the bottle, signed the chit, tipped the boy and mixed himself a reasonably stiff but not quite stupefying highball, thinking hard.

'Did you say "survival kit"?' he asked at last.

Harse was deep in the viewer again, but he looked away from it irritably. 'Naturally, survival kit. So that I can. Survive?' He went back to the viewer.

Mooney took a long, thoughtful slug of the drink.

Survival kit. Why, that made sense. When the Air Force boys went out and raided the islands in the Pacific during the war, sometimes they got shot down – and it was enemy territory, or what passed for it. Those islands were mostly held by Japanese, though their populations hardly knew it. All the aboriginals knew was that strange birds crossed the sky and sometimes men came from them. The politics of the situation didn't interest the headhunters. What really interested them was heads.

But for a palatable second choice, they would settle for trade goods – cloth, mirrors, beads. And so the bomber pilots were equipped with survival kits – maps, trade goods, rations, weapons, instructions for proceeding to a point where, God willing, a friendly submarine might put ashore a rubber dinghy to take them off.

Mooney said persuasively: 'Harse. I'm sorry to bother you, but we have to talk.' The man with the pale eyes took them away from the viewer again and stared at Mooney. 'Harse, were you shot down like an airplane pilot?'

Harse frowned – not in anger, or at least not at Mooney. It was the effort to make himself understood. He said at last: 'Yes. Call it that.'

'And – and this place you want to go – is that where you will be rescued?'

'Yes.'

Aha, thought Mooney, and the glimmerings of a new idea began to kick and stretch its fetal limbs inside him. He put it aside, to bear and coddle in private. He said: 'Tell me more. Is there any particular part of Brooklyn you have to go to?'

'Ah. The Nexus Point?' Harse put down the viewer and, snap-snap, opened the gleaming kit. He took out the little round thing he had consulted in the house by the cold Jersey sea. He tilted it this way and that, frowned, consulted a small square sparkly thing that came from another part of the case, tilted the round gadget again.

'Correcting for local time,' he said, 'the Nexus Point is one

hour and one minute after midnight at what is called. The Vale
of Cashmere?'

Mooney scratched his ear. 'The Vale of Cashmere? Where the
devil is that – somewhere in Pakistan?'

'Brooklyn,' said Harse with an imp's grimace. 'You are the
guide and you do not know where you are guiding me to?'

Mooney said hastily: 'All right, Harse, all right. I'll find it.
But tell me one thing, will you? Just suppose – suppose, I said –
that for some reason or other, we don't make it to the what-
you-call, Nexus Point. Then what happens?'

Harse for once neither laughed nor scowled. The pale eyes
opened wide and glanced around the room, at the machine-
made candlewick spreads on the beds, at the dusty red curtains
that made a 'suite' out of a long room, at the dog-eared Bible
that lay on the night table.

'Suh,' he stammered, 'suh – suh – seventeen years until there
is another Nexus Point!'

Mooney dreamed miraculous dreams and not entirely because of the empty bottle that had been full that afternoon.
There never was a time, never will be a time, like the future
Mooney dreamed of – Mooney-owned, houri-inhabited, a fair
domain for a live-wire Emperor of the Eons . . .

He woke up with a splitting head.

Even a man from the future had to sleep, so Mooney had
thought, and it had been in his mind that, even this first night,
it might pay to stay awake a little longer than Harse, just in
case it might then seem like a good idea to – well, to bash him
over the head and grab the bag. But the whisky had played him
dirty and he had passed out – drunk, blind drunk, or at least he
hoped so. He hoped that he hadn't seen what he thought he had
seen *sober*.

He woke up and wondered what was wrong. Little tinkling
ice spiders were moving around him. He could hear their tiny
crystal sounds and feel their chill legs, so lightly, on him. It
was still a dream – wasn't it?

Or was he awake? The thing was, he couldn't tell. If he was
awake, it was the middle of the night, because there was no light
whatever; and besides, he didn't seem to be able to move.

Thought Mooney with anger and desperation: I'm dead.
And: What a time to die!

But second thoughts changed his mind; there was no heaven and no hell, in all the theologies he had investigated, that included being walked over by tiny spiders of ice. He *felt* them. There was no doubt about it.

It was Harse, of course – had to be. Whatever he was up to, Mooney couldn't say, but as he lay there sweating cold sweat and feeling the crawling little feet, he knew that it was something Harse had made happen.

Little by little, he began to be able to see – not much, but enough to see that there really was something crawling. Whatever the things were, they had a faint, tenuous glow, like the face of a watch just before dawn. He couldn't make out shapes, but he could tell the size – not much bigger than a man's hand – and he could tell the number, and there were dozens of them.

He couldn't turn his head, but on the walls, on his chest, on his face, even on the ceiling, he could see faint moving patches of fox-fire light.

He took a deep breath. 'Harse!' he started to call; wake him up, make him stop this! But he couldn't. He got no further than the first huff of the aspirate when the scurrying cold feet were on his lips. Something cold and damp lay across them and it stuck. Like spider silk, but stronger – he couldn't speak, couldn't move his lips, though he almost tore the flesh.

Oh, he could make a noise, all right. He started to do so, to snort and hum through his nose. But Mooney was not slow of thought and he had a sudden clear picture of that same cold ribbon crossing his nostrils, and what would be the use of all of time's treasures then, when it was no longer possible to breathe at all?

It was quite apparent that he was not to make a noise.

He had patience – the kind of patience that grows with a diet of thrice-used tea bags and soggy crackers. He waited.

It wasn't the middle of the night after all, he perceived, though it was still utterly dark except for the moving blobs. He could hear sounds in the hotel corridor outside – faintly, though: the sound of a vacuum cleaner, and it might have been a city block away; the tiniest whisper of someone laughing.

He remembered one of his drunken fantasies of the night before – little robot mice, or so they seemed, spinning a curtain across the window; and he shuddered, because that had been no fantasy. The window was curtained. And it was mid-morning, at the earliest, because the chambermaids were cleaning the halls.

Why couldn't he move? He flexed the muscles of his arms and legs, but nothing happened. He could feel the muscles straining, he could feel his toes and fingers twitch, but he was restrained by what seemed a web of Gulliver's cords . . .

There was a tap at the door. A pause, the scratching of a key, and the room was flooded with light from the hall.

Out of the straining corner of his eye, Mooney saw a woman in a grey cotton uniform, carrying fresh sheets, standing in the doorway, and her mouth was hanging slack. No wonder, for in the light from the hall, Mooney could see the room festooned with silver, with darting silvery shapes moving about. Mooney himself wore a cocoon of silver, and on the bed next to him, where Harse slept, there was a fantastic silver hood, like the basketwork of a baby's bassinet, surrounding his head.

It was a fairyland scene and it lasted only a second. For Harse cried out and leaped to his feet. Quick as an adder, he scooped up something from the table beside his bed and gestured with it at the door. It was, Mooney half perceived, the silvery, jointed thing he had used in the truck; and he used it again.

Pale blue light screamed out.

It faded and the chambermaid, popping eyes and all, was gone.

It didn't hurt as much the second time.

Mooney finally attracted Harse's attention, and Harse, with a Masonic pass over one of the little silvery things, set it to loosening and removing the silver bonds. The things were like toy tanks with jointed legs; as they spun the silver webs, they could also suck them in. In moments, the webs that held Mooney down were gone.

He got up, aching in his tired muscles and his head, but this time the panic that had filled him in the truck was gone. Well, one victim more or less – what did it matter? And besides, he clung to the fact that Harse had not exactly said the victims were dead.

So it didn't hurt as much the second time.

Mooney planned. He shut the door and sat on the edge of the bed. 'Shut up – you put us in a lousy fix and I have to think a way out of it,' he rasped at Harse when Harse started to speak;

and the man from the future looked at him with opaque pale eyes, and silently opened one of the flat canisters and began to eat.

'All right,' said Mooney at last. 'Harse, get rid of all this stuff.'

'This. Stuff?'

'The stuff on the walls. What your little spiders have been spinning, understand? Can't you get it off the walls?'

Harse leaned forward and touched the kit. The little spider-things that had been aimlessly roving now began to digest what they had created, as the ones that had held Mooney had already done. It was quick – Mooney hoped it would be quick enough. There were over a dozen of the things, more than Mooney would have believed the little kit could hold; and he had seen no sign of them before.

The silvery silk on the walls, in aimless tracing, disappeared. The thick silvery coat over the window disappeared. Harse's bassinet-hood disappeared. A construction that haloed the door disappeared – and as it dwindled, the noises from the corridor grew louder; some sort of sound-absorbing contrivance, Mooney thought, wondering.

There was an elaborate silvery erector-set affair on the floor between the beds; it whirled and spun silently and the little machines took it apart again and swallowed it. Mooney had no notion of its purpose. When it was gone, he could see no change, but Harse shuddered and shifted his position uncomfortably.

'All right,' said Mooney when everything was back in the kit. 'Now you just keep your mouth shut. I won't ask you to lie – they'll have enough trouble understanding you if you tell the truth. Hear me?'

Harse merely stared, but that was good enough. Mooney put his hand on the phone. He took a deep breath and held it until his head began to tingle and his face turned red. Then he picked up the phone and, when he spoke, there was authentic rage and distress in his voice.

'Operator,' he snarled, 'give me the manager. And hurry up – I want to report a thief!'

When the manager had gone – along with the assistant manager, the house detective and the ancient shrew-faced head housekeeper – Mooney extracted a promise from Harse and left him. He carefully hung a 'Do Not Disturb' card from the door-knob, crossed his fingers and took the elevator downstairs.

The fact seemed to be that Harse didn't care about *aboriginals*. Mooney had arranged a system of taps on the door which, he thought, Harse would abide by, so that Mooney could get back in. Just the same, Mooney vowed to be extremely careful about how he opened that door. Whatever the pale blue light was, Mooney wanted no part of it directed at him.

The elevator operator greeted him respectfully – a part of the management's policy of making amends, no doubt. Mooney returned the greeting with a barely civil nod. Sure, it had worked; he'd told the manager that he'd caught the chamber-maid trying to steal something valuable that belonged to that celebrated proprietor of valuable secrets, Mr. Harse; the chambermaid had fled; how dared they employ a person like that?

And he had made very sure that the manager and the house dick and all the rest had plenty of opportunity to snoop apolo-getically in every closet and under the beds, just so there would be no suspicion in their minds that a dismembered chamber-maid-torso was littering some dark corner of the room. What could they do but accept the story? The chambermaid wasn't there to defend herself, and though they might wonder how she had got out of the hotel without being noticed, it was their problem to figure it out, not Mooney's to explain it.

They had even been grateful when Mooney offered hand-somely to refrain from notifying the police.

'Lobby, sir,' sang out the elevator operator, and Mooney step-ped out, nodded to the manager, stared down the house detec-tive and walked out into the street.

So far, so good.

Now that the necessities of clothes and food and a place to live were taken care of, Mooney had a chance to operate. It was a field in which he had always had a good deal of talent – the making of deals, the locating of contacts, the arranging of trans-actions that were better conducted in private.

And he had a good deal of business to transact. Harse had accepted without question his statement that they would have to raise more money.

'Try heroin or. Platinum?' he had suggested, and gone back to his viewer.

'I will,' Mooney assured him, and he did; he tried them both, and more besides.

Not only was it good that he had such valuable commodities to vend, but it was a useful item in his total of knowledge concerning Harse that the man from the future seemed to have no idea of the value of money in the 20th Century, *chez* U.S.A.

Mooney found a buyer for the drugs; and there was a few thousand dollars there, which helped, for although the quantity was not large, the drugs were chemically pure. He found a fence to handle the jewels and precious metals; and he unloaded all the ones of moderate value – not the other diamond, not the rubies, not the star sapphire.

He arranged to keep those without mentioning it to Harse. No point in selling them now, not even when they had several thousand dollars above any conceivable expenses, not when some future date would do as well, just in case Harse should get away with the balance of the kit.

Having concluded his business, Mooney undertook a brief but expensive shopping tour of his own and found a reasonably satisfactory place to eat. After a pleasantly stimulating cocktail and the best meal he had had in some years – doubly good, for there was no reek from Harse's nauseating concoctions to spoil it – he called for coffee, for brandy, for the day's papers.

The disappearance of the truck driver made hardly a ripple. There were a couple of stories, but small and far in the back – amnesia, said one; an underworld kidnapping, suggested another; but the story had nothing to feed on and it would die.

Good enough, thought Mooney, waving for another glass of that enjoyable brandy; and then he turned back to the front page and saw his own face.

There was the hotel lobby of the previous day, and a pillar of churning black smoke that Mooney knew was Harse, and there in the background, mouth agape, expression worried, was Howard Mooney himself.

He read it all very, very carefully.

Well, he thought, at least they didn't get our names. The story was all about the Loyal and Beneficent Order of Exalted Eagles, and the only reference to the picture was a brief line about a disturbance outside the meeting hall. Nonetheless, the second glass of brandy tasted nowhere near as good as the first.

Time passed, Mooney found a man who explained what was meant by the Vale of Cashmere. In Brooklyn, there is a very large park – the name is Prospect Park – and in it is a little planted valley, with a brook and a pool; and the name of it on the maps of Prospect Park is the Vale of Cashmere. Mooney sent out for a map, memorized it; and that was that.

However, Mooney didn't really want to go to the Vale of Cashmere with Harse. What he wanted was that survival kit. Wonders kept popping out of it, and each day's supply made Mooney covet the huger store that was still inside. There had been, he guessed, something like a hundred separate items that had somehow come out of that tiny box. There simply was no room for them all; but that was not a matter that Mooney concerned himself with. They *were* there, possible or not, because he had seen them.

Mooney laid traps.

The trouble was that Harse did not care for conversation. He spent endless hours with his film viewer, and when he said anything at all to Mooney, it was to complain. All he wanted was to exist for four days – nothing else.

Mooney laid conversational traps, tried to draw him out, and there was no luck. Harse would turn his blank, pale stare on him, and refuse to be drawn.

At night, however hard Mooney tried, Harse was always awake past him; and in his sleep, always and always, the little metal guardians strapped Mooney tight. Survival kit? But how did the little metal things know that Mooney was a threat?

It was maddening and time was passing. There were four days, then only three, then only two. Mooney made arrangements of his own.

He found two girls – lovely girls, the best that money could buy, and he brought them to the suite with a wink and a snigger. 'A little relaxation, eh, Harse? The red-haired one is named Ginger and she's partial to men with light-coloured eyes.'

Ginger smiled a rehearsed and lovely smile. 'I certainly *am*, Mr. Harse. Say, want to dance?'

But it came to nothing, though the house detective knocked deferentially on the door to ask if they could be a little more quiet, please. It wasn't the sound of celebration that the neighbours were objecting to. It was the shrill, violent noise of Harse's laughter. First he had seemed not to understand, and then he looked as astonished as Mooney had ever seen him. And then the laughter.

Girls didn't work. Mooney got rid of the girls.

All right, Mooney was a man of infinite resource and sagacity – hadn't he proved that many a time? He excused himself to Harse, made sure his fat new pigskin wallet was in his pocket, and took a cab to a place on Brooklyn's waterfront where cabs seldom go. The bartender had arms like beer kegs and a blue chin.

'Beer,' said Mooney, and made sure he paid for it with a twenty-dollar bill – thumbing through a thick wad of fifties and hundreds to find the smallest. He retired to a booth and nursed his beer.

After about ten minutes, a man stood beside him, blue-chinned and muscular enough to be the bartender's brother – which, Mooney found, he was.

'Well,' said Mooney, 'it took you long enough. Sit down. You don't have to roll me; you can earn this.'

Girls didn't work? Okay, if not girls, then try boys ... well, not boys exactly. Hoodlums. Try hoodlums and see what Harse might do against the toughest inhabitants of the area around the Gowanus Canal.

Harse, sloshing heedlessly through melted snow, spattering Mooney, grumbled: 'I do not see why we. Must? Wander endlessly across the face of this wretched slum.'

Mooney said soothingly: 'We have to make *sure,* Harse. We have to be sure it's the right place.'

'Huff,' said Harse, but he went along. They were in Prospect Park and it was nearly dark.

'Hey, look,' said Mooney desperately, 'look at those kids on sleds!'

Harse glanced angrily at the kids on sleds and even more angrily at Mooney. Still, he wasn't refusing to come and that was something. It had been possible that Harse would sit tight in the hotel room and it had taken all of the persuasive powers Mooney prided himself on to get him out. But Mooney was able to paint a horrible picture of getting to the wrong place, missing the Nexus Point, seventeen long years of waiting for the next one.

They crossed the Sheep Meadow, crossed the walk, crossed

an old covered bridge; and they were at the head of a flight of shallow steps.

'The Vale of Cashmere!' cried Mooney, as though he were announcing a miracle.

Harse said nothing.

Mooney licked his lips, glancing at the kit Harse carried under an arm, glancing around. No one was in sight.

Mooney coughed. 'Uh. You're sure this is the place you mean?'

'If it is the Vale of Cashmere.' Harse looked once more down the steps, then turned.

'No, wait!' said Mooney frantically. 'I mean – well, *where* in the Vale of Cashmere is the Nexus Point? This is a big place!'

Harse's pale eyes stared at him for a moment. 'No. Not big.'

'Oh, *fairly* big. After all –'

Harse said positively: 'Come.'

Mooney swore under his breath and vowed never to trust anyone again, especially a bartender's brother; but just then it happened. Out of the snowy bushes stepped a man in a red bandanna, holding a gun. 'This is a stickup! Gimme that bag!'

Mooney exulted.

There was no chance for Harse now. The man was leaping towards him; there would be no time for him to open the bag, take out the weapon . . .

But he didn't have to. There was a thin, singing, whining sound from the bag. It leaped out of Harse's hand, leaped free as though it had invisible wings, and flew at the man in the red bandanna. The man stumbled and jumped aside, the eyes incredulous over the mask. The silvery flat metal kit spun round him, whining. It circled him once, spiralled up. Behind it, like a smoke trail from a destroyer, a pale blue mist streamed backwards. It surrounded the man and hid him.

The bag flew back into Harse's hand.

The violet mist thinned and disappeared.

And the man was gone, as utterly and as finally as any chambermaid or driver of a truck.

There was a moment of silence. Mooney stared without belief at the snow sifting down from the bushes that the man had hid in.

Harse looked opaquely at Mooney. 'It seems,' he said, 'that in these slums are many. Dangers?'

Mooney was very quiet on the way back to the hotel. Harse, for once, was not gazing into his viewer. He sat erect and silent beside Mooney, glancing at him from time to time. Mooney did not relish the attention.

The situation had deteriorated.

It deteriorated even more when they entered the lobby of the hotel. The desk clerk called to Mooney.

Mooney hesitated, then said to Harse: 'You go ahead. I'll be up in a minute. And listen – don't forget about my knock.'

Harse inclined his head and strode into the elevator. Mooney sighed.

'There's a gentleman to see you, Mr. Mooney,' the desk clerk said civilly.

Mooney swallowed. 'A – a gentleman? To see me?'

The clerk nodded towards the writing room. 'In there, sir. A gentleman who says he knows you.'

Mooney pursed his lips.

In the writing room? Well, that was an advantage. The writing room was off the main lobby; it would give Mooney a chance to peek in before whoever it was could see him. He approached the entrance cautiously ...

'Howard!' cried an accusing familiar voice behind him.

Mooney turned. A small man with curly red hair was coming out of a door marked 'Men'.

'Why – why, Uncle Lester!' said Mooney. 'What a p-pleasant surprise!'

Lester, all of five feet tall, wispy red hair surrounding his red plump face, looked up at him belligerently.

'No doubt!' he snapped. 'I've been waiting all day, Howard. Took the afternoon off from work to come here. And I wouldn't have been here at all if I hadn't seen *this*.'

He was holding a copy of the paper with Mooney's picture, behind the pillar of black fog. 'Your aunt wrapped my lunch in it, Howard. Otherwise I might have missed it. Went right to the hotel. You weren't there. The doorman helped, though. Found a cab driver. Told me where he'd taken you. Here I am.'

'That's nice,' lied Mooney.

'No, it isn't. Howard, what in the world are you up to? Do you know the Monmouth County police are looking for you? Said there was somebody missing. Want to talk to you.' The little man shook his head angrily. 'Knew I shouldn't let you stay at my place. Your aunt warned me, too. Why do you make trouble for me?'

'Police?' Mooney asked faintly.

'At my age! Police coming to the house. Who was that fella who's missing, Howard? Where did he go? Why doesn't he go home? His wife's half crazy. He shouldn't worry her like that.'

Mooney clutched his uncle's shoulder. 'Do the police know where I am? You didn't tell them?'

'Tell them? How could I tell them? Only I saw your picture while I was eating my sandwich, so I went to the hotel and –'

'Uncle Lester, listen. What did they come to see you for?'

'Because I was stupid enough to let you stay in my house, that's what for,' Lester said bitterly. 'Two days ago. Knocking on my door, hardly eight o'clock in the morning. They said there's a man missing, driving a truck, found the truck empty. Man from the Coast Guard station knows him, saw him picking up a couple of hitchhikers at a bridge someplace, recognized one of the hitchhikers. Said the hitchhiker'd been staying at my house. That's you, Howard. Don't lie; he described you. Pudgy, kind of a squinty look in the eyes, dressed like a bum – oh, it was you, all right.'

'Wait a minute. Nobody knows you've come here, right? Not even Auntie?'

'No, course not. She didn't see the picture, so how would she know? Would've said something if she had. Now come on, Howard, we've got to go to the police and –'

'Uncle Lester!'

The little man paused and looked at him suspiciously. But that was all right; Mooney began to feel confidence flow back into him. It wasn't all over yet, not by a long shot.

'Uncle Lester,' he said, his voice low-pitched and persuasive, 'I have to ask you a very important question. Think before you answer, please. This is the question: Have you ever belonged to any Communist organization?'

The old man blinked. After a moment, he exploded. 'Now what are you up to, Howard? *You* know I never –'

'Think, Uncle Lester! Please. Way back when you were a boy – anything like that?'

'Of course not!'

'You're sure? Because I'm warning you, Uncle Lester, you're

going to have to take the strictest security check anybody ever took. You've stumbled onto something important. You'll have to prove you can be trusted or – well, I can't answer for the consequences. You see, this involves –' he looked around him furtively – 'Schenectady Project.'

'Schenec –'

'Schenectady Project.' Mooney nodded. 'You've heard of the atom bomb? Uncle Lester, this is bigger!'

'Bigger than the at –'

'Bigger. It's the *molecule* bomb. There aren't seventy-five men in the country that know what that so-called driver in the truck was up to, and now you're one of them.'

Mooney nodded soberly, feeling his power. The old man was hooked, tied and delivered. He could tell by the look in the eyes, by the quivering of the lips. Now was the time to slip the contract in his hand; or, in the present instance, to –

'I'll tell you what to do,' whispered Mooney. 'Here's my key. You go up to my room. Don't knock – we don't want to attract attention. Walk right in. You'll see a man there and he'll explain everything. Understand?'

'Why – why, sure, Howard. But why don't you come with me?'

Mooney raised a hand warningly. 'You might be followed. I'll have to keep a lookout.'

Five minutes later, when Mooney tapped on the door of the room – three taps, pause, three taps – and cautiously pushed it open, the pale blue mist was just disappearing. Harse was standing angrily in the centre of the room with the jointed metal thing thrust out ominously before him.

And of Uncle Lester, there was no trace at all.

Time passed; and then time was all gone, and it was midnight, nearly the Nexus Point.

In front of the hotel, a drowsy cab-driver gave them an argument. 'The Public Liberry? Listen, the Liberry ain't open this time of night. I ought to – Oh, thanks. Hop in.' He folded the five-dollar bill and put the cab in gear.

Harse said ominously: 'Liberry, Mooney? Why do you instruct him to take us to the Liberry?'

Mooney whispered: 'There's a law against being in the Park

at night. We'll have to sneak in. The Library's right across the street.'

Harse stared, with his luminous pale eyes. But it was true; there was such a law, for the parks of the city lately had become fields of honour where rival gangs contended with bottle shards and zip guns, where a passerby was odds-on to be mugged.

'High Command must know this,' Harse grumbled. 'Must proceed, they say, to Nexus Point. But then one finds the aboriginals have made laws! Oh, I shall make a report!'

'*Sure* you will,' Mooney soothed; but in his heart, he was prepared to bet heavily against it.

Because he had a new strategy. Clearly he couldn't get the survival kit from Harse. He had tried that and there was no luck; his arm still tingled as the bellboy's had, from having seemingly absent-mindedly taken the handle to help Harse. But there was a way.

Get rid of this clown from the future, he thought contentedly; meet the Nexus Point instead of Harse and there was the future, ripe for the taking! He knew where the rescuers would be – and, above all, he knew how to talk. Every man has one talent and Mooney's was salesmanship.

All the years wasted on peddling dime-store schemes like frozen-food plans! But this was the big time at last, so maybe the years of seasoning were not wasted, after all.

'That for you, Uncle Lester,' he muttered. Harse looked up from his viewer angrily and Mooney cleared his throat. 'I said,' he explained hastily, 'we're almost at the – the Nexus Point.'

Snow was drifting down. The cab-driver glanced at the black, quiet library, shook his head and pulled away, leaving black, wet tracks in the thin snow.

The pale-eyed man looked about him irritably. 'You!' he cried, waking Mooney from a dream of possessing the next ten years of stock-market reports. 'You! Where is this Vale of Cashmere?'

'Right this way, Harse, right this way,' said Mooney placatingly.

There was a wide sort of traffic circle – grand Army Plaza was the name of it – and there were a few cars going around it.

But not many, and none of them looked like police cars. Mooney looked up and down the broad, quiet streets.

'Across here,' he ordered, and led the time traveller towards the edge of the park. 'We can't go in the main entrance. There might be cops.'

'Cops?'

'Policemen. Law-enforcement officers. We'll just walk down here a way and then hop over the wall. Trust me,' said Mooney, in the voice that had put frozen-food lockers into so many suburban homes.

The look from those pale eyes was anything but a look of trust, but Harse didn't say anything. He stared about with an expression of detached horror, like an Alabama gentlewoman condemned to walk through Harlem.

'Now!' whispered Mooney urgently.

And over the wall they went.

They were in a thicket of shrubs and brush, snow-laden, the snow sifting down into Mooney's neck every time he touched a branch, which was always; he couldn't avoid it. They crossed a path and then a road – long, curving, broad, white, empty. Down a hill, onto another path. Mooney paused, glancing around.

'You know where you are. Going?'

'I think so. I'm looking for cops.' None in sight. Mooney frowned. What the devil did the police think they were up to? They passed laws; why weren't they around to enforce them?

Mooney had his landmarks well in mind. There was the Drive, and there was the fork he was supposed to be looking for. It wouldn't be hard to find the path to the Vale. The only thing was, it was kind of important to Mooney's hope of future prosperity that he find a policeman first. And time was running out.

He glanced at the luminous dial of his watch – self-winding, shockproof, non-magnetic; the man in the hotel's jewellery shop had assured him only yesterday that he could depend on its timekeeping as on the beating of his heart. It was nearly a quarter of one.

'Come along, come along!' grumbled Harse.

Mooney stalled: 'I – I think we'd better go along this way. It *ought* to be down there –'

He cursed himself. Why hadn't he gone in the main entrance, where there was sure to be a cop? Harse would never have known the difference. But there was the artist in him that wanted the thing done perfectly, and so he had held to the pretense of avoiding police, had skulked and hidden. And now –

'Look!' he whispered, pointing.

Harse spat soundlessly and turned his eyes where Mooney was pointing.

Yes. Under a distant light, a moving figure, swinging a nightstick.

Mooney took a deep breath and planted a hand between Harse's shoulder blades.

'Run!' he yelled at the top of his voice, and shoved. He sounded so real, he almost convinced himself. 'We'll have to split up – I'll meet you there. Now *run*!'

Oh, clever Mooney! He crouched under a snowy tree, watching the man from the future speed effortlessly away ... in the wrong direction.

The cop was hailing him; clever cop! All it had taken was a couple of full-throated yells and at once the cop had perceived that someone was in the park. But cleverer than any cop was Mooney.

Men from the future. Why, thought Mooney contentedly, no Mrs. Meyerhauser of the suburbs would have let me get away with a trick like that to sell her a freezer. There's going to be no problem at all. I don't have to worry about a thing. Mooney can take care of himself!

By then, he had caught his breath – and time was passing, passing.

He heard a distant confused yelling. Harse and the cop? But it didn't matter. The only thing that mattered was getting to the Nexus Point at one minute past one.

He took a deep breath and began to trot. Slipping in the snow, panting heavily, he went down the path, around the little glade, across the covered bridge.

He found the shallow steps that led down to the Vale.

And there it was below him: a broad space where walks joined, and in the space a thing shaped like a dinosaur egg, rounded and huge. It glowed with a silvery sheen.

Confidently, Mooney started down the steps towards the egg and the moving figures that flitted soundlessly around it. Harse was not the only time traveller, Mooney saw. Good, that might make it all the simpler. Should he change his plan and feign amnesia, pass himself off as one of their own men?

Or –

A movement made him look over his shoulder.

Somebody was standing at the top of the steps. 'Hell's fire,' whispered Mooney. He'd forgotten all about that aboriginal law; and here above him stood a man in a policeman's uniform, staring down with pale eyes.

No, not a policeman. The face was – Harse's

Mooney swallowed and stood rooted.

'You!' Harse's savage voice came growling. 'You are to stand. Still?'

Mooney didn't need the order; he couldn't move. No twentieth-century cop was a match for Harse, that was clear; Harse had bested him, taken his uniform away from him for camouflage – and here he was.

Unfortunately, so was Howard Mooney.

The figures below were looking up, pointing and talking; Harse from above was coming down. Mooney could only stand, and wish – wish that he were back in Sea Bright, living on cookies and stale tea, wish he had planned things with more intelligence, more skill – perhaps even with more honesty. But it was too late for wishing.

Harse came down the steps, paused a yard from Mooney, scowled a withering scowl – and passed on.

He reached the bottom of the steps and joined the others waiting about the egg. They all went inside.

The glowing silvery colours winked and went out. The egg flamed purple, faded, turned transparent and disappeared.

Mooney stared and, yelling a demand for payment, ran stumbling down the steps to where it had been. There was a round thawed spot, a trampled patch – nothing else.

They were gone . . .

Almost gone. Because there was a sudden bright wash of flame from overhead – cold silvery flame. He looked up, dazzled. Over him, the egg was visible as thin smoke, hovering. A smoky, half-transparent hand reached out of a port. A thin, reedy voice cried: 'I promised you. Pay?'

And the silvery dispatch-case sort of thing, the survival kit, dropped soundlessly to the snow beside Mooney.

When he looked up again, the egg was gone for good.

He was clear back to the hotel before he got a grip on himself – and then he was drunk with delight. Honest Harse! Splendidly trustable Harse! Why, all this time, Mooney had been so worried, had worked so hard – and the whole survival kit was his, after all!

He had touched it gingerly before picking it up but it didn't shock him; clearly the protective devices, whatever they were, were off.

He sweated over it for an hour and a half, looking for levers, buttons, a slit that he might pry wider with the blade of a knife. At last he kicked it and yelled, past endurance: 'Open up, damn you!'

It opened wide on the floor before him.

'Oh, bless your heart!' cried Mooney, falling to his knees to drag out the string of wampum, the little mechanical mice, the viewing-machine sort of thing. Treasures like those were beyond price; each one might fetch a fortune, if only in the wondrous new inventions he could patent if he could discover just how they worked.

But where were they?

Gone! The wampum was gone. The goggles were gone. Everything was gone – the little flat canisters, the map instruments, everything but one thing.

There was, in a corner of the case, a squarish, sharp-edged thing that Mooney stared at blindly for a long moment before he recognized it. It was a part – only a part – of the jointed construction that Harse had used to rid himself of undesirables by bathing them in blue light.

What a filthy trick! Mooney all but sobbed to himself.

He picked up the squarish thing bitterly. Probably it wouldn't even work, he thought, the world a ruin around him. It wasn't even the whole complete weapon.

Still –

There was a grooved, saddle-shaped affair that was clearly a sort of trigger; it could move forward or it could move back. Mooney thought deeply for a while.

Then he sat up, held the thing carefully away from him with the pointed part towards the wall and pressed, ever so gently pressed forward on the saddle-shaped thumb-trigger.

The pale blue haze leaped out, swirled around and, not finding anything alive in its range, dwindled and died.

Aha, thought Mooney, not everything is lost yet! Surely a bright young man could find some use for a weapon like this which removed, if it did not kill, which prevented any nastiness about a corpse turning up, or a messy job of disposal.

Why not see what happened if the thumb-piece was moved backward?

Well, why not? Mooney held the thing away from him, hesitated, and slid it back.

There was a sudden shivering tingle in his thumb, in the gadget he was holding, running all up and down his arm. A violet haze, very unlike the blue one, licked soundlessly forth – not burning, but destroying as surely as flame ever destroyed; for where the haze touched the gadget itself, the kit, everything that had to do with the man from the future, it seared and shattered. The gadget fell into white crystalline powder in Mooney's hand and the case itself became a rectangular shape traced in white powder ridges on the rug.

Oh, no! thought Mooney, even before the haze had gone. It can't be!

The flame danced away like a cloud, spreading and rising. While Mooney stared, it faded away, but not without leaving something behind.

Mooney threw his taut body backward, almost under the bed. What he saw, he didn't believe; what he believed filled him with panic.

No wonder Harse had laughed so when Mooney asked if its victims were dead. For there they were, all of them. Like djinn out of a jar, human figures jelled and solidified where the cloud of violet flame had not at all diffidently rolled.

They were alive, as big as life, and beginning to move – and so many of them! Three – five – six:

The truck-driver, yes, and a man in long red flannel underwear who must have been the policeman, and Uncle Lester, and the bartender's brother, and the chambermaid, and a man Mooney didn't know.

They were there, all of them; and they came towards him, and oh! but they were angry!

I Plinglot, Who You?

1

'Let me see,' I said, 'this is a time for the urbane. Say little. Suggest much.' So I smiled and nodded wisely, without words, to the fierce flash bulbs.

The committee room was not big enough, they had had to move the hearings. Oh, it was hot. Senator Schnell came leaping down the aisle, sweating, his forehead glistening, his gold tooth shining, and took my arm like a trap. 'Capital, Mr. Smith,' he cried, nodding and grinning, 'I am so glad you got here on time! One moment.'

He planted his feet and stopped me, turned me about to face the photographers and threw an arm around my shoulder as they flashed many bulbs. 'Capital,' said the senator with a happy voice. 'Thanks, fellows! Come along, Mr. Smith!'

They found me a first-class seat, near a window, where the air-conditioning made such a clatter that I could scarcely hear, but what was there to hear before I myself spoke? Outside the Washington Monument cast aluminium rays from the sun.

'We'll get started in a minute,' whispered Mr. Hagsworth in my ear – he was young and working for the committee – 'as soon as the networks give us the go-ahead.'

He patted my shoulder in a friendly way, with pride; they were always doing something with shoulders. He had brought me to the committee and thus I was, he thought, a sort of possession of his, a gift for Senator Schnell, though we know how wrong he was in that, of course. But he was proud. It was very hot and I had in me many headlines.

Q. (Mr. Hagsworth.) Will you state your name, sir?
A. Robert Smith.
Q. Is that your real name?
A. No.

Oh, that excited them all! They rustled and coughed and whispered, those in the many seats. Senator Schnell flashed his gold tooth. Senator Loveless, who as his enemy and his adjutant, as it were, a second commander of the committee but of opposite party, frowned under stiff silvery hair. But he knew I would say that, he had heard it all in executive session the night before.

Mr. Hagsworth did not waste the moment, he went right ahead over the coughs and the rustles.

Q. Sir, have you adopted the identity of 'Robert P. Smith' in order to further your investigations on behalf of this committee?

A. I have.

Q. And can you —

Q. (Senator Loveless.) Excuse me.

Q. (Mr. Hagsworth.) Certainly, Senator.

Q. (Senator Loveless.) Thank you, Mr. Hagsworth. Sir — that is, Mr. Smith — do I understand that it would not be proper, or advisable, for you to reveal — that is, to make public — your true or correct identity at this time? Or in these circumstances?

A. Yes.

Q. (Senator Loveless.) thank you very much, Mr. Smith. I just wanted to get that point cleared up.

Q. (Mr. Hagsworth.) Then tell us, Mr. Smith —

Q. (Senator Loveless.) It's clear now.

Q. (The Chairman.) Thank you for helping us clarify the matter, Senator. Mr. Hagsworth, you may proceed.

Q. (Mr. Hagsworth.) Thank you, Senator Schnell. Thank you, Senator Loveless. Then, Mr. Smith, will you tell us the nature of the investigations you have just concluded for this committee?

A. Certainly. I was investigating the question of interstellar space travel.

Q. That is, travel between the planets of different stars?

A. That's right.

Q. And have you reached any conclusions as to the possibility of such a thing?

A. Oh, yes. Not just conclusions. I have definite evidence that one foreign power is in direct contact with creatures living on the planet of another star, and expects to receive a visit from them shortly.

Q. Will you tell us the name of that foreign power?
A. Russia.

Oh, it went very well. Pandemonium became widespread:
much noise, much hammering by Senator Schnell, and at the
recess all the networks said big Neilsen. And Mr. Hagsworth was
so pleased that he hardly asked me about the file again, which
I enjoyed as it was a hard answer to give. 'Good theatre, ah,
Mr. Smith,' he winked.

I only smiled.

The afternoon also was splendidly hot, especially as Senator
Schnell kept coming beside me and the bulbs flashed. It was
excellent, excellent.

Q. (Mr. Hagsworth.) Mr. Smith, this morning you told
us that a foreign power was in contact with a race of beings
living on a planet of the star Aldebaran, is that right?
A. Yes.
Q. Can you describe that race for us? I mean the ones you
have referred to as 'Aldebaranians'?
A. Certainly, although their own name for themselves is
– is a word in their language which you might here render as
'Triops'. They average about eleven inches tall. They have
two legs, like you. They have three eyes and they live in cry-
stal cities under the water, although they are air-breathers.
Q. Why is that, Mr. Smith?
A. The surface of their planet is ravaged by enormous
beasts against which they are defenceless.
Q. But they have powerful weapons?
A. Oh, very powerful, Mr. Hagsworth.

And then it was time for me to take it out and show it to
them, the Aldebaranian hand-weapon. It was small and soft and
I must fire it with a bent pin, but it made a hole through three
floors and the cement of the basement, and they were very interested. Oh, yes!

So I talked all that afternoon about the Aldebaranians,
though what did they matter? Mr. Hagsworth did not ask me
about other races, on which I could have said something of
greater interest. Afterwards we went to my suite at the May-

flower Hotel and Mr. Hagsworth said with admiration: 'You handled yourself beautifully, Mr. Smith. When this is over I wonder if you would consider some sort of post here in Washington.'

'When this is over?'

'Oh,' he said, 'I've been around for some years, Mr. Smith. I've seen them come and I've seen them go. Every newspaper in the country is full of Aldebaranians tonight, but next year? They'll be shouting about something new.'

'They will not,' I said surely.

He shrugged. 'As you say,' he said agreeably, 'at any rate it's a great sensation now. Senator Schnell is tasting the headlines. He's up for re-election next year you know and just between the two of us, he was afraid he might be defeated.'

'Impossible, Mr. Hagsworth,' I said out of certain knowledge, but could not convey this to him. He thought I was only being polite. It did not matter.

'He'll be gratified to hear that,' said Mr. Hagsworth and he stood up and winked: he was a great human for winking. 'But think about what I said about a job, Mr. Smith. ... Or would you care to tell me your real name?'

Why not? Sporting! 'Plinglot,' I said.

He said with a puzzled face, 'Plinglot? Plinglot? That's an odd name.' I didn't say anything, why should I? 'But you're an odd man,' he sighed. 'I don't mind telling you that there are a lot of questions I'd like to ask. For instance, the file folder of correspondence between you and Senator Heffernan. I don't suppose you'd care to tell me how come no employee of the committee remembers anything about it, although the folder turned up in our files just as you said?'

Senator Heffernan was dead, that was why the correspondence had been with him. But I know tricks for awkward questions, you give only another question instead of answer. 'Don't you trust me, Mr. Hagsworth?'

He looked at me queerly and left without speaking. No matter. It was time, I had very much to do. 'No calls,' I told the switchboard person, 'and no visitors, I must rest.' Also there would be a guard Hagsworth had promised. I wondered if he would have made the same arrangement if I had not requested it, but that also did not matter.

I sat quickly in what looked, for usual purposes, like a large armchair, purple embroidery on the headrest. It was my space-ship, with cosmetic upholstery. *Zz-z-z-zit*, quick like that, that's all there was to it and I was there.

2

Old days I could not have timed it so well, for the old one slept all the day, and worked, drinking, all the night. But now they kept capitalist hours.

'Good morning, *gospodin*,' cried the man in the black tunic, leaping up alertly as I opened the tall double doors. 'I trust you slept well.'

I had changed quickly into pyjamas and a bathrobe. Stretching, yawning, I grumbled in flawless Russian in a sleepy way: 'All right, all right. What time is it?'

'Eight in the morning, Gospodin Arakelian. I shall order your breakfast.'

'Have we time?'

'There is time, *gospodin*, especially as you have already shaved.'

I looked at him with more care, but he had a broad open Russian face, there was no trickery on it or suspicion. I drank some tea and changed into street clothing again, a smaller size as I was now smaller. The Hotel Metropole doorman was holding open the door of the black Zis, and we bumped over cobblestones to the white marble building with no name. Here in Moscow it was also hot, though only early morning.

This morning their expressions were all different in the dim, cool room. Worried. There were three of them:

Blue eyes; Kvetchnikov, the tall one, with eyes so very blue; he looked at the wall and the ceiling, but not at me and, though sometimes he smiled, there was nothing behind it.

Red beard – Muzhnets. He tapped with a pencil softly, on thin sheets of paper.

And the old one. He sat like a squat, fat Buddha. His name was Tadjensevitch.

Yesterday they were reserved and suspicious, but they could not help themselves, they would have to do whatever I asked. There was no choice for them; they reported to the chief himself and how could they let such a thing as I had told them go untaken? No, they must swallow bait. But today there was worry on their faces.

The worry was not about me; they knew me. Or so they thought. 'Hello, hello, Arakelian,' said Blue Eyes to me, though his gaze examined the rug in front of my chair. 'Have you more to tell us today?'

I asked without alarm: 'What more could I have?'

'Oh,' said Blue-Eyed Kvetchnikov, looking at the old man, 'perhaps you can explain what happened in Washington last night.'

'In Washington?'

'In Washington, yes. A man appeared before one of the committees of their Senate. He spoke of the *Aldebaratniki,* and he spoke also of the Soviet Union. Arakelian, then, tell us how this is possible.'

The old man whispered softly: 'Show him the dispatch.'

Red Beard jumped. He stopped tapping on the thin paper and handed it to me. 'Read!' he ordered in a voice of danger, though I was not afraid. I read. It was a diplomatic telegram, from their embassy in Washington, and what it said was what every newspaper said – it was no diplomatic secret, it was headlines. One Robert P. Smith, a fictitious name, real identity unknown, had appeared before the Schnell Committee. He had told them of Soviet penetration of the stars. Considering limitations, excellent, it was an admirably accurate account.

I creased the paper and handed it back to Muzhnets. 'I have read it.'

Old One: 'You have nothing to say?'

'Only this.' I leaped up on two legs and pointed at him. 'I did not think you would bungle this! How dared you allow this information to become public?'

'How –'

'How did that weapon get out of your country?'

'Weap –'

'Is this Soviet efficiency?' I cried loudly. 'Is it proletarian discipline?'

Red-Beard Muzhnets intervened. 'Softly, comrade,' he cried. 'Please! We must not lose tempers!'

I made a sound of disgust. I did it very well. 'I warned you,' I said, low, and made my face sad and stern. 'I told you that there was a danger that the bourgeois-capitalists would interfere.

Why did you not listen? Why did you permit their spies to
steal the weapon I gave you?'

Tadjensevitch whispered agedly: 'That weapon is still here.'

I cried: 'But this report –'

'There must be another weapon, Arakelian. And do you see?
That means the Americans are also in contact with the *Aldebaratniki.*'

It was time for chagrin. I admitted: 'You are right.'

He sighed: 'Comrades, the Marshal will be here in a moment.
Let us settle this.' I composed my face and looked at him. 'Arakelian, answer this question straight out. Do you know how
this American could have got in touch with the *Aldebaratniki*
now?'

'How could I, *gospodin*?'

'That,' he said thoughtfully, 'is not a straight answer but it is
answer enough. How could you? You have not left the Metropole. And in any case the Marshal is now coming, I hear his
guard.'

We all stood up, very formal, it was a question of socialist
discipline.

In came this man, the Marshal, who ruled two hundred million humans, smoking a cigarette in a paper holder, his small
pig's eyes looking here and there and at me. Five very large men
were with him, but they never said anything at all. He sat down
grunting; it was not necessary for him to speak loud or to speak
clearly, but it was necessary that those around him should hear
anyhow. It was not deafness that caused Tadjensevitch to wear
a hearing aid.

The old man jumped up. 'Comrade Party Secretary,' he said,
not now whispering, no, 'this man is P.P. Arakelian.'

Grunt from the Marshal.

'Yes, Comrade Party Secretary, he has come to us with the
suggestion that we sign a treaty with a race of creatures inhabiting a planet of the star Aldebaran. Our astronomers say they
cannot dispute any part of his story. And the M.V.D. has as-
suredly verified his reliability in certain documents signed by
the late – (cough) – Comrade Beria.' That too had not been
easy and would have been less so if Beria had not been dead.

Grunt from the Marshal. Old Tadjensevitch looked expect-
antly at me.

'I beg your pardon?' I said.

Old Tadjensevitch said without patience: 'The Marshal asked about terms.'

'Oh,' I bowed, 'there are no terms. These are unworldly creatures, excellent comrade.' I thought to mention it as a joke, but none laughed. 'Unworldly, you see. They wish only to be friends – with you, with the Americans ... they do not know the difference; it is all in whom they first see.'

Grunt. 'Will they sign a greaty?' Tadjensevitch translated.

'Of course.'

Grunt. Translation. 'Have they enemies? There is talk in the American document of creatures that destroy them. We must know what enemies our new friends may have.'

'Only animals, excellent comrade. Like your wolves of Siberia, but huge, as the great blue whale.'

Grunt. Tadjensevitch said: 'The Marshal asks if you can guarantee that the creatures will come first to us.'

'No. I can only suggest. I cannot guarantee there will be no error.'

'But if –'

'If,' I cried loudly, 'if there is error, you have Red Army to correct it!'

They looked at me, strange. They did not expect that. But they did not understand.

I gave them no time. I said quickly: 'Now, excellency, one thing more. I have a present for you.'

Grunt. I hastily said: 'I saved it, comrade. Excuse me. In my pocket.' I reached, most gently, those five men all looked at me now with much care. For the first demonstration I had produced an Aldebaranian hand weapon, three inches long, capable of destroying a bull at five hundred yards, but now for this Russian I had more. 'See,' I said, and took it out to hand him, a small glittering thing, carved of a single solid diamond, an esthetic statue four inches long. Oh, I did not like to think of it wasted: But it was important that this man should be off guard, so I handed it to one of the tall silent men, who thumbed it over and then passed it on with a scowl to the Marshal. I was sorry, yes. It was a favourite thing, a clever carving that they had made in the water under Aldebaran's rays; it was almost greater than I could have made myself. No, I will not begrudge it them, it was greater; I could not have done so well!

Unfortunate that so great a race should have needed attention; unfortunate that I must now give this memento away; but I needed to make an effect and, yes, I did!

Oh, diamond is great to humans; the Marshal looked surprised, and grunted, and one of the silent, tall five reached in *his* pocket, and took out something that glittered on silken ribbon. He looped it around my neck. 'Hero of Soviet Labour,' he said, 'First Class – With emeralds. For you.'

'Thank you, Marshal,' I said.

Grunt. 'The Marshal,' said Tadjensevitch in a thin, thin voice, 'thanks you. Certain investigations must be made. He will see you again tomorrow morning.'

This was wrong, but I did not wish to make him right. I said again: 'Thank you.'

A grunt from the Marshal; he stopped and looked at me, and then he spoke loud so that, though he grunted, I understood. 'Tell,' he said, 'the *Aldebaratniki*, tell them they must come to us – if their ship should land in the wrong country . . .'

He stopped at the door and looked at me powerfully.

'I hope,' he said, 'That it will not,' and he left, and they escorted me back in the Zis sedan to the room at the Hotel Metropole.

3

So that was that and *z-z-z-z-zit*, I was gone again, leaving an empty and heavily guarded room in the old hotel.

In Paris it was midday, I had spent a long time in Moscow. In Paris it was also hot and, as the grey-haired small man with the rosette of the Legion in his buttonhole escorted me along the Champs Élysées, slim-legged girls in bright short skirts smiled at us. No matter. I did not care one pin for all those bright slim girls.

But it was necessary to look, the man expected it of me, and he was the man I had chosen. In America I worked through a committee of their Senate, in Russia the Comrade Party Secretary; here my man was a M. Duplessin, a small straw but the one to wreck a dromedary. He was a member of the Chamber of Deputies, elected as a Christian Socialist Radical Democrat, a party which stood between the Non-Clerical Catholic Workers'

Movement on one side and the F.C.M., or Movement for Christian Brotherhood, on the other. His party had three deputies in the Chamber, and the other two hated each other. Thus M. Duplessin held the balance of power in his party, which held the balance of power in the Right Centrist Coalition, which held the balance through the entire Anti-Communist Democratic Front, which supported the Premier. Yes. M. Duplessin was the man I needed.

I had slipped a folder into the locked files of a Senate committee and forged credentials into the records of Russian's M.V.D., but both together were easier than the finding of this right man. But I had him now, and he was taking me to see certain persons who also knew his importance, persons who would do as he told them. 'Monsieur,' he said gravely, 'It lacks a small half-hour of the appointed time. Might one not enjoy an aperitif?'

'One might,' I said fluently, and permitted him to find us a table under the trees, for I knew that he was unsure of me; it was necessary to cause him to become sure.

'Ah,' said Duplessin, sighing and placed hat, cane and gloves on a filigree metal chair. He ordered drinks and when they came sipped slightly, looking away. 'My friend,' he said at last, 'Tell me of *les aldebaragnards*. We French have traditions – liberty, equality, fraternity – we made Arabs into citizens of the Republic – always has France been mankind's spiritual home. But, monsieur. Nevertheless. *Three* eyes?'

'They are really very nice,' I told him with great sincerity, though it was probably no longer true.

'Hum.'

'And,' I said, 'they know of love.'

'Ah,' he said mistily sighing again. 'Love. Tell me, monsieur. Tell me of love on Aldebaran.'

'They live on a planet,' I misstated somewhat. 'Aldebaran is the star itself. But I will tell you what you ask, M. Duplessin. It is thus: When a young Triop, for so they call themselves, comes of age, he swims far out into the wide sea, far from his crystal city out into the pellucid water where giant fan-tailed fish of rainbow colours swim endlessly above, tinting the pale sunlight that filters through the water and their scales. Tiny bright fish give off star-like flashes from patterned luminescent spots on their scales.'

'It sounds most beautiful, monsieur,' Duplessin said with politeness.

'It is most beautiful. And the young Triop swims until he sees – *Her.*'

'Ah, monsieur.' He was more than polite, I considered, he was interested.

'They speak not a word,' I added, 'for the water is all around and they wear masks, otherwise they could not breathe. They cannot speak, no, and one cannot see the other's eyes. They approach in silence and in mystery.'

He sighed and sipped his cassis.

'They,' I said, 'they know, although there is no way that they can know. But they do. They swim about each other searchingly, tenderly, sadly. Yes. Sadly – is beauty not always in some way sad? A moment. And then they are one.'

'They do not speak?'

I shook my head.

'Ever?'

'Never until all is over, and they meet elsewhere again.'

'Ah, monsieur!' He stared into his small glass of tincture. 'Monsieur,' he said, 'may one hope – that is, is it possible – oh, monsieur! Might one go there, soon?'

I said with all my cunning: 'All the things are possible, M. Duplessin, if the Triops can be saved from destruction. Consider for yourself, if you please, that to turn such a people over to the brutes with the Red Star – or these with the forty-nine white stars – what difference? – is to destroy them.'

'Never, my friend, never!' he cried strongly. 'Let them come! Let them entrust themselves to France! France will protect them, my friend, or France will die!'

It was all very simple after that, I was free within an hour after lunch and, certainly, *z-z-z-z-zit.*

My spaceship deposited me in this desert, Mojave, I think. Or almost Mojave, in its essential Americanness. Yes. It was in America, for what other place would do? I had accomplished much, but there was yet a cosmetic touch or two before I could say I had accomplished all.

I scanned the scene, everything was well, there was no one.

Distantly planes howled, but of no importance: stratosphere jets, what would they know of one man on the sand four miles below? I worked.

Five round trips, carrying what was needed between this desert place and my bigger ship. And where was that? Ah. Safe. It hurled swinging around Mars: yes, quite safe. Astronomers might one day map it, but on that day it would not matter, no. Oh, it would not matter at all.

Since there was time, on my first trip I reassumed my shape and ate, it was greatly restful. Seven useful arms and ample feet, it became easy; quickly I carried one ton of materials, two thousand pounds, from my armchair ferry to the small shelter in which I constructed my cosmetic appliance. Shelter? Why a shelter, you may ask? Oh, I say, for artistic reasons, and in the remote chance that some low-flying plane might blundersomely pass, though it would not. But it might. Let's see, I said, let me think, uranium and steel, strontium and cobalt, a touch of sodium for yellow, have I everything? Yes. I have everything, I said, everything, and I assembled the cosmetic bomb and set the fuse. Good-bye, bomb, I said with affection and, z-z-z-z-zit, armchair and Plinglot were back aboard my ship circling Mars. Nearly done, nearly done!

There, quickly I assembled the necessary data for the Aldebaranian rocket, my penultimate – or Next to Closing – task.

Now. This penultimate task, it was not a difficult one, no but it demanded some concentration. I had a ship. No fake, no crude imitation! It was an authentic rocket ship of the Aldebaranians, designed to travel to their six moons, with vent baffles for underwater takeoff due to certain exigencies (e.g., inimical animals ashore) of their culture. Yes. It was real. I had brought it on purpose all the way.

Now – I say once more – now, I did what I had necessarily to do, which was to make a course for this small ship. There was no crew. (Not anywhere.) The course was easy to compute, I did it rather well; but there was setting of instruments, automation of controls – oh, it took time, took time – but I did it. It was my way, I am workmanlike and reliable, ask Mother. The human race would not know an authentic Aldebaranian rocket from a lenticular Cetan shrimp, but they *might*, hey? The Aldebaranians had kindly developed rockets and it was no great trouble to bring, as well as more authentic. I brought. And having completed all this, and somewhat pleased. I stood to look around.

But I was not alone.

This was not a fortunate thing, it meant trouble.

I at once realized what my companion, however unseen, must be, since it could not be human, nor was it another child. Aldebaranian. It could be nothing else.

I stood absolutely motionless and looked, looked. As you have in almost certain probability never observed the interior of an Aldebaranian rocket, I shall describe: Green metal in cruciform shapes ('chairs'), sparkling mosaics of coloured light ('maps'), ferrous alloys in tortured cuprous-glassy conjunction ('instruments'). All motionless. But something moved. I saw! An Aldebaranian! One of the Triops, a foothigh manikin, looking up at me out of three terrified blue eyes; yes, I had brought the ship but I had not brought it empty, one of the creatures had stowed away aboard. And there it was.

I lunged towards it savagely. It looked up at me and squeaked like a bell: 'Why? Why, Plinglot, why did you kill my people?'

It is *so* annoying to be held to account for every little thing. But I dissembled.

I said in moderate cunning: 'Stand quiet, small creature, and let me get hold of you. Why are you not dead?'

It squeaked pathetically – not in English, to be sure! but I make allowances – it squeaked: 'Plinglot, you came to our planet as a friend from outer space, one who wished to help our people join forces to destroy the great killing land beasts.'

'That seemed appropriate,' I conceded.

'We believed you, Plinglot! All our nations believed you. But you caused dissension. You pitted us one against the other, so that one nation no longer trusted another. We had abandoned war, Plinglot, for more than a hundred years, for we dared not wage war.'

'That is true,' I agreed.

'But you tricked us! War came, Plinglot! And at your hands. As this ship was plucked from its berth with only myself aboard I received radio messages that a great war was breaking out and that the seas were to be boiled. It is the ultimate weapon, Plinglot! By now my planet is dry and dead. Why did you do it?'

'Small Triop,' I lectured, 'listen to this. You are male, one supposes, and you must know that no female Aldebaranian survives. Very well. You are the last of your race. There is no future. You might as well be dead.'

'I know,' he wept.

'And therfore you should kill yourself. Check,' I invited, 'my logic with the aid of your computing machine, if you wish. But please do not disturb the course computations I have set up on it.'

'It is not necessary, Plinglot,' he said with sadness. 'You are right.'

'So kill yourself!' I bellowed.

The small creature, how foolish, would not do this, no. He said: 'I do not want to, Plinglot,' apologetically. 'But I will not disturb your course.'

Well, it was damned decent of him, in a figure of speech, I believed, for that course was most important to me; on it depended the success of my present mission, which was to demolish Earth as I had his own planet. I attempted to explain, in way of thanks, but he would not understand, no.

'Earth?' he squeaked feebly and I attempted to make him see. Yes, Earth, that planet so far away, it too had a population which was growing large and fierce and smart; it too was hovering on the fringe of space travel. Oh, it was dangerous, but he would not see, though I explained and I am Plinglot. I can allow no rivals in space, it is my assigned task, given in hand by the great Mother. Well, I terrified him, it was all I could do.

Having locked him, helpless, in a compartment of his own ship I consulted my time.

It was fleeing I flopped onto my armchair; *z-z-z-z-zit*; once again in the room in the Hotel Mayflower, Washington, U.S.A.

Things progressed, all was ready. I opened the door, affecting having just awaked. A chambermaid turned from dusting pictures on the wall, said, 'Good morning, sir,' looked at me and – oh! – screamed. Screamed in a terrible tone.

Careless Plinglot! I had forgot to return to human form.

Most fortunately, she fainted. I quickly turned human and found a rope. It took very much time, and time was passing, while the rocket hastened to cover forty million miles; it would arrive soon where I had sent it. I hurried. Hardly, hardly, I made myself do it, though as anyone on Tau Ceti knows it was difficult for me; I tied her; I forced a pillowcase, or one corner of it, into her mouth so that she might not cry out; and even I locked her in a closet. Oh, it was hard. Questions? Difficulty? Danger? Yes. They were all there to be considered, too, but I had no time to consider them. Time was passing, I have said, and time passed for me.

It was only a temporary expedient. In time she would be found. Of course. This did not matter. In time there would *be* no time, you see, for time would come to an end for chambermaid, Duplessin, senators and the M.V.D., and then what?

Then Plinglot would have completed this, his mission, and two-eyes would join three-eyes, good-bye.

4

Senator Schnell this time was waiting for me at the kerb in a hollow square of newsmen. 'Mr. Smith,' he cried, 'how good to see you. Now, please, fellows! Mr. Smith is a busy man. Oh, all right, just one picture, or two.' And he made to shoo the photographers off while wrapping himself securely to my side. 'Terrible men,' he whispered out of the golden corner of his mouth, smiling, smiling, 'how they pester me!'

'I am sorry, Senator,' I said politely and permitted him to lead me through the flash barrage to the large room for the hearings.

Q. (Mr. Hagsworth.) Mr. Smith, in yesterday's testimony you gave us to understand that Russia was making overtures to the alien creatures from Aldebaran. Now, I'd like to call your attention to something. Have you seen this morning's papers?

A. No.

Q. Then let me read you an extract from Pierce Truman's column which has just come to my attention. It starts, 'After yesterday's sensational rev –'

Q. (Senator Loveless.) Excuse me, Mr. Hagsworth.

Q. (Mr. Hagsworth.) '– elations.' Yes, Senator?

Q. (Senator Loveless.) I only want to know, or to ask, if that document – that is, the newspaper which you hold in your hand – is a matter of evidence. By this I mean an exhibit. If so, I raise the question, or rather suggestion, that it should be properly marked and entered.

Q. (Mr. Hagsworth.) Well, Senator, I –

Q. (Senator Loveless.) As an exhibit, I mean.

Q. (Mr. Hagsworth.) Yes, as an exhibit. I –

Q. (Senator Loveless.) Excuse me for interrupting. It seemed an important matter – important procedural matter, that is.

Q. (Mr. Hagsworth.) Certainly, Senator. Well, Senator, I intended to read it only in order to have Mr. Smith give us his views.

Q. (Senator Loveless.) Thank you for that explanation, Mr. Hagsworth. Still it seems to me, or at the moment it appears to me, that it ought to be marked and entered.

Q. (The Chairman.) Senator, in my view –

Q. (Senator Loveless.) As an exhibit, that is.

Q. (The Chairman.) Thank you for that clarification, Senator. In my view, however, since as Mr. Hagsworth has said it is only Mr. Smith's views that he is seeking to get out, then the article itself is not evidence but merely an adjunct to questioning. Anyway, frankly, Senator, that's the way I see it. But I don't want to impose my will on the Committee. I hope you understand that, all of you.

Q. (Mr. Hagsworth.) Certainly, sir.

Q. (Senator Loveless.) Oh, none of us has any idea, or suspicion, Senator Schnell, that you have any such design, or purpose.

Q. (Senator Duffy.) Of course not.

Q. (Senator Fly.) No, not here . . .

Oh, time, time! I looked at the clock on the wall and time was going, I did not wish to be here when it started. Of course. Ten o'clock. Ten thirty. Five minutes approaching eleven. Then this Mr. Pierce Truman's column at last was marked and entered and recorded after civil objection and polite concession from Senator Schnell and in thus wise made an immutable, permanent, in destructible part of the files of this mutable, transient, soon to be destroyed committee. Oh, comedy! But it would not be for laughing if I dawdled here too late.

Somehow, somehow, Mr. Hagsworth was entitled at last to read his column and it said as follows. Viz.

After yesterday's sensational revelations before the Schnell
Committee, backstage Washington was offering bets that
nothing could top the mysterious Mr. Smith's weird story of
creatures from outer space. But the toppers may already be
on hand.

Here are two questions for you, Senator Schnell. What were
three Soviet U.N. military attaches doing at a special showing at the Hayden Planetarium last night? And what's the
truth beyond the reports that are filtering into C.I.A. from
sources in Bulgaria, concerning a special parade scheduled for
Moscow's Red Square tomorrow to welcome 'unusual and
very special' V.I.P.'s, names unknown?

Exhausted from this effort, the committee declared a twenty-
minute recess. I glowered at the clock, time, time!

Mr. Hagsworth had plenty of time, he thought, he was not
worried. He cornered me in the cloakroom. 'Smoke?' he said
graciously, offering a package of cigarettes.

I said thank you, I do not smoke.

'Care for a drink?'

I do not drink, I told him.

'Or –?' he nodded towards the tiled room with the chromium
pipes; I do not do that either, but I could not tell him so, only,
I shook my head.

'Well, Mr. Smith,' he said again, 'you make a good witness.
I'm sorry,' he added, 'to spring that column on you like that.
But I couldn't help it.'

'No matter,' I said.

'You're a good sport, Smith. You see, one of the reporters
handed it to me as we walked into the hearing room.'

'All right,' I said, wishing to be thought generous.

'Well, I had to get it into the record. What's it about, eh?'

I said painfully (time, time!), 'Mr. Hagsworth, I have testi-
fied the Russians also wish the ship from Aldebaran. And it is
coming close. Soon it will land.'

'Good,' he said, smiling and rubbing his hands, 'very good!
And you will bring them to us?'

'I will do,' I said, 'the best I can,' ambiguously, but that was
enough to satisfy him, and recess was over.

Q. (Mr. Hagsworth.) Mr. Smith, do I understand that you have some knowledge of the proposed movements of the voyagers from Aldebaran?

A. Yes.

Q. Can you tell us what you know?

A. I can. Certainly. Even now an Aldebaranian rocket ship is approaching the Earth. Through certain media of communication which I cannot discuss in open hearing, as you understand, certain proposals have been made to them on behalf of this country.

Q. And their reaction to these proposals, Mr. Smith?

A. They have agreed to land in the United States for discussions.

Oh, happy commotion, the idiots. The flash bulbs went like mad. Only the clock was going, going, and I commenced to worry, where was the ship? Was forty lousy million miles so much? But no, it was not so much; and when the messenger came racing in the door I knew it was time. One messenger, first. He ran wildly down among the seats, searching, then stopping at the seat on the aisle where Pierce Truman sat regarding me with an ophidian eye, stopped and whispered. Then a couple more, strangers, hatless and hair flying, also messengers, came hurrying in – and more – to the committee, to the newsmen – the word had got out.

'Mr. Chairman! Mr. Chairman!' It was Senator Loveless, he was shouting; some one person had whispered in his ear and he could not wait to tell his news. But everyone had that news, you see, it was no news to the chairman, he already had a slip of paper in his hand.

He stood up and stared blindly into the television cameras, without smile now, the gold tooth not flashing. He said: 'Gentlemen, I –' And stopped for a moment to catch his breath and to shake his head. 'Gentlemen.' he said, 'gentlemen, I have here a report,' staring incredulously at the scrawled slip of paper. In the room was quickly silence; even Senaor Loveless, and Pierce Truman stopped at the door on his way out to listen. 'This report,' he said, 'comes from the Arlington Naval Observatory – in, gentlemen, my own home state, the Old Dominion, Virginia –' He paused and shook himself, yes, and made himself look again at the paper. 'From the Arlington Naval

Observatory, where the radio telescope experts inform us that an object of unidenified origin and remarkable speed has entered the atmosphere of the Earth from outer space.!'

Cries. Sighs. Shouts. But he stopped them, yes, with a hand. 'But gentlemen, that is not all! Arlington has tracked this object and it has landed. Not in our country, gentlemen! Not even in Russia! But –' he shook the paper before him – 'in Africa, gentlemen! In the desert of Algeria!'

Oh, much commotion then, but not joyous. 'Double-cross!' shouted someone, and I made an expression of astonishment. Adjourned, banged the gavel of the chairman, and only just in time; the clock said nearly twelve and my cosmetic bomb was set for one-fifeen. Oh, I had timed it close. But now was danger and I had to leave, which I did hardly. But I could not evade Mr. Hagsworth, who rode with me in taxi to hotel, chattering, chattering. I did not listen.

5

Now, this is how it was, an allegory or parable. Make a chemical preparation, you see? Take hydrogen and take oxygen – very pure in both cases – blend them and strike a spark. Nothing happens. They do not burn! It is true, though you may not believe me.

But with something added, yes, they burn. For instance let the spark be a common match, with so tiny you can hardly detect it, a quarter-droplet of water bonded into its substance – Yes, with the water they will burn – more than burn – *kerblam*, the hydrogen and oxygen fiercely unite. Water, it is the catalyst which makes it go.

Similarly, I reflected (unhearing the chatter of Mr. Hagsworth), it is a catalyst which is needed on Earth, and this catalyst I have made, my cosmetic appliance, my bomb. The chemicals were stewing together nicely. There was a ferment of suspicion in Russia, of fear in America, of jealousy in France where I had made the ship land. Oh, they were jumpy now! I could feel forces building around me; even the driver of the cab, half-watching the crowded streets, half listening to the hysterical cries of his little radio. To the Mayflower, hurrying. All the while the city was getting excited around us. That was the ferment, and by my watch the catalyst was quite near.

'Wait,' said Mr. Hagsworth pleading, in the lobby, 'come have a drink, Smith.'

'I don't drink.'

'I forgot,' he apologized. 'Well, would you like to sit for a moment in the bar with me? I'd like to talk to you. This is all happening too fast.'

'Come along to my room,' I said, not wanting him, no, but what harm could he do? And I did not want to be away from my purple armchair, not at all.

So up we go and there is still time, I am glad. Enough time. The elevator could have stuck, my door could have somehow been locked against me, by error I could have gone to the wrong floor – no, everything was right. We were there and there was time.

I excused myself a moment (though it could have been forever) and walked into the inner room of this suite. Yes, it was there, ready. It squatted purple, and no human would think to look at it that it was anything but an armchair, but it was much more and if I wished I could go to it, – z-z-z-z-zit, I would be gone.

A man spoke.

I turned, looking. Out of the door to the tiled room spoke to me a man, smiling, red-faced, in blue coveralls. Well. For a moment I felt alarm. (I remembered, e.g., what I had left bound in the closet.) But on this man's face was only smile and he said with apology: 'Oh, hello, sir. Sorry. But we had a complaint from the floor below, plumbing leak. I've got it nearly fixed.'

Oh, all right. I shrugged for him and went back to Mr. Hagsworth. In my mind had been – well, I do not know what had been in my mind. Maybe z-z-z-z-zit to the George V and telephone Duplessin to make sure they would not allow Russians or Americans near the ship, no, not if the ambassadors made of his life a living hell. Maybe to Metropole to phone Tadjensevitch (not the Marshal, he would not speak on telephone to me) to urge him also on. Maybe farther, yes.

But I went back to Mr. Hagsworth. It was not needed, really it was not. It was only insurance, in the event that somehow my careful plans went wrong, I wished to be there until the very end. Or nearly. But I need not have done it.

But I did. *Z-z-z-z-zit* and I could have been away, but I stayed, very foolish, but I did.

Mr. Hagsworth was on telephone, his eyes bright and angry, I thought I knew what he was hearing. I listened to hear if there were, perhaps, muffled kickings, maybe groans, from a closet, but there were none; hard as it was, I had tied well, surely. And then Mr. Hagsworth looked up.

He said, bleak: 'I have news, Smith. It's started.'

'Started?'

'Oh,' he said without patience, 'you know what I'm talking about, Smith. The trouble's started. These Aldebaranians of yours, they've stirred up a hornet's nest, and now the stinging has begun. I just talked to the White House. There's a definite report of a nuclear explosion in the Mojave desert.'

'No!'

'Yes,' he said, nodding, 'there is no doubt. It can't be anything but a Russian missile, though their aim is amazingly bad. Can it?'

'What else possibly?' I asked with logic. 'How terrible! And I suppose you have retaliated, hey? Sent a flight of missiles to Moscow?'

'Of course. What else could we do?'

He had put his finger on it, yes, he was right, I had computed it myself. 'Nothing,' I said and wrung his hand, 'and may the best country win.'

'Or planet,' he said, nodding.

'Planet?' I let go his hand. I looked. I waited. It was a time for astonishment, I did not speak.

Mr. Hagsworth said, speaking very slow, 'Smith, or maybe I ought to say "Plinglot", that's what I wanted to talk to you about.'

'Talk,' I invited.

Outside there was sudden shouting. 'They've heard about the bomb,' conjectured Mr. Hagsworth, but he paid no more attention. He said: 'In school, Plinglot, I knew a Fat Boy.' He said: 'He always got his way. Everybody was afraid of him. But he never fought, he only divided others, do you see, and got them to fight each other.'

I stood tall – yes, and brave! I dare use that word 'brave', it applies. One would think that it would be like a human to say he is brave before a blinded fluttering moth, 'brave' where there is no danger to be brave against; but though this was a human only, in that room I felt danger. Incredible, but it was so and I did not wish it.

I said, 'What are you talking about, Mr. Hagsworth?'

'An idea I had,' he said softly with a face like death. 'About a murderer. Maybe he comes from another planet and, for reasons of his own, wants to destroy our planet. Maybe this isn't the first one – he might have stopped, for example, at Aldebaran.'

'I do not want to hear this,' I said, with truth.

But he did not stop, he said: 'We human beings have faults, Plinglot, and an outsider with brains and a lot of special knowledge – say, the kind of knowledge that could get a file folder into our records, in spite of all our security precautions – such an outsider might use our faults to destroy us. Senate Committee hearings – why, some of them have been a joke for years, and not a very funny one. Characters have been destroyed, policies have been wrecked – why shouldn't a war be started? Because politicians can be relied on to act in a certain way. And maybe this outsider, having watched and studied us, knew something about Russian weaknesses too, and played on them in the same way. Do you see how easy it would be?'

'Easy?' I cried, offended.

'For someone with very special talents and ability,' he assured me. 'For a Fat Boy. Especially for a Fat Boy who can go faster than any human can follow from here to Moscow, Moscow to Paris, Paris to the Mojave, Mojave to – where? Somewhere near Mars, let's say at a guess. For such a person, wouldn't it, Plinglot, be easy?'

I reeled, I reeled; but these monkey tricks, they could not matter. I had planned too carefully for that, only how did they know?

'Excuse me,' I said softly, 'one moment,' and turned again to the room with the armchair, I felt I had made a mistake. But what mistake could matter, I thought, when there was the armchair and, of course, *z-z-z-z-zit*.

But that was a mistake also.

The man in blue coveralls, he stood in the door but not smiling, he held in his hand what I knew instantly was a gun.

The armchair was there, yes, but in it was of all strange unaccountable people this chambermaid, who should have been bounded in closet, and she too had a gun.

'Miss Gonzalez,' introduced Hagsworth politely, 'and Mr. Hechtmeyer. They are – well, G-men, though, as you can see, Miss Gonzalez is not a man. But she had something remarkable to tell us about you, Plinglot, when Mr. Hechtmeyer released her. She said that you seemed to have another shape when she saw you last. The shape of a sort of green-skinned octopus with bright red eyes; ridiculous, isn't it? Or is it, Plinglot?'

Ruses were past, it was a time for candid. I said – I said, '*Like this?*' terribly, and I went to natural form.

Oh, what white faces! Oh, what horror! It was remarkable, really, that they did not turn and run. For that is Secret Weapon No. 1, for us of Tau Ceti on sanitation work; for our working clothes we assume the shape of those about us certainly, but in case of danger we have merely to resume our own. In all Galaxy (I do not know about Andromeda) there is no shape so fierce. Seven terrible arms. Fourtten piercing scarlet eyes. Teeth like Hessian bayonets; I ask you, would *you* not run?

But they did not. Outside a siren began to scream.

6

I cried: 'Air attack!' It was fearful, the siren warned of atomic warheads on their way and this human woman, this Gonzalez, sat in my chair with pointing gun. 'Go away,' I cried, 'get out,' and rushed upon her, but she did not move. '*Please?*' I said thickly among my long teeth, but what was the use, she would not do it!

They paled, they trembled, but they stayed; well, I would have paled and trembled myself if it had been a Tau Cetan trait, instead I merely went limp. Terror was not only on one side in that room, I confess it. 'Please,' I begged, 'I must go, it is the end of life on this planet and I do not wish to be here!'

'You don't have a choice,' said Mr. Hagsworth, his face like steel. 'Gentlemen!' he called. 'Come in!' And through the door came several persons, some soldiers and some who were not. I looked with all my eyes; I could not have been more astonished. For there was – yes, Senator Schnell, gold tooth covered, face without smile; Senator Loveless, white hair waving; and – oh, there was more.

I could scarcely believe.

Feeble, slow humans! They had mere atmosphere craft mostly but here, eight thousand miles from where he had been eighteen hours before, yes, Comrade Tadjensevitch, the old man; and M. Duplessin, sadly meeting my eyes. It could not be, almost I forgot the screaming siren and the fear.

'These gentlemen,' said Hagsworth with politeness, 'also would like to talk to you, Mr. Smith.'

'Arakelian,' grunted the old man.

'Monsieur Laplant,' corrected Duplessin.

'Or,' said Hagsworth, 'should we all call you by your right name, Plinglot?'

Outside the siren screamed, I could not move.

Senator Schnell came to speak: 'Mr. Smith,' he said, 'or, I should say, Plinglot, we would like an explanation. Or account.'

'Please let me go!' I cried.

'Where?' demanded old Tadjensevitch. 'To Mars, Hero of Soviet Labour? Or farther this time?'

'The bombs,' I cried. 'Let me go! What about Hero of Soviet Labour?'

The old man sighed: 'The decoration Comrade Party Secretary gave you, it contains a microwave transmitter, very good. One of our *sputniki* now needs new parts.'

'You *suspected* me?' I cried, out of fear and astonishment.

'Of course the Russians suspected you, Plingiot,' Hagsworth scolded mildly. 'We all did, even we Americans – and we are not, you know, a suspicious race. 'No,' he added thoughtfully, as though there were no bombs to fall, 'our national characteristics are . . . what? The conventional caricatures – the publicity hound, the pork-barrel senator, the cut-throat businessman? Would you say that was a fair picture, Mr. Smith?'

'*I Plinglot!*'

'Yes, of course. Sorry. But that must be what you thought, because those are the stereotypes you acted on, and maybe they're true enough – most of the time. Too much of the time. But not *all* the time, Plinglot!'

I fell to the floor, perspiring a terrible smell, it is how we

faint, so to speak. It was death, it was the end, and this man was
bullying me without fear.

'The Fat Boy,' said Mr. Hagsworth softly, 'was strong. He
could have whipped most of us. But in my last term he got
licked. Guile and bluff – when at last the bluff was called he gave
up. He was a coward.'

'I give up, Mr. Hagsworth,' I wailed, 'only let me go away
from the bombs!'

'I know you do,' he nodded, 'what else? And – what, the
bombs? There are no bombs. Look out the window.'

In seconds I pulled myself together, no one spoke. I went to
window. Cruising up and down outside a white truck, red cross,
painted with word *Ambulance*, siren going. Only that. No air
raid warning. Only ambulance.

'Did you think,' scolded Hagsworth with voice angry now,
'that we would let *you* bluff *us*? There's an old maxim – "Give
him enough rope" – we gave it to you; and we added a little.
You see, we didn't *know* you came from a race of cowards.'

'I Plinglot!' I sobbed through all my teeth. 'I am not a
coward. I even tied this human woman here, ask her! It was
brave, even Mother could not have done more! Why, I sector
warden of this whole quadrant of the very Galaxy, indeed, to
keep the peace!'

'That much we know – and we know why,' nodded Mr.
Hagsworth, 'because you're afraid; but we needed to know
more. Well, now we do; and once M. Duplessin's associates get
a better means of communication with the little Aldebaranians, I
expect we'll know still more. It will be very helpful knowledge,'
he added in thought.

It was all, it was the end. I said sadly: 'If only Great Mother
could know Plinglot did his best! If only she could learn what
strange people live here, who, I cannot understand.'

'Oh,' said Mr. Hagsworth, gently, 'we'll tell her for you,
Plinglot,' he said, 'very soon, I think.'